TEENA - A HOUSE OF ILL REPUTE

by

JENNIFER JANE POPE

Published by **CHIMERA**
ISBN 9781780806198

Cover image by Barbara Jensen.

This novel is fiction - in real life practice safe sex.

Prologue
By Christeena Felicity Spigwell-Thyme

Hey, look! They've given me proper accreditation here, and about time, too. Which, of course, is what my story is all about - time.

For those of you who haven't met me before - and to refresh the little grey cells of those who have and who might have forgotten me, shame on you - I'm a time traveller and have been one since the tender age of eighteen, back in the mid nineteen-seventies. Yes, I'm sure you can do the arithmetic and, yes, that now makes me forty-six years old, although if you met me face to face (and no, that's not the real me on the cover of the book, silly) you'd think I was only about twenty-three.

No, I haven't had a lifelong addiction to plastic surgery, either. The secret of my apparent eternal youth lies somewhere in the phenomena of time travelling, as I explained in my second book. Don't ask me how it works... no, I *can* tell you *how* it works - the result, at least - but what I can't tell you is why, and what actually goes on. The results pan out something like this. Lucky old Teena gets whisked back in time at irregular intervals, spending irregular amounts of time in the bodies of my various ancestors. So far I've spent periods of time back in the past varying from little more than a few minutes to, as far as I've been able to calculate, several weeks.

However, no matter how long I seemingly go back for, whenever I return to my present day body, only a matter of seconds, minutes at most in the extreme cases, have actually elapsed. And that's not all. If I travel back for, let's say, a total of six months in any one given year, those six months apparently get credited to my physical account. In other words, and to make this more obvious, in the past twenty-seven years I've spent what must be a total of thirty one years back in antiquity, and so not only have I not aged physically in that time, but, and I'm guessing a bit here, I've already worked up a bit of credit.

I still don't look any older than I did when I was eighteen, and am unlikely to do so, at least for the foreseeable future. Okay, yes, I *did* say you would think I was twenty-something, but I can explain that, too. For a start, I'm well above average height for a girl, which tends to add a couple of years to the image. In addition, it's gotten to be impossible for a girl to live more than a quarter of a century in this world - let alone even more than that in various older worlds - without picking up a little *je ne sais quoi* that adds to her aura and gives her a special sort of maturity that has nothing whatsoever to do with age.

But back to my time travelling, which began one evening just after I had moved into the little cottage in Rowlands Castle, which had been left to me by a great-great-great aunt none of my immediate family had ever been aware I had, but of whom I turned out to be the eldest surviving female relative. In the loft, I discovered several boxes of clothing, underwear included, which although they clearly dated from some time in the Victorian era, appeared to be as fresh and clean as the day they were first made.

Tall though I am, I am not exactly heavily built, and thanks to one of the corsets I dug out of my trove, I was able to squeeze myself into one of the antique dresses. I was also able to fit my feet into the bootees, which at the time I hardly gave a

2

thought to, but which as my story unfolded, I realised was, to say the least, quite odd. Being tall I have feet that are not exactly tiny, and footwear made for a lady more than a century earlier should not have had a prayer where they were concerned. Call me thick, if you dare, but it was several weeks before I even considered this anomaly, and a while after that before the significance began dawning on me. But more of all that later, for the stage at which I left my adventure was prior to this...

Dressed in my old but new finery, I was prepared to settle into a night of relaxation, or as much relaxation as a tightly laced corset would allow, together with a bottle of wine, but whilst searching the kitchen for a corkscrew, I came across a gold pendant hidden at the back of a drawer. It was unremarkable as were the two tiny miniatures it held of a man and woman I guessed must have lived sometime at the beginning of the nineteenth century. That pendant was to prove the catalyst, and although its continued proximity was not, and is not, necessary for me to go for a jaunt in time, I remain convinced it was the initial trigger to something I cannot explain.

In the batting of an eyelid, I seemed to pass out and return to consciousness in a body that clearly was not mine, and in a time and place I quickly deduced was not my own. I had, in fact, journeyed back to some time late in eighteen thirty-nine, and the petite little blonde-haired frame in which I awoke had belonged to one Angelina Spigwell, now supposedly married to an archetypal dastard in the form of one Gregory Hacklebury, although in fact he had employed a doppelganger for the actual ceremony, as Angelina had steadfastly refused to say 'I will' and I wasn't about to gainsay that, I can tell you.

Gregory Hacklebury was a 'Sir', but he had little money, whereas Angelina had shed-loads of the stuff, all of which, by the laws of the day, would have become his upon their marriage. What would then have become of poor Angelina was anybody's guess, but to judge from her, and my, experiences in the short space of time following the mock wedding, I didn't think either of us wanted to be around to find out.

However, getting clear of Hacklebury was easier said than done, for if he was a bad'un, his so-called maid and housekeeper, Megan Crowthorne, was even worse. 'Mad Meg', as I thought of her, had her own designs on either Hacklebury or the estate he was after. She was determined to ensure that whilst he might have 'married' Angelina, he would not think of her as any sort of real wife. Rather, Meg was cunningly reducing Angelina, *me*, to the status of an animal, lacing me into an awful leather dog costume complete with snout and ears, and forcing me to walk around on all fours with cunning extensions inside the sleeves holding my forearms and paws fashioned at the end of each limb.

I was forced to live in a specially built stable-come-kennel in the grounds, and was watched over by a huge Viking type named Erik (I kid you not) whose chief duties - other than to make sure I didn't escape and that I was adequately fed and watered - consisted of walking me, whipping me and screwing me, the latter activity courtesy of just about the biggest rogering implement I have ever had the misfortune to encounter.

Now, I'm ashamed to say that, despite my predicament, I enjoyed Erik's dedication to that latter duty, initially blaming Angelina's body for betraying me, but gradually coming to realise the fault actually lay somewhere inside me, as Angelina herself had a tendency towards her own sex rather than the male persuasion. She had grown up in India with a native serving girl, Indira, who became her lover, but whom Hacklebury sold off to a bunch of soldiers heading back to the sub-continent.

Meanwhile, back in my own time during the periods when I reverted to my then present, I met up with Anne-Marie and her sort of stepbrother, Andy. They were an odd couple in every sense of the word. She was heavily into bondage scenarios with men and women alike, and he was just as heavily into dressing as a female, a role in which he was more than convincing as the sluttish Andrea.

Teena - or Teenie, as they preferred to call me - quickly became inveigled into their little game-playing, whilst at the same time the pair set about helping me trace my ancestral line back in time to see if I really was a descendant of the dreadful Hacklebury, or whether perhaps some other person may have fathered Angelina's eventual offspring, from which I was now certain I was descended. To further complicate matters, it seemed Anne-Marie was a Hacklebury descendant, though whether from the same Hacklebury or a different one we could not at first be sure. A visit to some of her distant cousins made me suspect she was indeed come down the line from the Gregory version, which I assumed quite probably accounted for most, if not all, of her curious sexual predilections, which she seemed determined to introduce me to at a breathtaking rate.

Coincidence? Fate? Either, both, or neither? Make up your own mind, for the gods do move in ways mysterious, and although I've met a good few historical figures during the course of my travels, I've yet to encounter a genuine deity face to face, so I make no claim to knowing myself either way. However, there was definitely more than a hint of good fortune in forming my new friendships, for Andy, having claimed to have fallen in love with me in nineteen seventy-five, suddenly turned up in eighteen thirty-nine in the body of the aforementioned Indira, and thanks to his/her intervention, we were both able to affect an escape, leaving a seething Megan trapped inside the dog suit and taking Erik with us at pistol point to drive the carriage in which we fled.

The final details of our getaway remain a mystery to me, other than snippets I gleaned from Erik later, for as we drove towards the gate, both Andy and myself found ourselves back in the present, doing what it was we had been doing at the moment we time-hopped. I'll leave you to guess what that was, reader...

And that was where we left things at the end of my last volume, but it was not how the story was going to leave me, nor me it, of that you can be as certain as I was then myself. There was unfinished business to be resolved, both in the past and in the present, and neither I nor the mysterious power transporting me back and forth in time was going to be satisfied until a resolution was achieved.

Believe it or not, as I lay back on the bed, perspiring and exhausted, I *wanted* to go back again. No, I *needed* to go back again, for my researches in my own time had more or less ground to a halt and I knew the answers to all my questions, all those answers which I knew I *had* to have, lay back in the first half of the previous century.

In nineteen seventy-five, during the space of a few short weeks, I had gone from being an arguably mature ex-sixth former to what most people would regard as a totally amoral slut, and I couldn't lay all the blame for that at Anne-Marie and

Andrea's feet, any more than I suspected it was anything for which I was wholly or consciously to blame. Either it was something genetic, or else it was something that had lain dormant through the decades and re-emerged in me to help steel me for the rigours I would have to endure in order to try to save Angelina. Or maybe it wasn't any of that and maybe we were all just bad at heart. Maybe there was nothing I could do to help Angelina, yet maybe there was and I had actually already done it. That's one of those things about every time travelling story I've ever read - when the time traveller goes back, is it merely to act out something he or she has already done, or is it to change the course of history?

If I went back and killed Hacklebury, would that mean I would then cease to exist back in my own time, assuming he had fathered the original child? If he hadn't, and I killed whoever was supposed to father it, would that alter things and kill off the line from which I was ultimately descended?

I lay back on the bed, closed my eyes and gently stroked Andy's naked shoulder. How the hell was I supposed to know any of the answers? I didn't even understand most of the questions. And then there were a lot of other things I wasn't even close to understanding and coming to believe I never would.

I sighed and opened one eye to peer across at my sleeping lover. He made a pretty girl, it was true, but he also made a lovely lad, and whilst he wasn't quite in the Erik league when it came to endowment, he hadn't been behind the door when that part of his anatomy was being given out. I sighed again and settled back to let sleep try to claim me, for I was totally exhausted, both physically and emotionally.

The questions could wait for now; they would come again in the morning, and with them, in time, would hopefully come at least some of the answers.

In time...

Chapter 1

Time was beginning to drag now for Maudie Taylor. As she sat at the bedroom window, looking out over the expanse of lawn running behind the back of the big house, she wondered just how much longer she would be expected to continue with this charade, and just how soon she would be able to collect the promised money and get back into the outside world again. An outside world that now, thanks to the hundred guineas she would pocket when she left, looked to hold far more prospects than it had only a few short weeks ago when Miss Crowthorne approached her in the market square in Salisbury.

Maudie turned away from the window at last, and as she did so, she caught sight of her reflection in the long dressing mirror standing in the nearest corner. She paused, and then took a step closer, unable still to resist the little thrill that passed through her every time she saw the picture she now presented to the world. No, not the world, she told herself as she stared into the glass, just this tiny fragment of it; a world that had constricted first from the house and garden down to the house, and then, these past two days, to just this one room with its adjacent dressing area.

And what a dressing room it was! Maudie, accustomed to a life where to own even two dresses - and those patched and darned - was a luxury, could hardly believe the wardrobe now at her disposal. Of course, she had known the upper classes owned clothes in abundance, but this was riches beyond anything she had ever expected, a dress almost for every day of the year, or so it seemed, for Maudie was not too good at counting above any number exceeding the number of fingers, thumbs and toes she possessed.

But it had to be close to that many dresses; there were three hundred and sixty-five days in the year and three hundred and sixty-six days every four years, that much she did know from the old rhyme, and that was lots and lots, and there were certainly lots and lots of dresses, so there had to be close to that many hanging in the wall closets, folded in the heavy trunk, or even hanging from the wheeled rail that stood across the narrow window of the dressing room.

And it didn't stop just with the dresses, for there were all the under-things - corsets, chemises, drawers and stockings, as well as drawers filled with gloves, chokers with little jewelled motifs, shoes and bootees enough to take care of a whole army of women.

Maudie stood before the mirror now, grinning at the way her bosom thrust out from the low neckline of the heavy velvet gown she was wearing; forced up and out by the strictures of the corset one of the two maidservants laced her into daily. A fresh corset every day, wicked boned garments forcing the very breath from her lungs as they presented her soft treasures for all to admire. Why, but even her nipples were all but visible - at least the darker brown circles that bounded them. She pouted her painted lips at the girl in the mirror that was really her, and winked at herself.

My, but it was incredible what the right clothes could do for a girl, she thought to herself. Dressed like this, she looked every inch the fine lady, certainly as much a fine lady as the one who was supposed to be ill and whose place Maudie had taken for that silly wedding ceremony. She still didn't quite understand why they had needed her to do that, but then, she reasoned in her uncomplicated way, she didn't have to understand. All she needed to think about was the hundred guineas, and maybe, just maybe, they might let her keep one or two of these fine dresses, and perhaps an odd corset and a pair of shoes. After all, she told herself as she looked across towards the dressing room door, they had so many of them here, and the real lady of the house would probably buy herself so many more long before she ever got around to wearing even half the things she already owned.

Maudie hoped the lady would be better soon, for the thought of her hundred guineas was beginning to wear on her. She had so many plans for all that money, so many ideas, so many hopes. No more working in the marketplace for Maudie Taylor, that much was certain. Oh no, there were so many other options for a pretty girl with money and the right clothes.

She turned again, relishing the swishing sound her petticoats and skirt made, and let out a little sigh of contentment. Time was dragging now, it was true, but she could afford to be patient. After all, she was only twenty years of age and she had plenty of time - all the time in the world, in fact...

'Time you two lazy buggers were stirring yourselves, or have you shagged yourselves silly all night?'

I opened one eye with some difficulty at the sound of Anne-Marie's voice, hoping my face didn't look as red as it was feeling, though why I should have felt any guilt at being found in bed with Andy I had no idea. It wasn't the first time we'd had sex, though perhaps it was the fact that this had been my first time with Andy, rather than with his alter ego Andrea, which made things seem so different.

'Good morning, sleepyhead,' Anne-Marie said, and I saw that she was smiling as she stood looking down at us from the doorway. 'I've got coffee on the go downstairs, if you're interested.'

'What time is it?' I mumbled, struggling to sit up from beneath the weight of Andy's arm, which lay across my chest.

'Half-eight,' she replied. 'I've been up and about since six, but then *I* had the benefit of a good night's sleep,' she added, grinning mischievously. She nodded down at my still unconscious bed partner. 'Looks equally good in or out of drag, doesn't he?'

'Yes,' I admitted uncertainly. I managed to sit upright finally. 'You don't mind, do you?'

Anne-Marie shrugged. 'Mind?' she echoed. 'Why should I mind? We don't do it together, you know. Even though we're not actually blood relations, well, it wouldn't feel right, if you know what I mean.'

I had to suppress a laugh at this. Anne-Marie's ideas concerning morality, or the lack of it, were curious to say the least. 'He told me he loved me,' I offered lamely.

Anne-Marie's smiled widened. 'I thought he might,' she said.

I had both eyes open now and both eyebrows lifted. 'I - I didn't think he'd said anything to you,' I stammered. 'He told me—'

'She hasn't said a word to me,' Anne-Marie assured me, raising a placating hand, 'but then he didn't have to. Our Andrea is as transparent as cellophane. I've known for days now, probably longer than she has herself.'

I didn't fail to notice how she referred to Andy in the feminine at first, despite his currently obvious male condition.

'Actually,' she continued, half turning to go, 'I think it's really sweet. Now I've got my two little slaves in love, which should make for some very interesting times.'

Interesting times, I reflected as the door closed behind her. The Chinese have a curse, *May you live in interesting times*, it says. Well, I thought as I shook my now slowly awakening lover, we certainly were living in interesting times at the moment. *Two* very interesting times, indeed.

I wondered what Anne-Marie would say when we told her that now Andy and I were not only lovers in the present, but also fellow travellers in time.

'Gone, you say?' Gregory Hacklebury slapped the palms of his hands down onto his desk with a crash that echoed around the library. 'Gone where?'

'I have no idea,' Megan Crowthorne replied, spreading her own hands, 'though I am already taking steps to find out. I have sent for Marjoribanks and he will arrive before noon. His people will find them quickly enough. The coach will be difficult to hide, to begin with.'

'And Erik has gone too, you say?' Hacklebury's features were contorted with barely suppressed anger. 'That's all the thanks you get from dragging the great oaf from the gutter.'

'I do seem to have misjudged him,' Megan admitted. 'I thought he was truly loyal to me, but then we do not yet know the circumstances. The girl may well have forced

him. There is a pistol missing that belonged to Garfield.'

'Garfield, yes,' Hacklebury said, frowning in concentration. 'I can't believe the bitch managed to get the jump on the fellow. Garfield has been a poacher and a gamekeeper for twenty or more years and yet he allows a slip of a girl to plunge a knife through his neck.'

'Presumably she managed to, er, distract him,' Megan suggested.

'Very resourceful for a peasant wench,' Hacklebury snapped. He leaned back in his chair and took a deep breath. 'And Angelina?' he asked after a moment.

Megan swallowed, trying to avoid his direct gaze. 'The bitch dog is safe in her kennel,' she replied quietly. 'I have left Burrows to watch over her in Erik's stead. She'll not be going anywhere, not until we want her to.'

'Good,' Hacklebury said. 'At least that's something. Without Maud, we may yet have need of little Angelina.'

'I think,' Megan began slowly, 'that it will be best if we avoid any situation where we might have need of Angelina. Short of drugging her into a stupor, she'll be of absolutely no use to us, for she'll hardly comply with your wishes now, will she?'

'No.' Hacklebury sighed. 'No, she'll certainly not.'

'Which makes her a distinct liability,' Megan continued, 'if not an outright danger to both of us.'

'Well, she'll not be doing much in the way of talking,' Hacklebury snickered, 'not in that little dog get-up you've put her in. Best you keep her that way for the foreseeable future, I reckon.'

'I'm not entirely sure that's a wise idea,' Megan disagreed. Her fingers twisted together in front of her as Hacklebury looked up in surprise.

'Well, we certainly cannot release her,' he protested.

Megan shook her head. 'No,' she agreed, 'that we cannot do, and I was not about to suggest we should.' She paused, looking down at the space between her feet and the desk. 'What I was going to suggest,' she went on, speaking very quietly, 'is that Angelina's usefulness is far outweighed by the danger she represents to us, especially if young Maud opens her mouth to the wrong people.'

'I cannot see Maud doing that,' Hacklebury asserted. 'The girl has committed murder, don't forget, and she'll know she'll be sure to swing for it if she's caught.'

'True,' Megan agreed, 'but as you say, she's little more than a peasant and we cannot be sure she will continue to use what brains she has. Besides, we still have to explain Garfield's death, and if the law then catches up with her, who knows what she might say about the goings on here? No, I think I have a better solution. A much better solution, in my opinion.'

'Which is?'

'Which is that we lay the blame for the killing on Angelina and Erik, or better still, solely on Angelina. That way the law will be looking for her, a woman they cannot possibly hope to find.'

'Unless they come here poking around. This place is big, but not that big.'

'They cannot find what isn't here,' Megan said firmly.

'You mean move her?'

'Not exactly. Once we've established that she has killed and fled with what is now rightfully your property, all your problems are over, just so long as she is never actually found and questioned. I suggest we take steps to ensure she is never found.'

She pursed her lips, and then set them in a taut line.

Hacklebury stared up at her for a few moments and then nodded slowly. 'Yes,' he said deliberately, his eyes narrowing. 'Yes, I believe you are right. However...'

'You need not trouble yourself over the details,' Megan put in hurriedly. 'I shall attend to those myself. It will be little different to disposing of any animal that has outlived its usefulness, I promise you.'

'Apparently not,' Hacklebury said. He stood up and deliberately stretched his long body. 'Then to you shall fall the duty, Meg, for there is none better suited, I reckon. However, talking of suited, perhaps I should take one last farewell of my little bitch hound?'

The corner of Megan's mouth twitched and she averted her gaze from his once again. She nodded. 'Yes,' she said, turning away towards the door. 'Yes, perhaps that would be appropriate.' She paused with one hand on the door handle. 'Allow me an hour or so, and I'll return for you once the bitch is in a suitable condition not to give you too much trouble. Then I think it will indeed be time for the master to bid his doggie a fond and final farewell.'

'Teenie! Teenie! What's the matter!'

I opened my eyes, blinked, and stared around me in some confusion, the now familiar surroundings of Anne-Marie's kitchen taking me somewhat by surprise. I gripped the edge of the table and blinked again, staring back at Andy in temporary bewilderment.

He reached out and placed a hand over mine. 'Did you go back again?' he asked, his voice unsteady. 'Only you went really blank there for a few seconds, just like before.'

Slowly, I shook my head. 'No, not this time,' I whispered, 'not as such, anyway. It was like the other time, only I wasn't there myself, but I could see and hear everything as though I was a fly on the wall.'

'What did you see?' Anne-Marie began filling a mug with coffee from the percolator. 'Hacklebury, I suppose? And Megan?'

I nodded. 'Yes, both of them. They were talking about me, Angelina, I mean, and about the girl they used for the fake wedding ceremony.' I paused, and then began relating the conversation I had somehow overheard from more than one hundred and thirty years earlier.

'But why would Mad Meg lie to him like that?' Andy demanded.

Anne-Marie let out a little snort of derision and rolled her eyes. 'Because, that way she gets rid of Angelina once and for all,' she said, with an edge to her voice that usually only harassed schoolteachers manage to perfect.

'By killing the girl Maud?' Andy protested. 'How does that get rid of Angelina?'

'It doesn't, not as such,' I said, 'but Hacklebury will *think* Angelina is dead and he won't be too bothered about trying to catch up with Maud, will he? He'll expect Maud to keep her head down, because as far as he's concerned, she's killed the gamekeeper fellow and stolen money and jewels from the house.'

'But Erik knows the truth and the real Angelina will still be out there somewhere,' Andy pointed out.

'Yes, but you can bet your woolly stockings Megan will move heaven and earth to catch up with them,' Anne-Marie said. 'And when she does, she isn't going to let them hang around to spill the beans, is she?'

'But meanwhile, the law will be looking for Angelina anyway,' Andy countered. 'What if they get to her first? She, *you*, can't go to them voluntarily. If only I'd got into Indira's body a few seconds earlier, she wouldn't have stabbed that bloke.'

'Well, it's a bit late to worry about that now,' I reasoned. 'All I know is that Hacklebury is going to let Megan kill Maud, thinking she's Angelina, so Megan will have a clear field for whatever devious plan it is she's hatching.'

'Well, whatever it is,' Anne-Marie said, 'it means she's got Hacklebury all to herself again.'

'I can't believe that one woman could be so bloody evil to another,' Andy declared. 'I mean, I knew from what Teenie said that she was a nutter, but to actually kill another person in cold blood...'

'After what she did to me,' I said, 'killing someone hardly seems that much. Dying would be preferable to spending years being treated like a damned dog. If you hadn't come to my rescue, who knows how many years Angelina and me might have spent trapped in that awful dog outfit. From the way Megan was talking before, I reckon it was meant to be a life sentence.'

'And now this other poor bitch has taken your place,' Anne-Marie said, 'although it looks like her life sentence is going to be a very short one.'

'Get that lacing tighter, Burrows.' Megan Crowthorne leaned back against the wall of the outbuilding, her mouth twisted sideways into the grin that was peculiarly her own. 'Come on, man, pull her gut in.'

The servant, Burrows, tugged dutifully on the laces that tightened the midriff section of the dog costume around the prone girl's body, and shook his head. 'Seems like she must have put on a bit of weight these past couple of days,' he muttered. 'Either that or that great oaf Erik was even stronger'n he looked.' He pulled again, and now there were the first signs of life returning to the drugged girl, for the head - which Megan had taken the precaution of enclosing in the dog-faced hood herself before summoning Burrows to help - began to stir, and faint groans emanated from within; groans made incomprehensible by the cunning gagging plate Megan had secured in place first.

Burrows still thought the girl he was preparing was Angelina. Only Tom Quickby, who had eventually not only found the body of Garfield, but had finally released Megan from the dog suit, knew the truth and he was temporarily out of the way, sworn to silence and despatched to bring the investigator, Marjoribanks, who Megan was certain would be able to track down the real Angelina and silence her as she herself intended to silence Maud.

She peered down at the helpless, brown-clad figure and its four curiously matched limbs with their artificial paws and the expressionless dogface, through which she could now see eyes finally beginning to open. She cut short a laugh, for it was uncanny how the dog suit removed all signs of individuality from its wearer, whoever she might be. Yes, Hacklebury would have his final moments of enjoyment with what he thought was Angelina, and he would never be any the wiser, if Megan had anything to do with it.

She grimaced and turned away towards the door, trying to shut out the memories of the hours she had spent within the suit's tight embrace, unable to speak and unable to stand other than on all fours, as she had been forced to stand while that brattish whore Angelina forced Erik to take her at pistol point. 'Just you wait, bitch!' she hissed beneath her breath as she emerged into the crisp afternoon sunlight. 'I'll repay you for that, be assured of it. No, I'll not have Marjoribanks kill you straight off, that I won't. Once the hue and cry has died down, methinks I'll have you back here for a little while longer. T'would be a shame to leave your nice kennel empty, that it would!'

'This whole thing is starting to get on my nerves now,' I said. We were sitting in the lounge and nearly two hours had passed since our belated breakfast - two hours during which we had discussed and debated the various events over and over, all of us promoting various theories and possibilities, but none of us coming even vaguely close to suggesting what our next course of action ought to be, nor even if there was a next course of action that would have any value in it.

For my own part, I was simply convinced the next course of action lay not in our own time, but back in the past, and that meanwhile I was merely going through the motions until I was whisked back again to continue whatever it was I had initially been taken back to do. Whether or not I once again might have an ally in Andy/Indira, of course I had no idea, any more than I could guess when my next time trip might happen.

It was a disconcerting feeling and one I have never quite managed to come to terms with, even now all these years later and after so many trips back to so many differing times and situations. It was also complicated by another feeling of unease caused by my new distrust of myself, for I was growing more and more convinced there was something within my psyche that was at least as bad as whatever it was that drove Hacklebury, though I fervently hoped it was not in the same league of depravity as whatever it was motivating Megan Crowthorne.

'It's just not fair,' I muttered, knowing I sounded about nine or ten years old as I said it. 'I didn't ask for any of this stuff and now I feel as if I'm no longer in control of my own life.'

'Join the club,' Anne-Marie smiled across at me. 'None of us are ever in control of our own lives.'

I didn't find her attempt at jocularity very funny and I pouted back defiantly. 'This is hardly the same,' I retorted pointedly. 'And it's getting worse. It was bad enough going back there and waking up as Angelina, but now these sort of flashback things on top of it all... it's too much, honestly it is!'

Andy, who was sitting in the armchair next to mine, reached across and gently stroked my forearm. 'Teenie, there's not much we can do about it,' he said soothingly. 'But maybe, if we can get to the bottom of what actually happened to Hacklebury and Mad Meg, maybe then it'll all stop.'

'Maybe it will,' I agreed, sighing, not sounding at all convinced. 'But just how do we go about finding out? Everything we've tried has either ended up at a dead end, or else given us bits and pieces that don't fit together. The only place we're likely to get any answers is back there, and I'm not sure I like the idea of going back there again. It was bad enough before, but now I know Megan is actually capable of murder. What about if she *does* catch up with Angelina? She may keep her alive for a while to torment her, but she can't risk keeping her around for too long. Even she'll realise that. If Hacklebury finds out she's been lying to him, there'll be one hell of a row. No, if Megan catches her, Angelina won't last long and what if I happen to be her when the time comes?'

'I don't think Mad Meg will be able to kill you,' Anne-Marie reasoned, 'not even if she does kill Angelina while you're in her body. If that does happen, then I reckon you'll just come straight back here and that'll be an end to it.'

'Oh, you *reckon*, do you?' I asked sarcastically. 'But can you *guarantee* it, eh?' I stared straight at her and Anne-Marie for once looked nonplussed. 'No,' I continued quietly, 'you can't guarantee anything any more than I can, and it won't be you that's at risk, either, will it?'

'No, it won't,' she agreed, shaking her head, 'and I wish there was something I could say or do that might help, but there isn't, not unless I get whisked back with you eventually.'

'And maybe turn up as a Hacklebury?' I suggested.

Anne-Marie smiled. 'Well, that would solve all the problems, wouldn't it?' she said. 'If I turned up as dear old Gregory, I'd simply whack Mad Meg over the head, dump her down the well, and that'd be an end to it. After all, you never lost your personality or real identity when you went back in Angelina's body, so there's no reason to suppose I'd end up as anything but myself, regardless of whatever body I was in.'

'But what's the likelihood of you going back in the first place?' I queried. 'I know Andy did, but that could be for a number of reasons, one of which you couldn't possibly duplicate, not with the best will in the world.'

'Maybe not duplicate, exactly,' Anne-Marie agreed, 'but who's to say it needs to be exact? There's something between all three of us, I reckon, and fate is a funny old thing.

'No, you're right, I can't guarantee much,' she went on, 'except that we're all going to get maudlin and miserable if we just sit around here doing nothing. I suggest we try taking our minds off it for a bit and let whatever's going to happen whenever and whatever. And I've got a few ideas that I *can* guarantee will distract you. In fact, they'll distract all three of us. No, don't ask, just trust me, it'll be a surprise.'

'Yes, well, I reckon I've had enough of surprises to last me a lifetime,' I sniffed.

Anne-Marie wasn't about to be deflected. 'There are good surprises and bad surprises,' she persisted, getting to her feet, 'and this one will be a good one, I promise. So, trust me?' She smiled down at me in her most disarming fashion and although I tried to resist, I knew I'd lost, at least for the moment.

'Call me a fool,' I replied, 'but yes, I trust you, though I reckon I'll end up wishing I hadn't!'

Maudie moaned softly and fought to open her eyes, her lids feeling as if they'd been weighed down. For a minute or so, as the vague patterns of light and shade struggled to form some vague semblance of order, she felt completely confused, wondering if this was just another of the weird dreams she had been experiencing since her arrival at the house. In those dreams her entire body felt tight, stiff and heavy and her limbs felt as if they were stuck in thick mud.

Very slowly her head began to clear and with it her vision, yet nothing she saw or remembered seemed to make any sense. The last thing she recalled was sitting at the small table by the bedroom window drinking the glass of wine the maid had brought in to her after her tea. She seemed to remember she had suddenly felt very tired, and that she then stumbled her way across the room to lie on the bed, but she most certainly was not lying on the bed now, for the surface beneath her felt hard and uncomfortable and, as things began at last to swim back into some sort of focus, she could see she was no longer even in the bedroom.

Instead, above her she saw rough-hewn timber beams, and above those what had to be dark tiles. Wherever she was it was not even inside the house, she realised, but rather some sort of outbuilding, too small to be a barn, but perhaps a storehouse or even a stable, for she could smell leather strongly now and from one side of her vision she could make out small heaps of straw.

Maudie made an attempt to lift her head, automatically moving her right arm to use her elbow as leverage. Except her right arm refused to bend, and her neck, when she tried to move it, felt stiff and awkward. At the same time she felt the 'thing' pressing down across her tongue, and when she tried to cry out, all she could manage was an incomprehensible animalistic squeal.

'Lie still for a while more.'

She blinked, her eyes darting around at the sound of Miss Crowthorne's voice, and she realised her field of vision was far more restricted than normal, even though things were more or less back in focus now. She blinked again, unable to believe what her eyes were telling her, but the pressure against her ears and cheeks and forehead provided further undeniable evidence. She was wearing some kind of hood, and the reason she could not see properly to either side was that she was looking out at the world through small holes cut in what her nose now told her was a thick leather hood.

With a concentrated effort, she managed to tilt her head slightly and found herself peering up at the haughty features of the woman who had originally brought her to the house. Miss Crowthorne was standing over her, smiling down, but there was something about her smile that brought a cold chill to Maudie's cramped stomach.

'No, don't try to get up,' the woman purred, 'and don't bother trying to speak, because you won't be able to. Just lie still for a while and I'll explain to you what is going to happen.' She gave a short sniff, and then coughed as if to clear her throat. 'You see, young Maudie, not everything about this life is pretty dresses and lolling about in comfort. Our lords and masters aren't like us, as you're about to find out. They like to play their little games and have their fun, just like naughty schoolboys, for I can tell you, that's near enough what they are and what they remain until the day they die. They never grow up, Maudie, not one of them, leastways, not one of them as I've ever known, and they let themselves be ruled too easily by what they have between their legs. Show a man something that stirs his loins and you can lead him easily by his cock for the rest of his life, and that, little Maudie, is exactly what we're going to do here.'

'This is a little game, you see my dear, and one that dear Gregory has come to enjoy. As you know, I brought you here to take the place of a certain little slut - his wife, as was supposed to be - and that's exactly what you're doing now, too. I made her into a docile little bitch for him and now I'm doing the same to you in her stead. It's a shame you can't see yourself just yet, but you make as fetching a dog as she did, and he'll never know the difference, excepting in one place, and we're about to take care of that before he comes calling. He's not that different from the rest of his sex, but even he might just notice that you're a bit tighter'n his original bitch, but I have a little something here that will attend to that.'

Her hand came into view and behind the mask, Maudie's eyes widened in horror, for although she had never yet been with a man, she'd had brothers and cousins and knew well enough what a man looked like underneath his breeches. Indeed, she had held a flesh-and-blood version of the object Miss Crowthorne was holding up for her, holding it and stroking it for her cousin Ned's best friend, Billy Smith, behind the barn at the smallholding where Cousin Ned lived with Uncle Walter, gripping and stroking it at Billy's behest.

She had known then what Billy Smith really wanted to do with that throbbing shaft, for her mother had explained to her clear enough only a few weeks before her illness finally took her, and her mother also warned her as to what could well happen as a consequence. Luckily, Maudie's ministrations had worked too well for Billy's intentions and he suddenly spurted his sticky mess all over her hand and arm, and then his proud shaft had quickly shrivelled and died again.

'I can see from your eyes that you know what this is, eh miss?'

Maudie swallowed with some difficulty and a small whimper escaped from between her dry lips.

'Well, this is a poor enough substitute for the real thing in some ways,' Miss Crowthorne continued, 'though there's many a man'd like to think he could match it for size!'

Indeed, Maudie thought, the leather pizzle she was now staring at certainly seemed a lot bigger than she remembered Billy's pink and purple weapon to be - bigger and far more sinister, glinting dully in the thin shaft of sunlight that suddenly pierced the half gloom of the chamber, its blackish surface seeming to come alight from within. She let out another squeal of alarm, this time a sort of mewling protest that came from the back of her throat, but this seemed only to amuse Miss Crowthorne.

'Get the bitch up into position,' the woman commanded, speaking to someone who was outside Maudie's current field of vision.

She heard a scrape of heavy boots, and then felt strong hands grasping her as dark shadows fell across her. All she could see momentarily was a buckle and part of a shirt, and then her world seemed to turn over as she was hauled up and twisted, other hands grasping her legs and arms. And then she was upright... but not exactly upright, for she was on all fours, crouched with her back parallel to the floor and staring down at arms that were hers and yet not hers, for they were far too long, dark brown in colour and ending in huge paws. She bowed her head further and peered back along the underside of her body. Sure enough, her stiffly braced back legs also had paws, and beneath her chest she could see two leather covered breasts that jutted down out of all proportion to the breasts she herself had.

'You'll soon get the idea,' she heard Miss Crowthorne telling her, and felt a tug at one side of her head. 'You see, for this game we've turned you into a little doggie girl. No, don't try to stand up!' This time there was a sharp slap of something that stung Maudie's behind, the pain dulled by the protective coating of the leather skin, but not so much that the sting did not make her jump and yelp.

'Dogs don't walk on two legs, missy,' a male voice growled close to her left ear.

14

'Mistress wants you down, so you stay down. Should I be putting a leash on the bitch now, Miss Crowthorne?'

'The nice red one, I think, Burrows, to match her pretty collar. Then you can attend to her and take her for a walk outside until the master is ready for her. Make sure she gets some water, too, and plenty of it. I found it amusing watching her when she peed. She's had her fun lolling and preening and trying to play the lady, now it's our turn. Here, you'll need this, and make sure you wash her thoroughly when you're through. The master isn't overly fussy whose hole he bores, but he does like 'em to be clean and sweet smelling, at least to begin with.'

I could at least pretend I didn't have any idea the sort of thing Anne-Marie had in mind, but of all the things I can be accused of, being a liar isn't one of them. No, I knew only too well that we were about to embark upon another round of her peculiarly devious and deviant little games, and if the truth be told even further and more bluntly, I welcomed the prospect. Not just as a diversion, for that craving little fire was beginning to grow ever more insistent within me. That little ember that may have first glimmered when I discovered the trunks of clothing in the loft space at the cottage was now something that burned whenever it was neglected for too long, and in attending to its needs, it seemed I was only adding to its appetite.

The one time well-balanced, healthy and energetic, dare I say normal teenager, seemed not only a thing of the past, but a thing from a past that was long gone, only distantly remembered and, if regretted at all in its passing, then regretted only in odd moments of self-recrimination that were becoming rarer by the day. In other words - and they were the only words I could think of back then - I was turning into a proper slut, transformed under the influences of both past and present, which banished innocence forever and left in its place an insatiable desire that needed appeasing.

Anne-Marie had already decided I was to once again become 'Teenie-slave', which meant the same outfit I had worn at the club, but first I had to bathe and shave away my stubble and present myself for her inspection. She duly looked me over with a close scrutiny, and nodded her approval.

'My soft little Teenie,' she murmured, using the diminutive still even though I would have been at least two inches taller than her had she not been wearing platform heeled shoes, whilst I was as yet still barefoot. 'Maybe one of these days we should try shaving your head, too,' she suggested. 'You don't like long hair anyway, so why not give it a try? I could get you a really authentic looking wig for normal wear and—'

'No!' I recoiled in horror, shaking my head wildly. 'No, not my head, not my hair. They did that to me then, don't forget, and it was awful.' Or was it? I tried not to remember the peculiar thrill I'd experienced when the cool air had played over my bald pate, and how the leather hood seemed to fit so much more snugly afterwards. Yes, it *had* been awful, but had it been awful truly, or had I merely been full of awe? I didn't really want to ask the question, let alone find the answer, and if I allowed Anne-Marie to do to me exactly as Megan Crowthorne had done, then there would be no hiding from the truth, no matter how unpalatable it might be.

'Okay, okay.' Anne-Marie held up her hands, sensing there was more than the obvious distaste in my reaction. 'It was only a suggestion. You know I'd never do anything to you I didn't think you'd like and want.'

But if I didn't know what I liked and wanted, how could *she* hope to? I didn't voice this doubt, but it was there all the same, and I wondered how far I would have resisted had she pursued the subject. Maybe not far enough, I suspected, and although I shivered slightly at the recollection and the possibility, I decided now was most definitely neither time nor place. I would be Teenie-slave willingly enough, but for the present, I would be Teenie-slave with hair.

As for the future, time alone would tell. As for the past...

Chapter 2

Maudie was still in a state of shock, but not shocked enough that she did not now know what was happening to her, and as the full realisation of the madness increased, she grew more and more terrified.

She had known from the very beginning this was an odd household. The master-servant relationship between Gregory Hacklebury and Megan Crowthorne was far from what Maudie would normally have expected, so much so that, on the few occasions when Maudie had seen the pair of them together, although Megan had been painfully polite and formal with her employer, Maudie had been left with the impression that it was really the woman who was pulling all the strings here and that Hacklebury only thought he was in charge.

There was also the mystery concerning the real Angelina. The reluctant bride was still very much alive, that much Maudie knew from snippets of conversation between the other servants she had overheard, but where she was Maudie had no idea. She presumed the girl was ill, for she had heard references to her being 'confined', but it had also occurred to her that maybe Angelina was actually already pregnant and was being kept out of sight until after her bastard was born. Maudie knew people from the better off classes could be so funny about things like that.

Now, however, she was far from sure either of her suppositions was anywhere near accurate, for Megan had made references to Angelina and this awful leather carcass into which Maudie had now been laced. She shook her head and tried to blink away the tears of terror and humiliation. Could they really have done something like this to one of their own kind? It was truly awful to think people could be so depraved, and the way in which Megan and Burrows had so calmly robbed her of her virginity earlier still seemed too horrible to be real.

She tried to turn herself around in order to see the doorway, backing in a circle to her left, shuffling awkwardly around the leash that was tethered to the floor ring and which kept her on all fours in the dog-like pose. The cool draft from the opening reminded her the dog suit did not cover her crotch area, which also felt even more vulnerable since Megan delighted in informing her that her pubic hair had been removed while she lay unconscious earlier.

Slowly, Maudie began to comprehend... Angelina had, indeed, been kept a prisoner in this hideous disguise, but something had happened to her and now Maudie was being used to take her place once again, only this time not as the lady of the house in luxurious surroundings and in fine gowns, but as a bitch dog with a hideously pug-snouted face and huge lopping ears attached to a hood that would ensure her real identity remained hidden.

Why it was so important that she appear like this, Maudie had no idea, but she was now convinced these people were both evil and sick, and that there was no love lost between Megan Crowthorne and the real Angelina. She had heard Megan muttering to herself from the doorway, and the threats the supposed maidservant had been mouthing had sent a chill of dread throughout Maudie's imprisoned body, so that even inside the leather skin she shivered uncontrollably.

The sound of approaching footsteps and muffled conversation made her freeze once more. The voices continued outside for several seconds, but with her ears covered by the thick leather, she could not identify them. She guessed, however, the female had to be Megan, and it was no surprise when the woman finally stepped into the room. Neither was it a surprise when Maudie saw that her companion was Hacklebury.

'You've said nothing, I trust?' he asked.

Megan Crowthorne shook her head. 'I don't have conversations with dogs,' she grunted. 'Dogs simply follow instructions, that's all. I've had her cleaned up and well watered. She'll be no more compliant than before, but I can give her a sound switching to remind her, if you like.'

'Thank you, but no,' Hacklebury demurred. 'I can take care of such things for myself. Pass me one of the crops from the rack, if you please. Yes, the shorter one, I think. There's not a lot of room in here.'

Maudie let out a low moan and tried to turn her head to see what was happening as Hacklebury moved behind her, but the stiff collar hampered her movements, and then Megan grasped her snout and pulled it around straight, stooping to stare into her eyes.

'Be still, bitch!' the woman hissed. 'Be still or anything the master does now I'll double up on afterwards. Unruly hounds need to be taught obedience and you are most certainly unruly.'

There was a brief swishing sound from behind Maudie, and suddenly a line of fire erupted across her buttocks. She let out a long, high-pitched howl and jumped forward, almost overbalancing on her stiffened legs and arms, but Megan had hold of her collar and held her fast and upright.

Again the swishing sound cut through the air and a second fireball exploded. Even with the protection afforded by the leather, which covered most of her buttocks, Maudie shrieked through her masked mouth and tried to rear up. Megan, however, was far too strong for her.

'Hold, bitch!' the cruel maidservant exclaimed. 'Be still, or t'will be all the worse for you. Have at her, Master Hacklebury. Bring the bitch to heel, sir.'

A third, fourth and fifth stroke fell and Maudie felt as though her whole rump was on fire. She sobbed uncontrollably and all four of her limbs trembled in fear and pain, but her tormentor was not prepared to allow her any respite. Once again Megan urged Hacklebury on, and once again he delivered a ferocious blow, the crop striking the taut hide with a resounding slap that seemed to echo around the bare-walled chamber. Tears streamed from Maudie's eyes, soaking the leather of her mask.

'Six will do,' she dimly heard Hacklebury announce. 'You can give her more later, if you like, Meg. But for me, I have something else to give her in the meantime. See if the bitch is ready for me. The damned buttons on these breeches are a curse and

no mistaking.'

Now Megan moved around behind Maudie and the poor girl stiffened as she felt cool fingers probing between her thighs for the unprotected area, feeling between the leather lips that framed her own nether ones. She heard Megan's low curse.

'Damn her, but she's dry as a bone!' she cried.

Hacklebury laughed from somewhere further behind. 'A change from before, I venture,' he observed. 'Last time the whip brought her on like an overflowing well.'

'Perhaps she's tiring, Master Hacklebury,' Megan suggested. 'But ne'er mind, my sweet laddie, I have the very thing here. Now hold, bitch and don't dare you move, else I'll have that crop to you again straight off.'

The cool fingers returned now, but this time they felt different. Maudie stifled a whimper as she realised what Megan was doing - prising her open and smearing something slippery into the mouth of her sex, working it in and massaging the interior of her passage, the slippery digits running back and forth across her nubbin, which refused to respond and even seemed to shrink, mirroring her terror.

Finally, the invaders slid clear and Maudie was aware of Megan standing up and moving back around beside her head.

'That will do it,' his devoted servant informed Hacklebury evenly. 'And she feels good and tight today, which should be all the better for you, my angel.'

'Aye, tight is good indeed.'

Maudie heard Hacklebury grunt, and then she felt something pressing against her sex. She closed her eyes, bracing herself for the inevitable she once again was powerless to prevent.

If Anne-Marie had noticed my latest 'flip-back', as I now privately thought of these curious dreamlike interludes, she gave no indication and I guessed that, as far as she and the present time were concerned, my 'absence' could only have lasted a second or two. In any case, Anne-Marie was far too intent on what she was doing to have taken much notice of me, other than as a sort of life-sized Barbie doll there for her personal amusement and distraction.

As before, the corset was like a vice as Anne-Marie tightened it about me, tugging mercilessly on the straps that adjusted the thick rubber, until I could once again barely breathe. My mind flickered back to that dreadful leather dog suit. Could that have been any tighter than this now was, or had that merely been imagination distorted by more than a century? I shifted and tried not to wince as Anne-Marie made another adjustment to the middle straps at the small of my back, drawing them, unbelievably, one notch more before passing them through the other sides of their respective buckles.

'D'you know,' she quipped, walking slowly round me, 'it's incredible how your body adjusts so easily. There's no way I could have gotten down this far before, no matter how hard I tried. It's almost as if you're made of rubber yourself, Teenie.'

I didn't feel as if I was made of rubber, merely encased and braced in it, now almost incapable of bending at the waist and forced to breathe in short, shallow gasps from the top of my lungs, which caused my pushed out breasts to rise and fall in a manner I knew would be irresistible to anyone who saw them.

Whereas before I had put on the latex stockings myself prior to Anne-Marie fitting me into the corset, now she attended to everything, dusting each limb lightly with talcum powder and adding a touch more of the white mist inside each stocking before she presented it to my foot. I shivered at the delightfully cool touch of the silky fabric, knowing that almost immediately that chilly kiss would begin to turn into a warming embrace in the same fashion as the corset was already beginning to bring up a heat within my torso.

'Boots next,' Anne-Marie whispered when the second stocking had been smoothed into immaculate, gleaming position and the final suspender tab attached to it. My toes were already beginning to feel damp as I dutifully raised one stocking-clad foot, sliding it into the depths of the long rubber boot and standing awkwardly while my beautiful mistress laced it tightly up towards the top of my thigh. She worked deftly and quickly and very soon I was balanced again - if balanced was the word to use regarding those heels - each foot atop a weighted four inch platform, each sole raised a further five inches on dagger-like, steel braced points.

Now I was indeed considerably taller than Anne-Marie, and yet she had that uncanny knack of appearing bigger and even more powerful than she was, a power that came from within and from her peculiarly fierce conviction that everything she did was right and the rest of humanity had somehow been put on this earth merely to pander to her whims.

'Oh, this does so prettily frame your sweet pussy,' she murmured, bending down to lightly caress my denuded mound and the lips beneath it. Her butterfly touch sent a jolt of lightning surging up my spine and for an instant I all but lost my balance. I heard her chuckle and then felt one hand cupping my naked left buttock.

'Steady, little Teenie-slave,' she cooed, 'plenty of time for that later. For now, let's just enjoy all this nice and easy.' She bent down and I felt the warmth of her mouth as her lips pressed gently against my nakedness. I braced myself, waiting for the invading tongue, but she must have realised that would have been too much, and she was not yet quite ready to reduce me to the helpless wreck we both knew I would eventually become.

Maudie stood trembling and swaying, her mind reeling with confusion and shame. She did not fully understand what had happened to her, but she was shrewd enough to have a very good idea, and she was horrified to think her body had so brazenly betrayed her.

Her breath came in short gasps, the tightly laced midriff section of the dog suit preventing her from using her diaphragm in the usual way, and each outgoing breath was accompanied by a low whining sound. She closed her eyes, trying to force the memories from her mind and to regain control of herself, but all that happened was that her body was once again wracked with spasmodic twitches even though it was now several minutes since Hacklebury had withdrawn from her, and he was now gone altogether.

She heard footsteps again, recognising Megan's lighter tread, and opened her eyes slightly, peering up as the woman loomed over her.

'Well, we'll postpone your next whipping, bitch,' Megan laughed. 'That was very good, very good indeed. He had no idea at all and that's excellent. He's off to London now as happy as a pig in shit and by the time he returns, as far as he'll be concerned, you'll be history.' She bent down in front of Maudie and grasped her beneath the chin, tipping the muzzled face up to her own.

'You see, Maudie,' she continued, lowering her voice, 'he thinks I'm going to kill you - put you down like a worn out old mutt, don't you see, but I think that would be a waste. Besides, I may have further use for you in the future, you never can tell. Of course, you'll need to be properly broken, but I reckon after a few months as my pet little bitch you'll do anything for me, isn't that so? Yes, we'll keep you on, doggie girl, at least for now, but not here. No, I've a much safer place to keep you. It's not that far from here, but it's somewhere nobody will ever go poking around and only I know where it is. So come, my little Maudie bitch. Let's go for a nice walk in the fresh air and go find your new kennel, eh?'

Again I was certain Anne-Marie had not noticed my 'flip'. In any case, by now she had the rubber helmet in place on me, and the tinted lenses would have made it difficult to see if my eyes had glazed over momentarily. I'd said nothing about the first of today's glimpses of the past, not wanting to disturb the mood that was beginning to build. I could say nothing about the second now, for the soft rubber gag filled my mouth completely and the only sounds I could make were sure to be misinterpreted by my eager mistress.

And so I stood stoically in my enforced silence as Anne-Marie completed my outfit, smoothing the gloves up my arms and attaching the wristbands, which she once again clipped to the belt encircling my waist over the stomach and lung-crunching corset.

'There!' she exclaimed finally, standing back and clapping her hands together in a gesture expressing intense satisfaction. 'Welcome back, Teenie-slave.'

I felt my stomach twitch as the rubber dildo inside me seemed to grow larger, but outwardly I managed to remain like a statue.

'We'll just take you out to the garage for the moment,' she continued, reaching up to clip a short leash to the front of my collar. 'I need to see to Andrea and then get myself ready. We're going for a little drive this afternoon and we won't be back until late tomorrow, so there are a few things I'll need to make sure we take with us. And in case you're wondering, we're all going to visit Carmen. She's having a very special party at her place and I know how keen she is to meet up with the two of you again. She was most impressed the other night, most impressed indeed. She even offered me a thousand pounds for each of you, but I told her I wouldn't part with either of you for a hundred times that much, silly woman. However, I think it will be nice to share you both, just for a few hours, don't you?'

I made no reply, obviously, but dutifully followed as she led me from the bedroom, down the stairs and out via the kitchen into the spacious double garage at the side of the house. Aside from a workbench area and some ladders hanging from the rafters, the building was empty and I was manoeuvred into the centre. Anne-Marie let go the leash briefly, crossed to the bench and returned with a length of cord, which she deftly threw up and over the main support rafter above my head.

She drew both ends together and threaded them through the leather handle of my leash, drawing them through, and then tying them off in a crude bow. I eyed the arrangement curiously, hoping my tenure here would not be an overly long one, for although there was enough slack in the cord and leash to enable me to walk about a little, I could see there would not be enough to allow me to sit or kneel. Until Anne-Marie decided otherwise, I would be a mute prisoner perched on my ridiculous heels, and already I imagined I could feel the protestations in my leg muscles.

I opened my eyes and straightaway knew I had gone back again, not as a nebulous observer this time, but once again into the body of the woman I was certain was my ancestor, Angelina Spigwell and supposedly also Hacklebury. I blinked several times and looked down at the black-haired head resting against my chest before turning my attention back to my latest circumstances.

We were inside a coach and for some reason it had stopped, although where I had no idea. Without disturbing my sleeping companion, I reached out and drew the blind to one side. It was still dark, although I realised suddenly this did not mean it was still the same night - the night we started to make our escape. Days, weeks even, might have passed since then, although something told me they had not.

We were obviously still somewhere out in the countryside, for I could see the dark outlines of trees and bushes, and there, off in the distance, a hill rose black against the night sky, barely perceptible on this moonless night. I shook my head, marvelling at how dark the night was compared to any I had, or would, experience in my own time. From outside came the faint sounds of shuffling horses and their laboured breathing, but aside from that, all was silence.

With a sudden start of realisation, I fumbled under the rug covering my lap and breathed a sigh of relief as my fingers closed around the pistol. Its solidity and weight felt very comforting, even though I had no idea whether or not I could make the damned thing fire. I carefully eased the sleeping Indira to one side, wondering whether Andy had returned with me this time, or whether, when she awoke, it would be as her own self. I wondered what she would make of all this, indeed what she must have made of it when Andy and I were finally being whisked back to our own century, and she returned to her senses to find that she and Angelina were already well on the way to escaping.

And what of Angelina? I reached out again and carefully unlatched the carriage door. Well, Angelina had certainly carried on with the escape plan, that much was certain, but in the meantime, where was Erik, and had she indeed taken the massive Scandinavian with them? I assumed she must have, for someone had to have been driving the coach.

Moving slowly, and wincing as the rustic coach springs creaked beneath my shifting weight, I stepped down onto what passed as the road, a rutted and pitted surface of mud and fine stones.

I closed the carriage door as quietly as I had opened it and raised the pistol in front of me, peering through the gloom towards the front of the carriage and to the dark shapes of the near motionless horses. Where the hell was Erik? And where exactly were we? Find one and I would, hopefully, find the answer to the second question. The darkness seemed to hug me like a cloak, but not a particularly comfortable one. I stepped sideways, moving away from the carriage and into the centre of the road.

'Erik?' I called his name quietly, for I had no way of knowing who else might be nearby. At the same time I fumbled with the pistol, drawing back the hammer until I heard a loud click. Whether pulling the trigger now would be enough, I had no way of knowing. My knowledge of old weapons was limited to what I'd seen and read in history books. All I did know was that, if this was the same pistol Indira/Andy had taken off the dead man back in the woods, at least it was some kind of flintlock, so there would be no need of a lighted fuse to discharge it.

'Erik?' I called again, this time a little more loudly, and began moving up alongside the horses. Suddenly, from out of the bushes to the right, he emerged, looming large and dark. I started and took a step back, raising the pistol towards him. 'Stop there!' I all but squeaked, and he seemed to freeze, motionless in the darkness. 'I've got the gun,' I warned, 'so no funny business.'

'Of the things this business is, funny is not one of them being,' I heard his lilting voice. 'And necessary the gun to be pointing at me it is not. Going off it may be, and then in Erik a large and messy hole there will be.'

'Exactly,' I agreed. 'So, like I said, no funny business. Now, where are we?' I sensed him relaxing in the darkness, but I was not about to follow suit.

'The road to Salisbury it is eventually leading,' he said, 'but another twenty miles still it will be. As I said before, the horses rest are needing for exhausted they be.'

'So, how long have we been stopped?'

He shrugged and waved his hands to either side. 'One half the hour, maybe more a little bit,' he replied. 'The horses needing the same again they will be, for driven them hard I have. Rest also we should now, for we must be going far on the morrow if Master Hacklebury and Miss Megan we wish to escape.'

'Huh, and what's with the *we* stuff? How do I know you aren't playing for time here in the hope that they catch up with us?'

'Not yet will they even know that gone we are,' he replied steadily. 'No one will miss her and soundly sleeping he will be until well after the dawn.'

'And how long until dawn?' I demanded, and saw his head tilt upwards as he scanned the sky above us.

'Maybe hours three more,' he said. 'Maybe a little less.'

'And how far have we come so far?'

'Perhaps miles twenty,' he replied, 'but in a straight line travelled we have not. Taking us in different directions have I been, as you told me I must.'

I nodded. It made sense to zigzag about rather than to stay on one straight road, and the condition of the track on which we now found ourselves suggested this was not a major highway. 'Where were you just then?' I demanded, switching tack myself. 'Just then, I mean, when I called to you.'

He gave a low, throaty chuckle. 'The call of nature was I answering,' he said, 'and urgent most was it, to be sure.'

'Oh,' I said, for from the way he had replied it was obvious he was telling the truth. 'So why didn't you just sneak off, or were you about to when I called, eh?'

He sighed. 'Telling you I was earlier that Erik is now your faithful servant,' he said. 'Much wrong have I done and sorry it is that I now am. Atonement for that will difficult be, but try I will. Miss Megan a bad woman is and Erik now knows that and will safe be keeping you from her if possible that is.'

'Oh,' I said again simply, disarmed, at least in the non-literal sense. 'So, you're on our side now, is that what you're saying?'

'On your side I am,' he confirmed. 'Erik staying with you will be and to a safe place to get you will be trying the damndest!'

'Oh,' I replied again. 'Right then, so be it. If the horses need another half hour, let's make use of the time to decide where we're going from here. Salisbury may be a bit too obvious, especially if it's the nearest large town, so what other choices do we have?' I raised my free hand to my head, letting my fingers slide across my smooth skull, suddenly remembering I had no hair in this time. 'We obviously need to find food, and probably water and feed for the horses,' I continued. 'I'm also going to have to do something about my head. I can't go wandering around looking like this, not unless I want to draw attention to us. I can probably make some sort of headscarf if I tear up one of... no, hang on. Did we bring other clothing with us in the end?'

'A trunk there is on the back,' Erik said. 'Dresses and other things are there inside it and shoes also.'

'Well, that's a start, at least,' I said with relief. 'Now, do we have a lamp somewhere? I want to take stock of whatever else we have. I remember I was intending to take money and any other valuables that were lying around, and I get the feeling we're going to need to make use of everything we've got, including, and especially, our brains!'

And what of Angelina? I turned back to the coach and Erik reached up beside the driver's seat to take down the lantern hanging there. It was obvious she had managed to take charge in my absence and that she had contrived to do as good a job of escaping as I could have hoped for, and this seemed curious to me, unless she had managed to remain in some way connected while I had control of her body and so was aware of what had been happening in her own 'absence'. If that was the case, I mused, in that way at least she had the advantage over me.

I opened the door and began pulling myself up. This adventure was difficult enough, I thought, without my having to play catch-up after every little episode. It would be much better if I could somehow stay back here in time until this little story had run its course, whether or not my own efforts and contribution were likely to change the ultimate outcome or not, but something told me that wasn't going to happen, at least not just yet.

I opened my eyes, and this time I was not at all surprised to find myself back in Anne-Marie's garage, standing as she had left me, with the leash from my collar hooked via the cord over the beam above my head. I sucked on the gag and managed to swallow with some difficulty, breathing in through my nose as deeply as the stringent corset permitted.

Inside my rubber costume I felt hot and clammy. Suddenly my fetish garb did not seem so exciting and I wanted to pull it all off and simply go and lie down for a while, but I knew there was no chance of that happening. Gagged as I was, there was no way I could convey my wishes to Anne-Marie and any physical show would only be interpreted wrongly.

I grunted in frustration and shifted my weight again. How long had I been 'out'? Probably only a few seconds, no more than a minute or two at most if previous experiences were anything to go by, and I had only been standing here for a matter of minutes prior to that. I groaned. By the time Anne-Marie had attended to Andy and herself, I would have had a long wait. I moved again and this time the dildo shifted and I felt it pressing against my clit. A shiver passed up and down my spine and I screwed up my eyes in an attempt to resist the inevitable, but I knew that even if I managed to hold myself in control at first, there was no way I could remain standing stock still for much longer. The extreme height of my heels made that sort of discipline impossible, and the moment I adjusted my stance again the rubber phallus would be about its work once more, this time with a swollen nub to work against, unless I was much mistaken.

Damn Anne-Marie, I thought fiercely. She knew me better than I knew myself and this seemingly careless desertion of me had been well thought out. I was willing to bet she was not exactly hurrying herself back in the house, and that she was banking on returning eventually to find me already a quivering wreck.

The pressures on my stomach and breasts seemed to increase as I stood contemplating my plight, and my entire body appeared to be undergoing a heightening in sensitivity. The dildo was growing inside me, too. No, I knew that was only my imagination, but knowing it didn't make the sensation go away. I could hear my heart beating loudly inside my chest; the steady pounding echoing inside my rubber covered skull and the sound of my rapid, shallow breathing grew louder with every minute that passed.

I swayed suddenly and had to take a hasty step in order to regain my balance. The inevitable happened and the shockwave surged through me again, this time stronger and more prolonged. I pressed my legs together, which was a big mistake. Despite the gag, my squeal echoed around the garage and I knew my first orgasm was only moments away.

It was impossible, terrible, an awful indictment of what I was becoming, and I was helpless to do anything about it. I wanted to cry, to scream, to beat myself for my weakness, but all I could do was stand there swaying like a dumb rubber doll, and surrender in abandoned solitude to my basest instincts and cravings.

My first visit to Arundel had been with my parents as a child of maybe nine or ten, and my second was as part of a school trip five or six years after that, when I would have been fourteen or fifteen. My third visit was three to four years later again, or one hundred and thirty years earlier, depending upon the way you want to look at it.

At first I did not recognise the sleepy little West Sussex town, for although the streets have changed relatively little in more than a century, the castle back in eighteen thirty-nine looked smaller, less impressive and not at all like the castle that stands there today. And then I remembered what we had been told during our school visit, that the Norfolk family effected a huge renovation on the edifice later in the eighteenth century, as did many of their landowning Victorian contemporaries, who altered, or even built from scratch, huge monuments to their wealth, power and egos.

As the coach swayed slowly down the hill towards the town centre, I let the door blind fall back into place and looked across to the opposite seat at the sleeping form of Indira. *Ye gods*, but that girl seemed to spend all her time sleeping and could drop off, it seemed, in the most awkward positions. I wondered if Andy had come back again this time, or whether I would once again be confronted by the voluptuous body's rightful tenant. During my earlier brief visit, the girl had woken up just long enough for me to understand she was indeed Indira and not my twentieth century lover. It had been a bitter disappointment, for with Andy around I felt much less vulnerable, or perhaps just a lot less on my own. Either way, I hoped it would be Andy inside her this time around.

I felt the coach slowing further, and then it finally came to a stop. I waited, feeling the slight lurch as Erik - at least I assumed it was Erik - jumped down from the driver's seat up front, and listened as his heavy boots scrunched on the ground. A moment later he opened the door and stood looking up at me.

'We are arrived,' he announced simply. 'There an hour or so before darkness still is, but an inn we should find without delaying further.' It was good advice, for the air outside was already icy and I knew the temperature would drop even more once night fell.

'Have you seen anywhere we might stay?' I asked, drawing my cape closer about my shoulders. Instinctively I reached up, and smiled as my fingers touched the soft fabric of a bonnet. Probably not quite in fashion by eighteen thirty-nine, I mused, but at least it would cover my hairlessness. Angelina must have continued with my plan in that regard, and I smiled again as I found myself wondering idly if she had any idea how she had come to be bald, or whether it had come as a shock to her when she returned to her body during the escape bid. Whatever the truth, she appeared to have been coping well in my absence, and I found myself forming a newfound respect for the little lady, who was obviously a lot tougher on the inside than she appeared on the outside.

'Three inns there are where staying the night I think we may be,' Erik said. 'Others there may also be, further along road, but the sign over there is saying that rooms there are.' He gestured across to the far side of the street, and I saw the hand painted notice propped against the wall of an inn, beneath a hanging sign that proclaimed the establishment was called the *Swan*.

'You had better go over and ask,' I instructed, and picked up the cloth bag that was on the seat at my side. 'I presume we have some money left?'

Erik looked at me oddly.

I quickly tried to make a joke of it. 'Just like a woman to get confused with cash,' I said, and felt hopefully inside the bag. To my relief, my fingers closed over a soft leather satchel, the weight and feel of which told me it contained several coins. 'You go ahead and see if they have two rooms,' I continued. 'They may find it a bit funny if a woman marches in on them unannounced.' As I've mentioned before, they had some odd notions back in eighteen thirty-nine. A woman's place was generally regarded as being in the home and, if she travelled from it, there was expected to be a man around, not merely to act as her protector, but to make all the arrangements and conduct any business, including the booking of rooms and meals.

As Erik trudged stiffly across the road - it must have been murder even on his muscles, for the weather seemed to have taken a sudden change for the worse and sitting up top the carriage in this cold autumn wind for hours at a time would have been no picnic - I drew out the money bag, pulled at the drawstring and emptied the contents into my lap. My eyebrows rose and I couldn't resist a grin of satisfaction as I saw the silver and gold glinting among the coppers. I picked out a few coins at random and held them up for a closer examination. They were unfamiliar to me, of course, but I soon identified guineas, shillings and florins - that's two shillings in old money - and a quick tot up revealed the coins amounted to nearly twenty pounds, a small fortune in those days.

A further examination of the larger bag showed our wealth did not end there, either. My hand emerged first with a wad of crumpled banknotes, which I flicked through eagerly, my mood improving as I totted up the pounds to more than two hundred. Angelina must have been to a few pawn shops or jewellers along the way, I thought, but she had far from exhausted the haul of valuables from the house, for next I found yet another smaller bag, inside which, wrapped in various pieces of cloth and paper, I discovered numerous pieces of jewellery ranging from rings to a heavy choker set with what were clearly very nice diamonds.

'Bloody hell,' I whispered aloud. 'We're rich!' And by the standards of the time, rich we were. Nearly two hundred and fifty pounds in cash and probably still several hundred pounds in reserve in the shape of these flashy baubles. Carefully, I rewrapped the pieces and replaced them in their bag, also tucking the notes away together with most of the coins, though I took a guinea piece and two shilling pieces and slipped them inside my bodice, wrapped in a piece of paper I had torn from one of the necklace wrappings for just that purpose. I didn't want to be flashing large amounts about in front of people. Arundel would have been a pretty civilised place compared to many, but you still had no idea whom you might meet.

I closed the bag, leaned forward and poked Indira in the ribs. 'Wake up, lazy bones, we've arrived!'

She gave an exclamation of protest, jerked convulsively and opened one eye. I stared at her, waiting for her to speak. 'Oh fuck!' she exclaimed. 'We're back here again, are we?'

I sat back again and started laughing. This time, there was no doubting the current inhabitant of the voluptuous body opposite me. 'Yes,' I said happily, 'we're back here, and here this time is Arundel, in case you're interested.'

The inn was most pleasant and welcoming inside. Two log fires burned at either end of the roughly L-shaped bar and dining area, and accommodation and meals for the three of us for one night did surprisingly little damage to our funds.

We ate heartily of a mutton stew with potatoes and fresh bread, accompanying this warming feast with two bottles of a rich red wine that started to go to my head well before we were halfway down the second bottle. We said little, keeping to ourselves at a corner table well away from the few other patrons in the establishment, not wanting to draw any unwarranted attention. Then, having purchased a third bottle of wine to take upstairs with us, we made our weary way up the stairs to our respective rooms.

'Sleeping shall I be over there,' Erik said, pointing to the room opposite the one I was to share with my companion. 'The door leaving open I shall be, but bolting yours securely should you be.'

'Oh, we shall,' I assured him.

He nodded and patted his jacket on one side, where the slight bulge betrayed the presence of a pistol, of which I had caught a fleeting glimpse earlier. I wondered just where and when he had obtained it, for my original weapon was still safe inside my bag. Obviously, he had managed to convince Angelina of his switch of loyalties and I hoped her, and now *my*, judgement was well founded.

'Early we should depart on the morrow,' he added. 'I shall the horses and coach have ready for eight. The fellow at the stable I have instructed on this.'

'Then perhaps you would knock on our door at seven,' I suggested. 'I can't guarantee to wake up, not without an alarm clock. No, don't bother to ask,' I added, seeing the quizzical look on his face, 'just give us a knock and make sure we're awake, there's a love.'

Inside the room, I stopped and looked around. There was a small hearth against the wall furthest from the window in which a small fire crackled, and I saw a box to one side in which there was coal and a couple of sizeable logs. At least we would stay warm overnight and the bed looked welcoming, a heavily framed construction with a half tester, a canopy over one end and a high, elegantly carved footboard made of what I was fairly certain was honest to goodness English oak.

I was quite ready to simply flop down and surrender to sleep, but Indira/Andy seemed to have other ideas. She quickly began stripping off her clothing, until she was left standing in front of the dressing table mirror clad only in a thin shift, over which she had kept on her tightly laced corset. As I sat on the side of the bed, she began slowly fondling both her breasts, which bulged freely over the top of the corset boning, straining fiercely against the thin cotton that only covered their lower reaches.

'Amazing!' she breathed, her eyes wide. 'I always wondered what it would feel like to have real boobs.'

'And now you know,' I said dryly. 'Does it beat the padded ones you usually wear?'

She nodded gravely. 'I'll say, though it feels funny having nothing down *there*.' She dipped her head, nodding towards her groin area.

'Well,' I said, 'you've had this fetish about being a woman for so long, you might as well enjoy the experience while it lasts, though it may turn out to be not all you've been expecting. For a start, this Indira girl wasn't exactly under endowed, and those things are going to make your shoulders ache if you don't keep them well supported. Just hope you don't get to come back in that body again in another twenty years. Unless I'm mistaken, those boobs are going to sag something rotten as Indira gets older, poor bitch.'

The brown fingers were circling the nipples now and the twin peaks had reacted dramatically, for I could see them clearly outlined as two jutting points under the shift. Andy's brown eyes had suddenly taken on a sort of glazed appearance.

I shook my head and managed not to smile. 'Come here,' I said quietly, crooking my forefinger.

She turned, and her pink tongue slid across her lower lip.

'C'mon,' I urged. 'Or do you just want to play with those boobies all by yourself?'

She didn't need any second bidding now the penny had dropped, but she still approached me hesitantly, surprisingly shy considering some of the things we had indulged in back in our own time.

'Just relax,' I whispered as she stopped in front of me. Still sitting, I reached up and tugged at the thin ribbon holding up the shift. It slipped undone easily and I eased the garment back and down over her shoulders, letting it hang about her upper arms, but revealing now the full glory of those perfect brown melons. I blinked at the size of the nipples as they were exposed, for I had never seen any so large and long. Certainly they made anything I had, either in this body or in my own, look insignificant and puny.

'Wow!' I said. 'What a pair of absolute beauties!' They rose together as Indira drew in what, in her corset, passed for a deep breath. 'Oh yes!' I exclaimed, and reached out with both hands to gently squeeze those two nipples between forefingers and thumbs.

The effect on Indira was electric. She let out a tiny little squeal that could barely have been within the human audible range, and her back arched forwards.

'Oh lordy,' I muttered, gently rolling the stiffening flesh. 'This is going to be quite something...' I cupped my hands more, though still without releasing my two little prisoners, so I was now half supporting the heavy globes and could knead them as I played with the nipples. Indira groaned and staggered slightly, and I had to pause for a few seconds while she regained both balance and some semblance of composure.

She stared down at me and a languid smile spread across her beautiful face. 'My mistress,' she sighed, and I saw her hands move around to the front of her shift, where her fingers immediately began gathering up the loose folds towards her waist, exposing first her stocking-clad legs, and then her coffee-cream thighs, and finally the closely trimmed little triangle beneath which I could see a dark pink nubbin already starting to force its way out from between glistening lips.

I released one of her nipples and used my freed hand to guide all the material into her left hand, all the time taking the greatest care not to touch her exposed flesh. I had other ideas where that was concerned, at least for the moment, and once I had organised her own right hand free of the encumbrance of holding up her shift, I guided that towards the inviting target.

She made a small noise in the back of her throat and looked down at me uncertainly.

I smiled encouragement. 'It's okay,' I assured her, 'you just need to find out a few of these things for yourself. It's not only lads who like to masturbate, you know. We girls do it just as much, some of us even more,' I added, for I had gone through a year or so in my middle teens when I had been able quite happily to lose myself in my own fantasies and without either the fumbled musings of some inexperienced lad or the danger of falling pregnant and shocking my father back into sobriety.

She touched herself, gingerly at first, and I shaped her hand so her middle finger bent in separately and pressed firmly against the swollen lips. A little more pressure from me, and the finger disappeared inside without meeting any resistance. A moment or two later, following just the briefest digital hint from me, Indira was away, frigging herself enthusiastically while I once again turned my full attention to higher matters, two higher matters, as it happened.

Her first orgasm as a woman - Andrea's that is, for I doubted whether the original inhabitant of this lovely body was a stranger in that department - came quickly, and with a shattering effect that took me as much by surprise as it evidently did her. She let out a loud shriek, her eyes bulged as if she were being strangled and she lurched forwards, knocking me sideways before rolling off me onto her back atop the bed, the invading finger still going nineteen to the dozen and her stocking-clad feet kicking at the air.

Almost immediately there was an urgent knocking on the door, followed by the sound of Erik's voice. I had forgotten all about our protector, who must have thought Indira's scream of passion was something else. I rolled off the bed and staggered across the room, leaning against the door. Behind me Indira was beginning to subside, but I noticed that her self-ministrations continued, if now at a slightly less frenetic pace.

'It's all right, Erik,' I called out. 'I just stubbed my toe on the end of the bed. Sorry if I alarmed you.'

He grunted something in his native tongue, and then in English asked if I was sure I was all right.

I assured him I was and that he could safely go back to bed, and then listened as I heard his footsteps retreating across the landing.

'Well, miss,' I said, turning back to Indira, who now lay motionless, her right hand trapped out of sight between her thighs, 'I reckon we'll have to consider gagging you before we try that again, otherwise you'll have the entire town awake.'

The shift happened, as ever, without warning. One moment I was lying alongside Indira, both of us now naked and gently cuddling and exploring each other's bodies, and the next I was back in the garage again, only this time I was no longer alone, for Anne-Marie was standing in front of me and beside her was Andy, or at least I assumed it was Andy, for not only had our devious mistress effected the usual transformation into Andrea upon him, this time she had gone even further.

Like me, my transvestite lover was dressed from head-to-toe in rubber, starting from the bottom with thigh-high boots from which the sleekly polished legs of the cat suit emerged. Above this, and over the cat suit, a rubber corset, mostly black, but with piping and frilled dark-red latex edges at the top and bottom, constricted his waist and supported a pair of heavy artificial breasts that sat in moulded cups inside the suit.

Again, like me, Andrea had been hooded, but this was a hood with a difference, and for a moment I thought the face part had been left exposed, until I realised the flesh-coloured portion was as much a part of the thing as the black hooding section, and that the features had been formed from the rubber itself, giving the effect of a large pouting mouth, a wide nose and huge, staring blue eyes emphasised with what appeared on the surface to be extravagantly applied make-up and a pair of the longest, heaviest eyelashes I had ever seen.

'Meet Andrea the love doll,' Anne-Marie said.

I stared at the face in awe, and then looked down again, just to check that what I thought I had seen the first time was really there. It was, and what a contrast to the face and the rest of the body, for from the triangular crotch piece attached to the bottom hem of the corset jutted a massive black phallus complete with unbelievably large black testicles hanging beneath. The effect of this monster when set against and contrasted with the undoubtedly feminine appearance of its owner was truly spectacular and quite unnerving.

'Lovely, isn't she?' Anne-Marie chuckled.

Andrea, of course, said nothing and I assumed that beneath the facemask she had been effectively gagged, as was Anne-Marie's preference for most of her little scenarios. The doll face regarded me dispassionately and I saw the eyes were some kind of tinted lens. I wondered whether Andrea could see anything from behind them, for they certainly hid her eyes from anyone on this side of them.

'I thought I'd bring this for you, too,' Anne-Marie said. She held up what at first I thought was a black wig, until I saw there was rubber attached to it, some black, some pink, and as she released her grip on Andrea's arm and stretched the thing out for me to examine more closely, I saw there were features in the pinkish part, although hanging limply as they still were, they had a grotesque and distorted appearance.

'Gives a whole new meaning to the expression *putting your face on*, doesn't it?' Anne-Marie said, and giggled. She placed the hood-wig to one side and quickly began removing my original hood, though she made no effort to take my gag out, for I would have protested that I had changed my mind now and preferred just to spend a quiet night in. That, of course, was not to be, and a few minutes later I was standing there in my new face and hair, staring out at a world that had taken on a greenish hue, courtesy of the tinted lenses now covering my eyes.

'Brilliant,' Anne-Marie declared when she had finished fastening the neck and tucked it beneath my collar. She teased my hair about my dolly face. 'I only had the one with hair attached, as they were out of stock, but if we find a hat for Andrea, she won't attract any attention in the car. Besides, we shan't be driving through any built-up areas, so no one will get that close a look at the pair of you.

'Even so, though,' she continued, turning back towards the door leading into the house, 'I'd better find you both something to wear over that little lot, just in case. Now you just stand there like the two good dollies I know you are and I'll be right back.'

Chapter 3

This time the switch really did take me by surprise, firstly because it came so quickly after my latest return, and secondly because I dropped straight back into that inn bedroom apparently only minutes after I had left it, for I was still very much entwined with Indira, who was nuzzling greedily between my thighs and bringing me towards an orgasm of my own with a tongue that would have qualified for a Queen's Award for Industry had there been such a thing back in eighteen thirty-nine. Whether this was Indira or whether she was Andy inside Indira again I had no way of telling, because her mouth was currently occupied on business other than talking, but I wasn't really in a state to worry which was which just then.

Instead I reached across, twisting myself around and alongside her, so that even though she did not have to break the intimate contact, we were now lying on the bed in opposite directions. Whichever of the two was in control, they got the message immediately, and the soft brown thighs parted willingly for me to return the compliment. She tasted sweet as my tongue dipped into her and the reaction was immediate. I sucked on her clitoris, which although already engorged grew with astonishing rapidity. At the same time I felt her beginning to tremble violently, and her thighs clamped over my ears in a spontaneous reaction, but with such power that I would have had trouble trying to break free, had I been so inclined. However, breaking away was the last thing on my mind, especially as that wicked tongue of hers had redoubled its efforts. I felt the wave building and building. At last it broke with all the ferocity of a North Atlantic storm, and but for the muffling effect over my mouth, I'm sure I should have brought Erik running once more.

All too soon, though perhaps not in some ways, it was over. I fell back exhausted and shivering, my right arm hanging loosely over her body, which seemed to have lost all life save for a slight twitching of the legs. I closed my eyes and tried to control my breathing, which was ragged, almost tortured.

'Bugger!' exclaimed a tired voice, and I knew then Andy had indeed come back with me.

I kept my eyes closed and made no response, not yet willing to trust my own voice, nor even my brain, to organise intelligible speech.

'Oh sheesh!' she said, and I felt her shifting position beneath my arm. 'If that's what it's like as a girl, I reckon I wouldn't mind making the swap permanently.'

'It has its disadvantages as well,' I muttered, finally breaking my silence.

'Name one,' came the response.

I let it go, knowing there was no way I could as yet make Andy, even as Indira, understand what I was getting at. Besides, I rationalised, probably a good few men experienced a similar loss of all control over their bodies and it wasn't just women. Fleetingly, I did wonder if it wasn't even a woman thing, but if it was something peculiar to me, and my current companion in lust, of course.

'We should try to sleep,' I suggested, wriggling around until we were both more or less facing the same way. I raised myself up on one elbow and looked down into that beautiful face and those bottomless pits of eyes. 'We're going to have a long day ahead of us tomorrow,' I added.

Those eyes looked back at me quizzically. 'We don't need to have,' came the reply. 'If this is Arundel, then we're something like eighty miles from the Hacklebury stately pile and they don't have the faintest idea which way we've gone. We could afford to rest up here for another day or two and then decide where we're going.' She struggled into a sitting position and finally closed her legs, but then she changed her mind and drew them up into a cross-legged position. 'Let's say that Hacklebury didn't find out about our escape until late the following day, which is what you seem to have seen and heard. Meg's also got a few loose ends to tie up, including this Maudie party, and she's got to wait until this other guy turns up. That's given us about a two day start and, like I said, they still have to try to work out where we've gone. Yes, we could just get underway again in the morning and keep travelling, but where are we travelling to? Even assuming we could just keep running, what sort of life would that be, and eventually the money will run out, won't it?'

'That's true,' I conceded. We were currently pretty well set up, but even our little fortune could not last forever. Inns were cheap enough, but an inn every night, plus stabling and feed for the horses, that would gnaw away at our funds over a prolonged period.

'Besides,' she continued, and echoed another thought that had begun to invade my mind, 'I don't think we were brought back here just to go on the run. We need to settle Hacklebury's hash and Mad Meg's, too, and the sooner we work out a way of doing that, the better.'

'And I suppose you've got a plan, have you?'

'Nope, I haven't.' The beautiful features broke into the most disarming smile imaginable. 'But I'm sure we'll think of something soon enough. In the meantime, this is a nice warm place and the food is decent enough, so why don't we give ourselves some thinking time, maybe take a look around the area and consider our options.'

'You could have a point,' I replied slowly. 'Perhaps I should wake Erik and let him know, otherwise he'll be up getting the carriage ready before first light.'

Indira/Andrea nodded. 'Yes, you do that,' she said, 'and then you come back here - straight back here, that is.'

I looked down at her again and now it was my turn to smile. 'Why, I do believe you're jealous,' I teased, pinching one large nipple gently. 'Getting a bit paranoid because you don't have the only cock any more, are we?'

'Huh!' she snorted. 'It's not a case of not having the only cock, I don't have one at all at the moment.'

'You see,' I chuckled, 'I told you there could be disadvantages.'

'Maybe,' she sniffed, 'but you forget, I've already learned you don't need a cock to satisfy a woman. Being Andrea taught me that often enough, being Indira ain't going to be any different.'

I snaked out a hand and probed between her thighs, eliciting a sharp gasp from her as my fingers found their hard to miss target first time. 'Wanna bet on that?'

We finally slept, after I had woken Erik to inform him of the change of plans, and he undertook to inform the landlord early next morning we would be staying at least one more night.

I woke late, but I was still ahead of Andrea, who was snoring gently as she slept the sleep of the innocent, which she hardly qualified for. Outside it was already daylight and a watery sun was struggling gamely into the sky, which was all but cloudless. The fire had nearly died in the hearth and the air felt chill as I crawled out from beneath the covers. Records indicating that winters had been colder in the previous century were not exaggerated, I thought, grabbing my cape to wrap about my shoulders as I raked through the embers and tried to cajole them back into life by adding several of the smaller pieces of coal.

I looked around the room, noting the trunk now containing our spare clothing, which Erik had hauled up the previous evening, and sniffed. I smelled of stale sweat and felt sticky, despite the cold. What I wouldn't have given for a shower or even a modern bath, but I knew there was no chance of finding the former, and that arranging for anything approximating the latter would probably be quite a feat. I decided to settle for a wash-down, using the water that had been placed in the tall jug on the washstand, but not, I thought, until the temperature in the room improved. I glanced back across at the fireplace and was gratified to see the new fuel was starting to burn. Another few minutes and I would be able to add one of the large logs.

Meantime my mouth felt terrible, as if something had crawled inside and died during the night. On the small table in the corner, I found a junior version of the washstand jug and two thick glasses. I poured a little water into one of them and tasted it, somewhat suspiciously. To my surprise it seemed perfectly drinkable and not at all stale, so I poured more, rinsed my mouth a couple of times, and then took a longer drink.

'What year is it?'

The sleepy groan from the direction of the bed made me start, and I almost choked on the final mouthful of water. I spun round to find my lover peering over the top of the blankets, her black hair looking more like something a bird would have felt at home in. 'I didn't expect you to stir for ages yet,' I said accusingly. 'A minute ago you were snoring your head off.'

The eyes twinkled back at me. 'I was having a lovely dream,' she sighed. 'It was quite amazing really. I had this body, but I also had a cock that grew out when I needed it. Best of both worlds, if you know what I mean.'

'Wishful thinking,' I retorted. 'Be content with what you've got, same as the rest of us.'

'Except the rest of you haven't had the chance to try both sides,' Andrea/Indira grinned. 'Bloody hell, but it's cold in here!'

'You should have tried it ten minutes ago,' I said, indicating the fire now beginning to flicker encouragingly. 'That may not look like much, but it was all but dead when I woke up. I think it'll be okay to put one of the logs on now. No, don't you bother your lazy little body, I'll see to it. Having boobs seems to have made you idle.'

'Well, it's having all the extra weight to carry around,' she retorted cheekily, and then let out a small groan of satisfaction as she began massaging her chest beneath the covers. 'Well, this seems to prove I didn't dream everything that happened last night,' she sighed contentedly.

It took not a little willpower to resist crawling back into bed with my exotic, big-breasted lover, but I knew if I did, we would not only waste - maybe that's not the right word, but what the hell? - a good couple of hours, I would also feel completely exhausted again before the day had even begun properly. So instead, once the fire built up and the room temperature with it, I washed and dried myself and selected a suitable change of clothing.

For a few seconds I considered allowing myself the luxury of going without a corset, but I quickly dismissed the idea, for even this slender frame was not going to fit into any of the available dresses without something to compress the waistline even further. As I stood and grimaced while Andrea/Indira laced me in, I wondered how she was going to cope. She was no taller than me, but her figure was considerably fuller and there had been no dresses in the box that would fit her easily. All she had was what she stood up in, plus a short cape.

Obviously, Angelina had not seen fit to take time out to acquire clothing for Indira, and if she had been wearing the same dress for three or four days... well, I preferred not to think about that. My eyes narrowed as I studied her, now completely at ease in her nakedness and evidently enjoying her new body to the full.

'I suppose we could try lacing you a bit tighter,' I suggested. 'The blue corset looks as if it might be smaller than the others.'

'You're joking, I hope,' she said. 'Even the one I had on last night was crushing the life out of me.'

'Well, you won't fit into any of Angelina's clothes,' I pointed out. 'It's not like modern stuff, no stretchy materials and all buttons and hooks. We'll have to get you something new, always assuming they have some sort of dress shop hereabouts.'

'I'll just put the original dress back on,' she said.

I shook my head. 'No you won't. That needs a good wash, especially in this sort of place. Heaven knows how many fleas and bed buggy things there are. No, you can wait here and I'll get Erik to take me out to have a look around.'

'Oh great!' she exclaimed. 'And what am I supposed to do in the meantime?'

I eyed up her voluptuous curves, recalling her wonderment as she explored them the previous evening. 'I'm sure you'll think of something to distract yourself,' I replied, smiling.

I was beginning to think we were out of luck as far as getting new clothes for Andrea/Indira was concerned, but then we found a shop down near the river. The choice wasn't fantastic - most women who could afford decent clothing still tended to have it made to their individual requirements - but it would do, if only because it had to and there were no other choices to be had at the moment.

The proprietor was a weedy looking male, probably in his late fifties, assisted by a younger woman who turned out to be his wife. I explained I needed at least two new dresses for my companion, and that she was a little more generously proportioned than I was. The woman, who looked as though she might have at one time been quite pretty, but who was now fading fast even though she was probably not yet forty, smiled and said she had some things in the storeroom she thought would fit my requirements. As long as they fit Andrea, I thought grimly, and followed her through.

We found three dresses, all fairly plain, of the sort of everyday design the lower class women wore out during the day. I could imagine Andrea's reaction when she saw the dowdy garments, but she was in no position to argue, and so I paid for all three, plus another corset, some under-drawers, some new shifts and four pairs of silk stockings, which were all the shop had in stock. I had hoped for some shoes, but the woman replied there was a cobbler on the far side of the river and I should try there.

The shoemaker offered a greater choice when we finally found him, and I realised he probably supplied footwear for all the classes, not just for the workers. He was quite a craftsman and some of his creations were real masterpieces of feminine delicacy. I decided it might help soothe Andrea's feelings if I treated her to something really pretty, and settled upon a pair of red leather shoes with pointed toes and surprisingly high heels reminiscent of the Louis Quinz period in France.

'Made those back about five years ago now,' said the shoemaker, whose name according to the sign outside was Milton Faraday. 'They were supposed to be for George Middlemiss's young French bride, but the poor lass took with the fever and died. Great shame that was, her being barely twenty years old, but then these things happen all too often.'

I paid for the red shoes, and also for a black pair with much less formidable heels and a pair of doeskin ankle boots, the latter being for myself, Angelina being light in the footwear department.

'I can offer a nice line in proper stout outdoor boots, too,' Faraday assured me. 'If you're thinking of doing much walking around these parts at this time of the year, then you'll be needing something with a bit of wear in them.' I opened my mouth to assure him I didn't intend to do any walking, not in these nor in any other parts, but then I stopped myself and considered again.

'That's very kind,' I replied. 'Perhaps you have something you could show me.'

Of course, he did, and I left with two pairs of very functional looking ladies' boots, the one pair slightly larger, for I had noticed Indira's feet were at least a full size bigger than Angelina's and that Andrea had only just been able to force her feet into the shoes in which she had escaped.

'So now what?' Andrea asked as I finished buttoning her into the least awful of the new dresses.

'Well, I haven't eaten yet this morning and neither have you,' I reminded her, 'so I reckon we should go down and organise some food, and then maybe we could take a little walk.'

'You've come up with a plan, then? She twirled around once, and then wrinkled her nose in disgust. 'Bloody awful taste, these country peasants,' she muttered.

'No, not really,' I replied in answer to her question, 'but I thought about what you said last night and we certainly can't just keep on running. So we'll need to find somewhere to stop, and Arundel could be as good a place as any. If we ask around, we may find a house or cottage that's up for sale or for rent.'

We didn't have to ask far, for a brief mention to the landlord downstairs elicited the information that there were two or three potential properties, and all within a mile of the town centre.

'Up Mill Road there's a cottage for rent,' he informed us. 'Belongs to the Tamworth family and was lived in by the old aunt up until just before Christmas, when she passed on, rest her soul. Mind you, she was nearly ninety, so she couldn't complain. Then there's Banks Cottage, over yonder on the far side of the river. Used to be part of the Beasley estate, but that's been split up since the old man died and the two sons are happier living up in the city. I don't think that's been sold yet, but you could check with their lawyer, Bartlett. His office is just up the High Street. He'll also be acting for John Goring, selling off the old mill house. It's not been used these past ten years or more and John's moved down to Brighton now. Place'll probably need some attention, but it's sound enough in construction and it ain't about to fall down.' He looked around at the three of us. 'Thinking of settling then, are you?' he asked.

I smiled my sweetest smile at him. 'My doctor suggested I should find somewhere with pleasant country air,' I replied. I patted the top of my chest. 'I've been unwell, you see, and the air in London these days... well, I'm sure you know what I mean.'

'Indeed I do, mistress,' he replied. 'Only been there a couple of times meself, mind, but that was more'n enough. Dirty, smelly place London. Don't see why people carry on living there. Wouldn't surprise me if they didn't have another outbreak of the plague there, and that's a fact.'

I suppose I had a picture of a quaint little cottage leaning against a larger and possibly now derelict mill building before we set out to view the old mill house, but what we found when we arrived was quite different. For a start, this particular mill had not been situated along Mill Road, which would have taken us past a pub and inn called the *Black Rabbit*, which is still there to this day, but rather it was on the further, eastern bank of the Arun and more than a mile further upstream. Don't bother looking for it now, however; I've been back since and there's no obvious signs of where it once stood, only the remains of what passed for foundations back then, which are hard enough to find even when you know exactly where to search.

'Wow!' I exclaimed, as I stepped down from the carriage.

Erik, who had already alighted from his seat in front, towered over me as usual, but even he seemed impressed. 'Large it is,' he agreed, nodding sagely.

'Bet it's bloody draughty though,' Andrea/Indira commented from the doorway of the coach.

'Probably,' I agreed, 'but at least all the windows seem intact. Not much in the way of mindless vandalism these days, I'd say.' I pushed open the gate standing in the middle of a low picket fence along the front of the house. It bounded a narrow strip of lawn, in which someone had cut and tended two flower beds, although these currently contained nothing more than the withered remains of some former summer plants and a couple of hardy weeds. I stood and stared up at the three-storey edifice, noting there were even dormer windows in the roof, which effectively added a fourth floor.

'It's massive,' Andrea declared, trudging up behind me. She was still sulking because I had insisted we wear our most sensible footwear for this expedition. 'Far too big for what we need,' she added.

I pursed my lips, my mind stepping up a couple of gears. 'Maybe,' I said half to myself, 'and then again, maybe not. The main thing is, it's cheap.'

'And stuck miles up this god-awful track,' Andrea observed. 'This might just as well be the backend of beyond.'

'Yes.' I smiled. 'It might.'

By the time Anne-Marie led us outside to the car it was already dark, and even through the layers of protective rubber I could feel the drop in temperature. My mind went immediately back to Arundel in the autumn of eighteen thirty-nine, from where I had returned only moments earlier. Incredibly, although this was now February and that had probably only been October, as far as I could make out, it had been far colder there and I marvelled at how the ordinary people had managed to brave the extreme conditions of winters past for so many generations.

From a distance, and away from any street lighting, there would have been little about Andrea and myself to draw the attention of the casual observer, though up close our appearance might have caused the odd raised eyebrow. For although the long rubber capes Anne-Marie had draped about us hid the more bizarre features of our outfits, they did not conceal the extreme nature of our heels, and neither, I suspected, would our rubber faces pass close inspection.

However, once we were inside the car and seated side-by-side in the back, there was little chance of our condition being observed, nor of anyone realising that beneath the capes our arms were bound helplessly behind us.

'What a well-behaved pair of dollies you are,' Anne-Marie enthused as she adjusted the rubber folds across our chests and fastened seat belts over them. 'Now you just sit there nice and quiet and we'll go for a nice little drive together.'

The journey was relatively uneventful, although every time the tyres hit any unevenness in the road's surface I squirmed as the dildo pressed deeper. Alongside me Andrea also seemed to be experiencing some embarrassments, and I assumed her one orifice had been similarly treated. The trip, which was probably not much more than forty-five minutes in reality, began to take on the proportions of an epic voyage, with me struggling to fight against the inevitable, not wanting to have to admit, not even to myself, that I could be so easily brought to orgasm by the combination of an inanimate rubber phallus and a bouncy car seat. Needless to say I lost the contest, not once, but four times, the final three climaxes coming virtually one after the other just after we turned off the main road and began a winding descent along a narrow country lane.

Carmen's house was set back even from this rustic piece of road, but thankfully, after one lurching bump over a rut just across the gateway, the approach was well maintained and offered a mercifully smooth final cruise of a few hundred yards. The building itself was nowhere near as impressive as the approach suggested, a nineteen-twenties or thereabouts structure of two storeys with a single storey extension of later vintage projecting from one end, to one side of which I could make out a double garage, and behind that what was either a large shed or small barn, though the exterior lights enabling me to get a decent view of everything else did not really penetrate that far back.

Anne-Marie drove slowly towards the garage although the open doors showed there were already two vehicles in residence, but at the last moment she veered to the left and negotiated the narrow gap between the side of the building and the end of the house extension. We emerged on the edge of a wide expanse of lawn, the lights from the house windows, and from a moon that emerged conveniently from behind the clouds, illuminating enough for me to see it was well tended and bounded on three sides by cordons of high trees.

'Right then, dolly girls,' Anne-Marie said, switching off the engine and hauling on the handbrake, 'we've arrived and now the fun can begin.' She got out, opened the rear door on Andrea's side and unfastened her seat belt. It then needed quite a lot of effort on both their parts for Andrea to climb out, and the same applied when it came to my turn, but eventually we were standing on the edge of the grassy area, caped, masked and our hands still bound. I looked around, expecting to see some sign of our hostess coming out to welcome us, but if anyone in the house had witnessed our arrival, they gave no indication of it.

I should at this juncture perhaps give a brief description of Anne-Marie's attire, for although it was in no way as bizarre as ours - she had to drive, after all, and might possibly have had to get out of the car, one never knows - she was still striking in tight leather jeans tucked into high-heeled knee-high boots, and tightly hugging her torso was a zipped leather jacket cut to emphasise her generous figure, bosom and buttocks alike. She also wore black leather gloves, so that only her face and head remained uncovered, giving her an aura of power and control that would have remained even had the two of us not been bound and gagged as we were.

'Now we have to walk down there through the trees,' she said, clipping leashes to each of our collars. 'Andrea's been here before, but Teenie, go very carefully. The path isn't all that level in places and there are usually bits of odd branch and twig all over the place, especially at this time of the year.'

And she wasn't kidding, I soon realised, for once we had crossed the lawn the trees closed in on both sides, blocking out almost all the light, a condition made even worse by my tinted lenses. I kept my eyes firmly on Anne-Marie's silhouette as she walked just in front of us, my right shoulder rubbing and bumping against Andrea's in the darkness, my feet occasionally landing on dry twigs that cracked beneath them, or stumbling against larger branches that fortunately were not so big they didn't kick out of my way. It was so overwhelmingly dark the only way I knew we were on a path at all was because Anne-Marie had told us we were. I was mightily relieved when, a few hundred yards or so further on, we emerged into a large clearing.

The moon had ducked for cover again during our perilous trek, but it chose to make a second reappearance a moment later, revealing an impressive looking stone structure about thirty yards in front of us. I say impressive because it was solid and high, but a second inspection showed there were several chunks of it missing, not surprising given that I quickly estimated it had to be several hundred years old.

'Welcome to Finton Priory, Teenie-slave,' Anne-Marie said.

I gawped up at the massive stone pillars and the heavily carved balustrade that had largely survived, although of the original roof only a couple of heavy beams now remained silhouetted against the night sky.

'Don't worry,' Anne-Marie continued as if sensing my misgivings, 'it's all perfectly safe. Nothing's fallen off these past few years and Carmen has a builder check it every few weeks. Besides, where we're going is more secure than an air-raid shelter.'

She wasn't kidding, either, for once we had entered through the arched doorway and trotted obediently in her wake up a central aisle that must once have been polished by the feet of generations of monks or nuns or both, we approached a huge carved block at least five feet high and ten feet from side to side. And we saw, as we moved around the side of it, it was at least a good eight feet from front to back. I immediately thought of an altar, but it had been built for more than just that purpose, because at the rear, a section of the stone had been swung away to reveal a doorway and stone steps leading down into the ground, their unevenness revealed by a pale light filtering up from somewhere deep below.

'You'll need to watch your head at the top here, Teenie,' Anne-Marie warned, 'but it's higher once you get down the first half dozen steps.' And it was, but in my towering heels I still felt as though my head was about to scrape on the rough-hewn ceiling. Anne-Marie went first, walking in a sideways fashion so she could keep an eye on my progress, but I didn't fancy her chances if I toppled forward on to her, nor my chances if Andrea, who was bringing up the rear, fell on top of me. Thankfully, however, the steps grew wider as we descended and we finally made it to a level area some twenty-five feet below ground level and maybe even more, for I had completely lost count of the number of steps I had negotiated.

We found ourselves grouped together in a rectangular antechamber, which I guessed had to be about ten feet by eight feet and which was illuminated by electric light units fitted on each of the longer walls. The roof here was higher than on the stairway, but even now it could not have been more than a foot above my head, and the overall effect was therefore quite claustrophobic.

'C'mon,' Anne-Marie urged, gathering our leashes and giving them a sharp tug. 'The best bit is yet to come.' She turned and made her way towards a sturdy looking door set in the far wall, and opened it to reveal a short passageway with a vaulted ceiling. A single lamp hanging from this ceiling burned about midway along its approximate twelve-foot length, showing a second door at the far end. Anne-Marie paused before it and knocked three times.

We waited in silence, but only for a few seconds, then there was the sound of a bolt being withdrawn and the door swung open. Standing close behind Anne-Marie my initial view of what lay beyond was very much obscured, but as she moved forward again and I passed through the door, what I saw was almost enough to take away what little breath my tight corset allowed me.

I realised straight away that my estimate as to how far beneath the ground we had come had been much too conservative, for the long chamber into which we now emerged stretched upwards for what had to be at least thirty feet, with stone vaulting supported by huge pillars set near to the side walls along its length forming natural alcoves at ground level. At the furthest end was a wide raised area like a stage, at the back of which several arches were lit by blue and red lights, giving an eerie backdrop to a scenario that looked as though it had been well underway for some time.

Roughly in the centre of the 'stage' stood a huge wooden wheel, against which a featureless rubber figure was bound in a spread-eagle position, straps securing it at wrists, elbows, shoulders, chest, waist, thighs and ankles, so that as the wheel turned slowly, the figure did not sag with its own shifting weight, but remained stiff and unmoving, like yet another doll. As we came closer I saw the rubber skin stretched over firm breasts and wide hips, but I knew that was no guarantee the victim was actually a female, any more than Andrea's initial outward appearance meant that she was actually a girl.

The wheel seemed to be driven by some kind of motor unit I could see standing behind the support beam on which it spun, and the rest of the stage area was deserted, although to either side there were matching empty pillories I guessed would be filled before the night was over. So engrossed was I at the sight of the slow spinning mannequin, that we had walked halfway along the main hall before I realised that the dozen or so dark recesses formed by the pillars on either side each contained a similarly garbed and equally silent figure.

I shivered slightly wondering just who they all were and how long they had been there, before another thought struck me and I tried to look harder at the next figure. Maybe they weren't real, living people at all. Perhaps they were simply the statues they resembled, placed there for theatrical effect. I peered through the gloom that persisted at this end of the hall, trying to identify and sort out straps or manacles that might be binding arms and legs, but the lenses made seeing clearly difficult enough even in good light, and this low level of illumination most certainly wasn't helping my vision.

'Good evening, girls.'

I recognised Carmen's voice, but otherwise the tall figure that emerged from the shadows as if by magic could have been anyone, for her face was hidden by a black leather mask and hood, the eyes and lips of which had been picked out in white for a truly devilish effect. The leather bodysuit was similarly decorated, the white piping lines emphasising breasts and waist and running down the outside of each long leg. The gloves and boots that encased her hands and feet were, I saw, part of the main cat suit, extensions connected to the end of each limb so that when she moved, Carmen appeared like some sort of dark insect, deadly on her spiked heels with glinting steel talons attached to the tips of her fingers.

Anne-Marie was clearly very impressed with the effect. 'Oh, now that I do like!' she enthused. 'Expensive though, I should think?'

'A present from an admirer,' Carmen replied. She nodded towards the illuminated stage area. 'As you can see, I'm rewarding him this evening for his generosity.' She turned back and appeared to study Andrea and me with a critical gaze, although her actual eyes were barely visible through the slits in her mask. 'The Dolly twins!' she exclaimed at last. 'Very sweet, I must say. Which one is which? No, don't tell me, I'll try to guess, and it'll be such fun finding out later on. Perhaps we could have a sort of competition among the guests? And don't for one moment think I'm going to be influenced by that one's big rubber cock. I know you only too well, Annie. That could just as easily be your idea of a joke.'

'Is anyone else here yet?' Anne-Marie asked, smiling confidently back at our hostess. 'We're a bit early, but I always prefer to be early rather than late.'

'There are a few here already,' Carmen replied. 'I had two mistresses and a master as houseguests last night and they're busy freshening up their slaves just now. Two of them spent fifteen hours together in one of the old penitence cells, so we thought it best to give them a bath and a fresh outfit for tonight.'

I felt the squelching sensation between my toes as I shifted my weight, and glumly wished that maybe someone would think about affording me that luxury, though I suspected it wasn't going to happen, at least not for some few hours yet.

'You want to run a brothel?' The huge brown eyes looked larger and rounder than ever.

I grinned. Well, at least Andy was still back here with me, so we must have made the last hop together. 'Not a brothel, exactly,' I countered, although there really wasn't another description for it. I opened my mouth to speak again, but then paused. 'Hang on a sec,' I said, after thinking for a moment. 'I only just remember being back here and I'm sure I never got as far as making that suggestion. Come to think of it, I'm not sure it *was* entirely my suggestion. I mean, a sort of idea was forming when we were looking around the house, but then the last thing I remember was starting back in the carriage, and then suddenly we were back with Anne-Marie again.'

'Then how—?'

I interrupted, quickly trying to put into words all the suspicions and theories suddenly doing an impression of a tumble inside my head. 'Angelina,' I concluded. 'She must have some way of knowing what I'm thinking, saying and doing when I'm here, and Indira must be retaining some of your memories and you some of hers. I know I didn't mention anything to you, so Angelina must have said it to her in the moment just before we came back here from the present.'

'You must be kidding,' my astonished lover snorted. 'Angelina prepared to run a bloody brothel? Doesn't sound like her, not from what I've heard from you, anyway.'

'But I don't really know that much about her,' I rejoined. 'I made a load of assumptions, but that's all they were. Maybe she's just prepared to go along with what she thinks I'm thinking.'

'Like running a brothel?'

'I wish you wouldn't call it that,' I complained. 'That's not what I have in mind, not if you mean a simple whorehouse where any old Tom, Dick or Harry can go for a quick leg-over. No, I was thinking about something a lot more sophisticated than that, something that would cater to the less usual tastes.'

'Oh my, we should have Anne-Marie back here if that's what you're thinking, but then I don't suppose they had rubber gear back here, did they?'

I shook my head. 'Not as far as I know, but there's plenty of leather - the dog suit and other things they used on me are proof of that - plus all the usual lace, silk, satin and so on. What they don't have is nearly a century-and-a-half of other people's inventiveness to benefit from, and they almost certainly don't have an Anne-Marie.'

'Well, I hate to point out the obvious,' Andrea drawled, 'but neither do we, not unless you reckon she's going to suddenly start time hopping with us.'

'Well, if we had a real need for her,' I replied slowly, considering this possibility, 'I wouldn't discount the idea. After all, you popped up in this time at a very opportune moment for me and I'm far from convinced that was just some sort of lucky coincidence.'

'But,' I went on thoughtfully, 'we don't actually need Anne-Marie, do we? I mean, we've both experienced her cunningly inventive little mind, you especially, so all we have to do is make use of what she's already taught us, and maybe change a few things to suit our own particular circumstances. I'm sure between us we could conjure up something the right people would be more than willing to pay handsomely for.'

'But why?' Andrea protested.

'Well, for a start there's the money angle,' I replied. 'Our funds won't last forever. Besides, as I said before, I don't think we've been brought back here just to play hide-and-seek with Hacklebury and Meg.'

'So instead you want to start a new career as a Madame, is that it? And I suppose you think I'm going to be happy to play the whore for you? I don't think that'll sit well with Indira when she's back in her body.'

'I'm sure there will be female clients soon enough,' I said. 'And I reckon we could recruit a couple of girls easily enough, especially if Erik goes up to London with a few quid in his pocket.'

'Ugh!' Andrea looked disgusted. 'I've heard about London whores in Victorian times!'

'So, we get Erik to rescue a couple of young girls, bring 'em back here and scrub 'em up and get them some decent things. Afterwards we can give them enough money so they don't have to go back on the street again, which means at least someone else will get something good out of all this.'

'After what?' Andrea demanded.

I winked. 'After we've settled Hacklebury's hash, and hopefully Megan's, too.'

'And how are we going to do that and run a brothel at the same time?'

'I think I prefer the term *House of Ill Repute*, actually.' I smirked. 'And that's all part of the plan.'

'Oh well, that's all right then,' she muttered, 'just as long as you have a plan. Silly me for thinking you were just making this up as we go along, but if there's a plan, well, who am I to argue?'

'Well,' I admitted, 'I only have part of the plan so far, but I'm working on it and I'm sure it'll all come together, no pun intended.'

Andrea pursed those full Indira lips and stared hard at me. 'Would it be too much to ask you to share this part plan with me, or is it going to be a surprise?'

'Only for Hacklebury and Megan,' I assured her, 'but if I tell you, you've got to promise to trust me, because this is likely to be just a bit tricky and perhaps more than a bit dangerous.'

She continued to stare at me for a moment, and then heaved a long sigh of resignation. 'How come that's not a complete surprise to me?'

Unless you've experienced it for yourself, it's more than just a bit difficult to understand how much of a struggle it can be to come to terms with a time-shifting habit that always lands you back in your own century mere seconds after you left it, but which deposits you back in the past almost at random. One time I would go back only seconds after I had last left eighteen thirty-nine, yet another time it might be days, even weeks later, when I next turned up there, and it would take me a good few hours to catch up and fill in the blank bits.

But I digress and, in any case, this particular stay in the past turned out to be quite a lengthy one, so much so that when I was finally whisked back to that huge underground crypt at Carmen's, I had all but forgotten what had been happening when I was originally there. But more of that in a while...

For the particular moment - that is in eighteen thirty-nine - I set about preparing to put my half formed plan into action, not anywhere near sure of how the thing would eventually be executed and yet somehow certain I would think of something when the time came. For now there were simply basic things that had to be done, and so I set about making sure they were dealt with.

I started by negotiating a price for two of us - Andrea/Indira and myself - to remain at the inn for anything up to a month, which was the time I calculated it would take to make the old mill house at least partially habitable. I then despatched Erik to find a local builder who was prepared to undertake the work needed. Then, having haggled for an afternoon with one Mister Jonas White and finally settled on a figure, I sent our giant Viking to London with sufficient funds to accomplish the task of finding our first recruits, and with a diamond necklace to sell for the best price he could get.

The next several days were really quite boring, although my sweet little Andrea/Indira was becoming adept at finding new ways to distract me and pass the chilly evenings. Initially, I was expecting to be thrown forward to my own time at almost any moment, for our last few time-shifts had been of short duration and taken place with rapid regularity. Now, for some reason, it seemed I was destined to spend a protracted period as Angelina, which considering we had fallen into quite a boring routine struck me as curious. However, *ours was not to reason why*, as Tennyson was to write a few years hence, so I contented myself with daily visits to the house to keep an eye on the builders (believe me, builders haven't changed much in the past century-and-a-half) and with finding a local dressmaker who could give substance to one or two of my own particular designs, and who I could trust to keep quiet about their uniqueness.

I also spent some hours with the shoemaker, who was more than happy to accommodate some of my more extreme ideas and even came up with a few modifications and improvements of his own. A very creative and perceptive man was Milton Faraday, and a craftsman who took the most impressive pride in the finished quality of his work.

'The ladies who wear these,' he said, presenting me with one pair of very long and particularly high-heeled boots, 'must be very special indeed. I would very much like to meet them,' he added with a sly smile.

'Oh, you shall,' I promised him, 'and I just know they will be especially delighted to thank the man whose work they are so certain to enjoy.' That particular penny was anything but slow in the dropping, and resulted in an immediate ten percent discount not only on the boots in question, but on everything else I proceeded to commission.

I had arranged with Erik for him not to return to Arundel for at least three weeks, for I did not want to attract undue attention by billeting two or three additional 'ladies' at the inn, and he could not have timed it better. Twenty-three days into the project, our builder had succeeded in getting the kitchen serviceable, the first sitting room at least draught proof, and two of the bedrooms up to a stage where they needed only rugs and furniture. He was also able to direct me to an auction at a farm about ten miles away where the grand total of six pounds purchased four beds, three chests of drawers, an assortment of curtains and a selection of floor coverings, all of which the sales agent agreed to have delivered the following day for an additional three shillings. As I said, the timing couldn't have been better.

The same afternoon my purchases were installed, our carriage trundled into the High Street with Erik perched on top, and when it finally came to a halt, it disgorged three rather unusual lady passengers. I had given Erik explicit instructions, which he had carried out meticulously, and so the girls did not immediately appear to be what they were. However, a good bath and decent clothing will only cover so many sins, so I thought it best to move them on to the house without further delay.

As they filed into the one usable sitting room, I had to admit Erik had done well, for they were indeed young and, in their new finery, more than passably pretty. They told me their names in turn and then I selected aliases for each of them.

'Best no one knows who you really are,' I explained, and they all nodded knowingly. Even at their tender ages, and with their careers still in the equivalent of the nursery stage, they were experienced enough to know a good idea when they heard it, and so Milly, Molly and Mandy came into being.

Milly was the eldest, though she was only just twenty-one, a tall brunette with a narrow waist and slender neck. She had large green eyes and a ready smile and in many ways reminded me of my real self, except that even I wouldn't have used some of her language under the severest provocation. I resolved to work on that part of her and without wasting too much time, either.

Molly and Mandy were actually cousins, as it turned out, both nineteen and with only three or four weeks between them. Neither was entirely sure of her actual birth date, but that didn't seem to worry them so I decided it shouldn't worry me. One was blonde and the other a sort of reddish-brunette. Both were pretty enough, although Mandy had one slightly chipped tooth, and both were bright and alert, causing me to wonder what a decent educational system might have made of them. I suspected that if my plan eventually worked and I was able to send them on their way with a decent nest egg, then the world outside might have to look to itself.

And speaking of nest eggs, Erik had excelled himself with the necklace. Four hundred pounds he gave me, and well pleased he was, too.

'Five different places tried I,' he explained proudly. 'One man fifty pounds did he offer, but fooled was I not. The eyes were giving it away, for greedy they were and too anxious he was to go up to seventy when first said I not. Knew I then that more was it worth.'

'You've done really well, Erik,' I said, standing on tiptoe to kiss his cheek.

He blushed, and then beamed like a child.

I found it all but impossible to accept that this was the same man who, only a few weeks earlier, had been... but then you already know about that, so I won't go into it again. Suffice it to say that Erik really did appear to be bent on atonement, and I decided there and then he was due at least some sort of special reward I could also use to introduce my little bed companion to a few joys of which she was as yet totally ignorant.

'Right,' I said, looking around at my five companions, 'in the morning we start cleaning and organising the usable rooms, and over the next week we should be able to get the rest of the house in order. After that, once I figure out the best way to get the word out in the right places, we start getting down to business.'

A moment later I found myself back in the crypt again, surrounded by flickering lamplight and a gathering crowd of fetishists who would have frightened the very life out of their Victorian ancestors.

Chapter 4

I suffered the distinct impression I had been out of my own body for more than a few seconds, perhaps not all that long in relative terms, but definitely my absence had to be measured in minutes, for the crypt was beginning to fill with figures. There had to be at least fifty people present now, not including the alcove statues, whose claim to humanity I had not yet been able to establish.

That mystery was not long in being resolved, for as I watched I saw the lanterns were now giving at least a semblance of illumination to the main nave area. They were being carried on curious curved frames strapped to the backs of a number of rubber-clad forms, that rose up in sort of large shepherd's crook shapes so the lamps hung about twelve inches above their heads as they moved about, with their arms strapped behind them in a peculiar single-sleeve arrangement.

A group of less hampered rubber figures was busily attaching the harnesses and frames, moving along one side of the wall and pulling forward each of the statue-like alcove figures in turn to adapt them as lamp holders. The green-tinted filters in front of my eyes gave the whole scene an even more surreal aura than it already possessed, making the black silhouettes milling about the place look like predatory alien insects. I glanced up towards the stage area. The figure was still strapped to the slow turning wheel and the red and blue lighting behind it was a reassuring contrast to what was happening nearer to me, which was beginning to feel more like a dream with every passing minute.

I felt a hand caressing my buttocks and instinctively tried to turn my head, but the stiff collar about my neck meant I had to more or less swivel my entire body from the hips up. I saw Carmen's skeletal mask, the white-rimmed lips drawn back into a permanent grimace, her eyes shining dully behind the slotted leather above.

'I have plans for you two dollies this evening,' she hissed, her mouth close to my ear, 'but first I have to win the rights to you. I love your mistress dearly, but she is so naive at times, I think I need to take a hand in the next stage of her education. When I win our little wager, I'll have not two, but *three* love dollies for the night and maybe for most of tomorrow and tomorrow night as well.'

My eyes widened upon hearing this. I knew Carmen had been impressed with Andrea and myself at the club, for we had excelled ourselves - if that is the right term for our wanton show of abandonment - but now it seemed she wanted to take things further. I looked around for Anne-Marie, but could see no sign of her anywhere.

As if sensing what I was thinking, Carmen spoke again. 'She's gone to get properly dressed,' she said. 'Soon we shall have a little contest, Anne-Marie and I, and the winner will take all. I have two slaves of my own I have staked against you, but Anne-Marie and I are also part of the wager. The loser will join you dollies as part of tonight's entertainment for the guests. I'll not spoil things by telling you more yet, but you can be sure I have no intention of losing, so it should be great fun.'

She laughed and patted my backside before turning away and moving off between other figures, not at all concerned at leaving me alone, but then I realised she had no reason to worry. I was gagged, bound, and unlikely to risk the stairs unaided, even if whoever guarded the inner door would let me pass, which I doubted. Besides, I was hardly going to leave without Anne-Marie, and neither could I warn my mistress that she was almost certainly being set up. I wondered just how Carmen was intending to fix the coming contest, but I had to wait at least another hour to find out, an hour during which, separated not only from Anne-Marie, but now from Andrea as well, I was forced to wander aimlessly amidst the growing throng, a target for every prying, probing hand. I was groped, spanked and even kissed upon my inanimate lips by an assortment of the most bizarrely clad and curious people anyone could ever want to encounter in one place.

As at the club, the numbers were divided fairly clearly between what Anne-Marie had explained to me were 'tops' and 'bottoms', that is, dominants and submissives, or masters and mistresses and their slaves. Almost all were clad in either leather or rubber, the 'tops' mostly, though not exclusively, in the former, the 'bottoms', or slaves, mostly in the latter, although there were a few submissives whose outfits seemed to consist merely of leather harnesses that were both decorative and restrictive at the same time.

Many of the slaves were obviously with their masters and mistresses, either leashed or sometimes just connected to them by means of chains attached to belts or wrists, but others, like myself, were left to roam on their own, at the mercy of anyone who wanted to exploit their helplessness, though I noticed no one took any really undue advantage of me, merely contenting themselves with patting and pinching and the odd playful spank.

My doll face, however, seemed to draw more attention than most. Of course, like the majority of the other slaves here, my identity was hidden behind it, but unlike the others, my face did have features, no matter how inanimate. I was a sort of 'halfway' creature, and apparently quite a novelty, for there were several comments made, including one or two to the effect that they would have to find out where they could purchase similar masks for their own slaves.

Behind my mask I sucked and chewed the gag in frustrated silence. I wanted to find some way of warning Anne-Marie, but of course there was none, and neither would there be until well after it was too late. I groaned inwardly and tried to ease my way into the shadows between two of the pillars, backing up against the stonework in an effort to remain as inconspicuous as possible. Not that it would make any difference in the long run, I knew, and all I could do was continue waiting until the inevitable happened. I just hoped Carmen wouldn't carry out her threat to keep us all here until after the following night, for although I could still find my enforced bondage arousing, to endure it for perhaps another day-and-a-half was not a prospect I relished.

If conditions in the original kennel building had been harsh, those in which Maudie now found herself were positively grim. The rough cell in which she was incarcerated was barely six feet by six feet, and hidden away beneath the remains of an old watchtower the locals still referred to as Scartley Manor, although there were none now still alive who could remember a time when there had been a house on the small knoll on which it stood, nor even any who could recall when the tower itself had been more than the rubble-strewn ruin it now was.

Maudie herself had previously only seen the dark outline from the top of Tanley Hill, a good two miles away, across the marshland that was the result of a major shift in the courses of two local rivers, a phenomena legend had it was a warning from God to Henry VIII, whose soldiers, under Sir Hector Scartley, sacked several monasteries in the area some three centuries earlier. As a result, the Manor had been left on a small islet, cut off from the rest of the country by treacherous bogs and whirlpools and reachable only by boat. Over the ensuing century, the house had been left to fall into disrepair and eventually dismantled for salvage, leaving only the tower, which had steadily crumbled under the onslaughts of successive seasons.

It had therefore come as a surprise to Maudie that there was actually a way of reaching the tower by land, although how Megan was able to negotiate the winding pathway was beyond her, for there were no obvious signs among the reeds and swamp grass clusters, and several times they were actually wading through several inches of muddy water even though the ground beneath them remained firm enough.

'They'll not find you here, my little bitch,' Megan assured her, as she drew aside the trailing branches to reveal the dark entrance to what Maudie saw was a flight of stairs leading down into the earth. 'There are only three people who know the way out here and Master Hacklebury ain't one of them.'

The keeper, Burrows, however, obviously was, and it was he who visited Maudie daily in her subterranean cell, removing her mask and gag so she could eat and drink, and then replacing them and leading her above ground for a brief exercise walk around the outside of the tower. But always only when it was dark, so there was no danger of their presence being detected by anyone on the hills stretching into the distance on both sides of the marsh.

'Please, master,' she begged on her second night of captivity, 'can you not take pity on me?' She nodded towards the dog's head mask he had set aside on a large piece of stone rubble that had somehow found its way below ground and now stood against one wall of the cell. 'Must I endure that beastly thing when you are not here? Even if I cried out, there would be none to hear me, and I cannot escape from this dreadful place, for the door seems as stout as the day it was first made.'

'Aye, well, this particular door was only made about a year back,' Will Burrows retorted, 'and a bugger of a job it was to get it all the way out here, I can tell you.'

'Then you need not use that horrible thing on me, must you, sir?' Maudie whined.

Burrows threw back his head and guffawed cruelly. 'And if her high and mightiness comes out here and finds you not as she expects, what then, eh? She'll make my life a bloody misery, and like as not she'll thrash your arse for talking me into such disobedience of orders.' He picked up the mask and held it between them, but he made no move to pick up the metal tongue strip that made such an effective gag. 'I'll make do with just this, but only for the night,' he said. 'If she does come out here, you keep your tongue still. If she does find out, I'll have to tell her your tongue was looking a bit raw and hope she wears that, but don't you go taking no chances, wench, else I'll beat you meself.'

'I shan't, sir, I swear it,' Maudie whimpered. It was better than nothing and, indeed, the metal did chafe her tongue at the slightest movement.

Burrows, however, intended to exact his price. 'Of course,' he grinned, drawing the mask over her head and adjusting it carefully, 'I expect something in return, if you know what I mean?' He finished tightening and knotting off the laces and then walked slowly around to stand before Maudie, who remained as ever on all fours, her head level with his waist.

'What is it you want of me?' she asked, her voice muffled by the extended snout in front of her nose and mouth, although she knew the answer, for Burrows had already begun opening his breeches and his weapon quickly burst forth in a state of eager anticipation.

'I reckons this'll reach far enough in,' he chuckled, stroking his erection enthusiastically to encourage the last drop of blood into its tissues. 'Enough for you to give me a nice little doggie suck, and then maybe I'll even mount you and you can pretend I'm a bloody great wolfhound, if you like.' He threw back his head and let out a mock howl, which disintegrated into a raucous laugh.

Maudie blinked away tears, but inside her snout she dutifully parted her lips, and then extended her head meekly towards him.

I saw Andrea again just before Carmen and Anne-Marie reappeared. She had been cornered by a mistress in a figure-hugging red leather dress and matching red boots and gloves, who already appeared to own two diminutive female slaves whose outfits consisted of white leather masks, white leather thigh-high boots and gloves, and a series of straps and buckles that hid nothing and emphasised plenty. Their features and hair were hidden, of course, but the colouring of their skin suggested they might well be of Oriental origin, and so well matched were they with their pert breasts and tiny feet that I suspected they might even be sisters.

Such a pairing ought to have been sufficient for anyone's tastes, I thought, but no, the red leather woman was evidently attracted to the contrast between her petite charges and the much taller and, apparently, more heavily endowed Andrea. From somewhere the mistress had produced a chain leash at one end of which was a broad red leather band she had buckled around Andrea's jutting cock-piece and was using to parade her around, making her stand between her other two charges and talking animatedly to everyone she encountered. Trying not to attract too much attention to myself, I sidled along the wall and watched her progress for several minutes, wondering at the audacity of the woman at taking over control of someone else's slave in such a way. I suspected Anne-Marie would be furious when she found out, but then I remembered it was unlikely Anne-Marie would long remain in any sort of position to voice her objections. Perhaps, I thought, the red leather witch was in league with Carmen and already knew what was going to happen. It was a suspicion that was to prove well founded and I didn't have to wait much longer to discover the truth.

Until now, apart from the gradually growing level of conversations and the odd smacks of leather on rubber and vice-versa, the vault had been fairly quiet. That may sound like a contradiction in terms, I know, but the truth is those voices that were able to communicate had been doing so at a muted level, and the high ceiling and the echoing effect of the unsympathetic walls had contrived to carry most of the sound away, leaving only a sort of eerie background noise, which through the rubber skin covering my ears was generally little more than a low hum.

Now, however, hidden speakers burst into life, a brass fanfare over a thunderous bass guitar beat erupting into an ear-shattering lead guitar riff that was painfully loud even through the protection of my hood. And then, just as suddenly, the music stopped and a tall figure strode across the front of the stage area, microphone in hand held up to a mouth that was the only visible feature in a deep purple leather mask, that matched the cape he wore over what appeared to be a black leather cat suit. A ragged cheer rose from the assembled onlookers, or at least from that percentage of them who retained the use of their mouths.

'Ladies and gentlemen!' His deep voice resonated around the walls. 'Ladies and gentlemen, be welcome!' He raised his arms in the air and there was an enthusiastic round of applause, joined in, I noticed, even by those slaves whose arms were not fettered.

'Thank you, thank you!' the kinky MC continued, lowering his arms. 'And thank you all for coming this evening for what I hope will be a very enjoyable gathering. Nice to see so many familiar faces,' he quipped, and I saw the mouth twist into a grin. The humour of the remark was lost on no one and laughter broke out amongst all the masked figures slowly organising themselves into a more disciplined group before him. As they shuffled and edged for position, the figure began listing several entertainment highlights planned for the night. Many of the terms he used were new to me, but I gathered the slaves who had been brought along were in for a strenuous few hours, at the very least.

'But first,' he continued, 'we have a very special feature to kick off tonight's festivities, a contest between two well-known mistresses.' A cheer went up at this announcement even though he had not mentioned any names as yet, and I suspected he didn't need to and that many, if not the entire crowd, already knew what was coming.

'Our charming hostess, Mistress Carmen, has placed herself and two of her most devoted slaves as a stake, and Mistress Anne-Marie, one of our newer friends it must be said, has accepted her challenge. The winner will take all. I'm sure you all understand the rules where that's concerned?'

There was a ripple of laughter at this, and I wondered how many other masters and mistresses had themselves engaged in similar wagers over the years, and what tales these walls could tell had they but the means to do so.

Another fanfare ripped the air, and then two spotlights lit up circular areas on either edge of the stage into which stepped the two contestants, heads erect and arms behind their backs. They were dressed identically and I could only tell which was which because Carmen, I knew, was a good three inches taller than our own mistress, and I could see that the platform stiletto-heeled boots they wore were of identical height. Apart from the boots, which were so high they hid whatever stockings were attached to the suspender straps bisecting the fronts of their pale thighs, each wore a tight-fitting leather corset that left her breasts bare, long leather gloves and all-encompassing hood masks terminating in broad studded collars about their necks. Their eyes seemed to be protected and half hidden by clear lenses, to judge from the glinting reflections of light off them, their mouths framed by the dark leather painted a bright crimson colour. It was only after I had taken in all these details that I realised neither combatant wore any form of panty, nor even gusset, and that both had been carefully clean-shaven above their glistening sexes.

The MC turned to each of the mistresses in turn and executed a stiff little bow, which they returned, and as they did so, I realised their wrists were connected behind their backs by means of two broad leather cuffs and a short length of chain. Inching forward along the right hand wall, I peered towards Anne-Marie, who was on the farther side, trying to determine if there was any way in which she might have been handicapped, save for the obvious difference in height, but I could see nothing untoward. However, my observations did not give me any cause to relax; something suspicious was going on here, of that I was convinced. My brief acquaintance with Carmen had convinced me she was not a personality who would risk losing, especially not before an audience of her admiring guests. Silently, I cursed Anne-Marie for her blind confidence, which ranked as stupid arrogance as far as I was concerned.

'We have as our arbiter for this contest,' the MC continued, 'your friend and mine, Lady Davina of the Sisterhood of Barbara. Please give her a huge welcome, ladies and gentlemen!'

It was no surprise to me when the red leather mistress emerged from the throng to mount the stage, and I was mildly amused at the title she had been announced under, for I recalled that Barbara, who had eventually been canonised, was famous in myth for having been tortured for her beliefs, and that her would-be executioner had been struck down by lightning. A suitably dramatic background for a very dramatic lady, assuming she really was female underneath that brilliant red skin.

She waited alongside the MC until the applause and cheering died down again, and then she turned to her right, nodding and beckoning. I realised there had to be doorways off in the 'wings' on either side of the stage area, for now two slender acolytes appeared, one after the other, dressed in long white rubber gowns, hooded and gloved in rubber of the same colour, and carrying before them large red cushions, upon each of which lay what at first looked like an amorphous tangle of white straps. An air of expectancy settled over the audience, myself included, and I could hear my pulse beating inside my head like a drum heralding a condemned prisoner's approach to the scaffold.

Lady Davina beckoned the first acolyte to her and began carefully extracting objects from amongst the straps. My heart missed a beat as I identified a double dildo in its harness, and I understood why the two contestants had been left with their sexes naked. Satisfied she had everything more or less the right way around, Davina approached Carmen first.

The tall mistress did not flinch, nor did she hesitate. Obligingly, she moved her booted feet apart and bent her legs slightly at the knees, probably as far as they could bend in those boots, I suspected. Davina crouched down and presented one of the dildos to Carmen's slit and I saw it enter her easily, with barely a push from without. Guiding it in to the hilt, Davina quickly adjusted the harness and buckled it securely in place, so that when she straightened up and stepped back, a white rubber cock jutted up fiercely in front of Carmen's lower abdomen, starkly highlighted against the black of her corset. Slowly, the tall mistress drew her legs back together, and I thought I detected a slight smile form on her lips, although the mouth opening in her mask mostly hid them from view.

A few minutes later Anne-Marie had been similarly dealt with, and I felt a stupid surge of pride at the way in which she mimicked the older mistress's poise and dignity in accepting the invading phallus. Obviously she thought she was engaged in a contest of wills, as much as in one that might require other abilities, and she was not about to hand the psychological advantage to her opponent at the very outset. I blinked away tears that inexplicably formed in my eyes, and stared hard at the two shafts. I wondered just what purpose they were actually intended for, but then, as Davina moved back towards Carmen once again and took up the remaining white strap assembly, I knew the answer. Almost at the same time I guessed exactly what was really going on and how Carmen intended to win the coming battle. She stood motionless as the gag was presented to her mouth, stretching her lips wide to take what at first I took to be an abnormally thick penis gag. It was only when Davina finished tightening all the straps on the bridle-styled head harness, and stepped clear, that I was able to see the truth, at which time the first penny dropped, followed a moment later by the second. It was not a solid gag at all, I saw now, but a hollow tube attached to the straps, a tube that would hold the wearer's mouth open and available, in this case available to accept the white rubber dildo of her opponent. Therefore, I realised, the aim of the game had to be to see which woman could plug her opponent's mouth first, a test of strength, cunning and flexibility, if ever there was one.

Except, I suddenly knew with a blinding flash of insight, this was never intended to be a fair and true test, for as Anne-Marie opened her mouth and Davina moved in on her, I realised it would not require very much to tip the odds in Carmen's favour. The two dildos and the two gagging tubes looked identical enough, it was true, but half a millimetre or so extra girth on Anne-Marie's rubber penis, and the same again as a reduction on the diameter of Carmen's gag hole, and the odds would be well and truly affected. Doubtless it would still be possible for Anne-Marie to effect the necessary penetration, but for either woman to do so would require a high degree of accuracy when it came to the necessary angle of attack. A millimetre or so overall difference could, and would, mean several additional degrees of tolerance. It might take a while before Carmen achieved the correct positioning, but she would probably have four or five times the chances of success Anne-Marie had, and as they began eventually to tire, sufficient opportunity was bound to present itself.

I prayed fervently that Anne-Marie might get a lucky break early on and take Carmen by surprise. After all, one fortunate thrust was all it would need, but then it quickly became apparent Carmen herself was aware of that, and when the contest finally began I saw she was taking no early chances, contenting herself with avoiding her opponent's attacks and allowing her to exhaust herself all the quicker.

Both women started from the kneeling position, and deprived of the use of hands and arms, they were soon rolling around and crawling about all over the stage area, whilst the front row of the audience formed a crouching barrier preventing them from rolling over the front edge and dropping the three feet or more to the main floor below.

The two dominants used their elbows and knees and even their heads as weapons, each in turn aiming for soft spots, although the stiff corsets protected their most vital regions. They nudged, battered and butted at each other's bodies, though I was quick to notice that neither protagonist targeted the head area, nor did they use any part of their legs beneath the knee. Obviously there was no kicking and no gouging allowed. With their arms cuffed behind them and with their eyes protected behind the plastic lenses, there was no chance of infringing the latter rule. Presumably they had to rely on each other's sense of the rules concerning the former, or else there was more likely a strict disqualification rule in force for the first to transgress.

After the first few minutes Anne-Marie was definitely trying to take the initiative, and twice I thought she had Carmen, knocking her flat on her back and scrambling awkwardly to sit astride her shoulders, thrusting her pelvis forward in an attempt to locate the tip of her weapon in the target orifice. Each time, however, the angle was wrong, and as she leaned further forward in an attempt to correct this the wily Carmen bucked suddenly, thrusting her solid bosom up beneath Anne-Marie's buttocks and launching her headfirst back over her own head.

The second tumble was disastrous for our mistress, for she landed awkwardly, banging the side of her head as she fell, and despite the protection of her helmet she was clearly stunned and somewhat disorientated. In a flash Carmen went on the attack for the first time proper. She scrambled forward, raising herself off her knees into a crouching position, and then dropped, all her weight falling onto Anne-Marie's chest. I heard a stifled moan as the breath was driven from my mistress's lungs, and I saw her flailing legs stiffen as the paralysing effect of a blow to the solar plexus took its toll.

Carmen was already on the move again, anticipating the effect of her crushing attack. She scrambled around until she was crouching at Anne-Marie's head, raised herself again, and leaned carefully over her face, gauging the distance carefully. Then, with a gurgled howl of triumph, she plunged down, her dildo finding its target with unerring accuracy.

A great shout went up from the audience and they began a slow handclapping. Carmen, lying across Anne-Marie, who had ceased all attempts at movement, began to raise and lower her hips in time to the clapping. For a few seconds I began to panic, thinking that perhaps Anne-Marie must be seriously hurt, but I could see her chest rising and falling and understood there was probably some sort of rule that prevented the loser from trying to wriggle free once her mouth had been impaled. Later, much later in fact, I learned my assumption was correct.

Meanwhile, Carmen was humping her victim's face with evident enthusiasm, but there was one final act to come. Turning her head sideways towards the audience so the glint of triumph in her eyes was unmistakable even through the covering lenses, she then turned back to Anne-Marie's dildo, drew her face back several inches whilst arching her back, and guided her mouthpiece towards the waiting tip. Then, with a single thrust of her neck and head she impaled her own mouth, to the rapturous applause and ringing cheers of the entire audience, or at least that part of the audience able to clap and cheer.

My heart sank. It was not only a defeat for Anne-Marie, but a conclusive one, and I had no doubt Carmen would exact her prize with as much enthusiasm as she had displayed in winning it. I looked around for Andrea, wondering if she was experiencing the same feeling of dreadful anticipation, only to see her already being escorted away by a featureless rubber figure. A moment later, I felt strong hands grasping my shoulders.

Arundel again, only this time the transition through time was accompanied by violent feelings of nausea and a complete sense of having been detached from everything for several seconds. My head cleared slowly and I opened my eyes to find myself sitting on a padded sofa in the first sitting room. Then suddenly, and for several more seconds, I experienced a blinding headache and for a moment I thought I was going to black out. But then again, miraculously, my head cleared, except I found it now contained a set of crystal-clear memories I knew had not been there before.

'Amazing!' I gasped, but there was no one else in the room to hear me. Slowly I stood up, not sure whether to trust to my balance yet, but I discovered there was absolutely nothing to worry about. I felt steady, focussed and, above all, I knew and remembered exactly what had been happening during the twenty-six days of my last absence from this time. Yes, I even knew I had been away and back in my own time only for an hour or two, and yet that I had been away from here, in this time, for four weeks, give or take a day or two.

I swallowed, licked my lips, and quickly took stock of things, beginning with myself. I was wearing an emerald-green dress, tight at the waist as usual, the corset beneath reminding me of its efforts on behalf of my figure. The neckline was low, exposing the top inch or so of what passed as Angelina's bust, not a spectacular sight, even though my cruel undergarment was striving to make the most of my bosom. I saw also that I was wearing a ruby necklace, and remembered it was one of the pieces I had put aside not to be sold unless circumstances became extremely tight.

I reached up and ran one hand over my head, my hair having now gone just beyond the stubbly stage to where it felt velvety to the touch, though it was still far too short not to draw attention to me should I venture out in public with it uncovered. As I was thinking this, my eyes caught sight of the two wigs standing on the dressing table by the window. I remembered the dressmaker and her second cousin who lived in Brighton, and how the wigs arrived a week after she wrote to her. I tottered uncertainly to the dressing table, studied the two hairpieces - one very dark, the other blondish with dark-red highlights, both carefully coiffed, the semi-buns beribboned, with teasing curls dangling on either side - and selected the darker and less ostentatious version.

I raised it slowly, ducked my head slightly and lifted it into place, settling it carefully with both hands. It was a good fit, but with no way of fastening it and no modern elasticised base, I felt certain it would slip off if I made too violent a movement. I would need, I decided, to use some sort of bonnet with a ribbon fastening beneath the chin if I was going to risk wearing either of the wigs out of doors. Indoors I would either find a lighter version of the same, or else I would have to make sure I didn't toss my head about too much.

Slowly, and with as much dignity as I could muster, I crossed the room and found the bell pull behind one of the heavy curtains covering the window alcove. I tugged it hard twice, and was rewarded with the sound of a distant bell ringing somewhere in the house. I turned again and regarded myself from across the length of the room, in the gilt-framed mirror now adorning the wall to the left of the fireplace. I made an impressive picture, if I do say so myself.

'Right then, boys and girls,' I said, though there was still no one to listen to my announcement, 'it's time we went to work properly. Everything is more or less in place, so let's get this house of ours open.'

I wasn't sure how it was that I could remember everything from those missing four weeks, but remember everything I could, and I did not intend to waste too much time in trying to figure out the whys and the wherefores. I suspected that in some way my mind now held part of what had once been Angelina's - possibly *was* still hers, for all I knew - but I had no way of proving my theory. Nevertheless, what was important was that I knew exactly what had been achieved in my absence, exactly how far my, *our* plan had progressed, and so also knew we were more or less ready to move on to the next and, for the moment, most important phase.

The intention was, dear reader, in case you haven't worked it out for yourself, to use what I termed my *House of Ill Repute* as irresistible bait for Hacklebury and, with luck, for Mad Megan Crowthorne as well. However, in order for the bait to be successful and for them to enter the trap unsuspectingly, there was a lot of work to be done in order to establish a set of credentials that would not arouse suspicion in minds I knew were only too naturally suspicious by nature.

Credentials. My *House of Ill Repute*, or bordello or brothel, call it what you will, my whorehouse, speciality whorehouse indeed, but whorehouse nonetheless, needed credentials. I already had my three whores, so now I needed to establish a clientele - and the right clientele especially.

The sitting room door opened and Indira appeared. I say Indira because I had no way of knowing if Andrea had come back as before, but I also knew it hardly mattered at the moment. If Angelina was going along with my idea then so would her faithful lover, and besides, I had already caught sight of the figure standing out in the hallway behind her.

'Mr Julian Corner-Browne, mistress,' she announced, bowing slightly. I noticed she was wearing a *sari* and immediately remembered ordering fabric from the dressmaker for her to make them, except it had been Angelina who had ordered the material, not I. Not that it mattered, I thought, and suppressed a smile.

'Show him in, girl,' I ordered in my best 'lady of the manor' voice, and turned away to resume my position on the sofa, while at the same time adjusting the heavy veil obscuring my features attached to my wig.

Julian Corner-Browne, eldest son of one of the two brothers who between them owned a very successful merchant bank in the city of London. Ex-Eton, ex-Harrow, sent down from both and forced to finish his education in one of the minor public schools, and only able to do that thanks to a generous bursary from his family, which the ailing establishment had been only too willing to accept in return for overlooking the young Corner-Browne's previous record of indiscretion and debauchery.

I wondered how I knew all this, or rather I *knew* how I knew, but I wondered how Angelina had managed to find it out. Then I recalled the little man Marsh and the discreet service he offered to those with the ability to pay. Some things never change, regardless of the year or the century, and it was as amazing then as it is now what one can source through the personal advertisement columns of even the most respectable national newspapers. Simeon Marsh I paid, Julian Corner-Browne I hoped would pay me, and quite lavishly, unless I was much mistaken.

I smiled, though whether the smile could be seen from behind the veil I had no idea, and gestured to one of the vacant armchairs opposite me. And as the first of my wannabe clients moved to take a seat, I forced my expression to remain totally impassive, trying even harder not to feel like a spider who is about to envelop an unfortunate and stupid fly in its web.

Thanks to the efforts of Simeon Marsh, whose investigative powers and circle of contacts would have earned him a fortune with the tabloids a century or so later, we were now beginning to build up quite a dossier on Gregory Hacklebury, though even Marsh hadn't as yet been able to find out much about Megan Crowthorne, who remained very much a mystery woman. However, it was Hacklebury I wanted and needed to concentrate on, establishing a list of his closest associates and initially avoiding any direct contact with any name on that list when it came to building up our clientele. We needed to establish ourselves first and ensure our girls were capable of fulfilling the roles for which we had recruited them. After that, it would be time to infiltrate the Hacklebury network and finally snare the big buck rabbit himself.

Milly, Molly and Mandy were a revelation, and Erik found himself much in demand as the only male currently in the household. Our 'guests', when they started arriving, would not be disappointed, I thought, although I conceded we had to do a little work on the trio in order to smooth out some of their rougher edges, especially in their vocabulary. I also resolved to put each of them through their paces with a member of their own sex, as I was sure we would have female clients, even if they formed a minority.

Meanwhile, there was Indira, and for the moment it really was the Indian girl, for Andrea remained back in our own time, presumably alongside a temporarily vacant version of me as we awaited Carmen's dubious pleasure. I tried to put that scenario from my mind. I would find myself back in it soon enough, I knew, but for the moment there was plenty here to occupy me, including the regular nocturnal presence of my little brown-skinned lover.

'You really would do anything for me, wouldn't you, Indy?' I whispered to her as we lay snuggled together after a languid session of lovemaking.

She raised her head, leaned across me and kissed my right nipple.

My hand trailed idly through her thick black tresses.

'I would die for you, mistress,' she whispered. 'You know I would.' She peered up at me and I saw there was a depth of concern in her huge eyes.

I kissed her forehead. 'No one is going to do any dying,' I assured her. 'Hacklebury and his witch-bitch aren't at all nice people, but now we're in the driving seat and as long as we're careful, that's the way it'll stay.'

'Perhaps we should just kill them,' Indira suggested, and I knew she was being deadly serious.

I shook my head. 'Murder is murder,' I said, 'no matter how justified it might seem. Besides, we'd only be descending to their level then, wouldn't we? No, I don't mind playing them at their own game if no one gets hurt, but we don't want to do anything that might end up with us getting an appointment with the hangman.

'Besides,' I continued, 'I don't think Meg's ultimate punishment is destined to be a quick death.' I thought back to the story we had heard about the mad woman roaming the hills and humping a chunk of rock in the dead of night. 'No, I think fate has something else planned for our dear Miss Crowthorne.' I looked into Indira's eyes again and decided it was time I said something I had been avoiding during the four days since my latest return. 'Indy,' I began, 'do you remember everything that's happened since we escaped that night?'

She lowered her eyelids. 'You mean the man I killed?'

'No, not that, though that *could* become a problem. Megan saw you, so it's quite possible they've told the authorities, though I've got a funny feeling they may have changed their minds on that. They won't want the law too closely involved in their doings, so they'll be using other means of trying to find us. No, I mean all the things that have happened since? Do you remember them all?'

'Mostly,' she replied. Her small hand began slowly stroking my stomach. 'Yes, I remember, mostly, though some of it *has* been like watching the world through the smoke of a cooking fire.'

'A bit like you weren't really there at all, you mean?'

'Yes, like a dream, like I was doing things and saying things, but that at the same time it was not I who was in control.' The hand reached my smooth mound and I drew in a deep breath.

'And what about me?' I asked. 'Do I seem to have changed at all?'

There was a silence of several seconds before Indira spoke again. 'I think you have,' she replied, 'but then so have we all, and those evil people did much to you that was very bad, so that would change you as it would change anyone.' She fell silent again.

I did not speak, for I could sense she was trying to find the right way to say something more.

'But there is something else, too,' she continued at last, 'something I cannot explain, as if there is a spirit with you now, perhaps a spirit from the past. I feel that, too, as if my ancestors are watching over me.'

'Or as if one of them has perhaps come back to help you?' I suggested. 'Would that be so hard to explain? Or perhaps you are one of your ancestors reborn? You believe that in your religion, don't you?' I thought perhaps this was a better way of trying to deal with things than simply diving straight in and telling this probably uneducated girl that I had actually dropped back from the next century, and that a friend of mine was doing the same thing and taking over her body for days, and even weeks at a time. But the suggestion was based on two false premises and her reaction to it took me completely by surprise.

'My religion?' she snapped, suddenly sitting up. Her brown eyes were now alight with a mixture of anger and suspicion. '*My* religion is the same as yours!' she said.

'And your parents were my godparents and they were there when I was baptised a Christian as my parents were baptised and their parents before them!' She pushed herself along the bed until she was perched against the footboard, as far from me as she could be without getting down on the floor. 'Now,' she continued, looking me straight in the eyes, 'there are many things that one might forget, but I think that would not be one of them, and I believe in reincarnation about as much as you would believe in fairy folk.'

'I... well... err...' I simply couldn't think of anything to say. In assuming Indira was a Hindu, I was guilty of a crass assumption, and in thinking of her as uneducated I was guilty of an even worse mistake.

'I want to know who you really are,' she said quietly, but fervently. 'I mean, who you *really* are and why it is you act so strangely at times, and how you seem able to make me think and act strangely, too. Perhaps you are a demon, is that it?' Her expression was hard, but then it suddenly softened again. 'No, you are no demon, angel mistress, but I think you know something far more than you are telling me. I feel there is some power at work here, but I think it is not of the devil.'

'I don't think it is, either,' I said, pulling myself up into a sitting position. 'Though for all I know it could be, because for the life of me I can't explain it.'

'Then explain what you can,' Indira suggested. 'Tell me what it is you know and maybe I can shed a little light.'

And so I sat there and told her everything, everything about Teena Thyme and the twentieth century and about my several times over great aunt who left me the cottage, money and trunks of what I assumed were her clothes, and about the pendant I found and how I initially believed it was responsible for my time hopping, but that I had not seen it here in eighteen thirty-nine since my first trip back.

'I still have it back in my own time,' I said, 'but it's locked safely away. What happened to it here after Meg took it from me I have no idea, though.'

'*I* have it,' Indira announced. 'I found it in the house when we were looking for clothing and money. Look, I will show you, and you should have it back, for it is yours after all.' She jumped down from the bed and padded across to where her clothing was piled on one of the bedroom chairs. After a few moments of rummaging in the folds, she turned and came back to me holding out her hand, which she opened to reveal the pendant.

I took it from her as if I was handling the most delicate and precious object in the world.

'The portraits are of your parents,' she explained, sitting alongside me. 'Or should I say that they were the *real* Angelina's parents, but then I think maybe you had guessed that yourself?'

I nodded. 'I thought they had to be,' I agreed. 'Funny, even though Angelina has managed to make me aware of what's been happening here at the house, I still have no memories of her mother and father.'

'Perhaps that is because she knows you do not need to have any,' Indira suggested sagely. 'I do not pretend to understand any of this any more than you do, but there are some things that should always remain precious to the individual.'

'Then you do believe everything I've told you?' I asked.

She nodded. 'It would be too ridiculous a story to make up, and the Angelina I know, sweet as she is, well, let's just say her imaginative talents lay in other directions.' She grinned at me, and suddenly I just wanted to hug her. She must have sensed something, for she reached out a hand and traced a soft line around my left nipple. 'My talents lie in similar directions,' she whispered.

'Yes,' I smiled, 'I *had* noticed. But now that you know, do you—?'

'My Angelina is still a part of you,' she replied, 'as you are now a part of her. For whatever reason you have been brought back here, and whatever the outcome of all this, in the meantime there is no reason for other things to change.'

Quite why Andrea was not making a reappearance this time I could only surmise, not that I was in particular need of her support, but I had to tread a little diplomatically where the real Indira was concerned, now it was time to start schooling our little troupe of girls in the different ways I envisaged we would need to employ in order to make our establishment unique. All the time Erik was sating himself with the girls and attending to their more base needs, Indira was quite content that this left the two of us free to enjoy one another, but I knew I would need to take a hand in their education, and how my brown-skinned lover would react to that, I had no idea.

As gently as I could, I broached the subject the following evening, and was most surprised when Indira showed not the slightest sign of jealousy; rather, she seemed very interested in what I was proposing and even eager to help me.

'What must be done must be done,' she said simply, 'and the faster and the better it is done, then the better our chances of succeeding, for I am worried they might find us before we are ready.'

'There is always that chance,' I agreed, 'but I am almost certain that I'll in some way have warning if we are in that sort of danger. We are well out of the way here, and the few people who might be able to identify us are earning too much from our project to talk to strangers. The story I've been using is that I fled from a violent French husband, and memories of the war with France are still fresh enough for all good Englishmen and women to mistrust the French, not to say hate them.'

In truth, I had used this cover story with the innkeeper, the dressmaker and the shoemaker. Our builder lived well outside town and would not have been the obvious person for any would-be spy to question, and besides, when I saw he had taken a shine to Molly, I took the precaution of asking her to allow him the enjoyment of her charms every few days. The lascivious minx, not particularly given to being selective in the past, and now quite happy to find herself with clients who were not likely to slap her about in a drunken rage, not only serviced Jonas White, but also took care of his two assistants rather than recruiting her two fellow whores to the cause.

'We must still not waste any time,' Indira stated firmly. 'I do not know exactly what it is you are planning, but if your intention is to attract the likes of Gregory Hacklebury, then I can well imagine. However, with that type of person we must be very careful.'

'Yes, I know,' I agreed, 'though the likes of Hacklebury as such are thankfully rare. Those men I have seen so far are not even pale imitations. They are simply looking to act out fantasies, and just so long as we provide the right theatricals for them, they will be happy enough to pay up and return to their wives and families.'

'So, this is to be a theatre?' Indira nodded thoughtfully, pursing her lips. 'And we shall all become good actresses. Yes, I think I shall make a good actress and so shall you.'

'*You?*' I said incredulously.

She looked at me, wide-eyed. 'And why not?'

'But you don't *like* men.'

'Not the sort of evil scum Hacklebury handed me over to, no, but then they are the only men I have known in that way, so I cannot make a fair judgement, can I? It would be like someone who has never seen a potato saying they don't like potatoes, wouldn't it? Besides, there will be many roles and many characters and I need not have to suffer a man inside me, not unless we find a particularly pretty man, that is.'

I immediately realised there was probably a whole lot more to Indira than I had originally suspected, and that the real Angelina had almost certainly not known her lover as well as she thought. In her company, the Indian girl would have likely acted the demure role expected of her in this age, whereas with me, who had spent much of the past twenty-four hours telling her about the world from which I had come, she was starting to express a different side of her personality.

'Right then,' I said, standing up and straightening my dress. 'Time we got to work. Mr White has not yet quite finished in the cellar, but we can use the large bedroom at the back of the first floor for our rehearsals. I have placed some of the props we will need in the small room next to it, so let's go and see what we'll need.'

'And we shall start with Molly, perhaps?' she suggested.

I turned to her and nodded. 'Yes,' I said, 'we'll start with Molly, and then use her to demonstrate to the other two girls.'

'Good.' She smiled radiantly. 'And I should like to be the one who introduces her to the feel of a cane across her backside. The girl has far too much to say for herself and is most disrespectful to me when you are not within earshot.'

'She'll not have so much to say once we get a gag in her mouth,' I declared. 'Our friend the shoemaker's talents extend far beyond footwear, and his flair has improved upon a couple of basic designs I gave him. Which reminds me, we shall have to add him to our client list, though on a preferential basis.'

Molly eyed the black leather corset suspiciously, but then that was hardly surprising, for not only did the hide and its colour lend it a sinister air, the sheer narrowness of the waist made it obvious it was designed without the slightest concern for the comfort of the wearer, and even more so than the standard foundation garments of the day.

'You'll never get me into that thing!' she gasped.

I eyed her naked body and shook my head, but not in agreement with her, for she had a slender build that belied her ample breasts. 'It will fit you,' I assured her, 'with a little persuasion. Why, I've worn much more rigorous things. Now, come over here you silly wench, and let's get it on you. Remember, you will end up as quite a wealthy young woman when this adventure is finally finished, unless you've changed your mind, in which case you can get dressed and leave in the morning.'

The promise of the money and the threat of losing it was more than enough to persuade our reluctant heroine, although I could see she was very nervous as I began hooking the garment about her.

'Relax,' I said, stroking her neck when the final fastening had been closed. 'It's not so bad. Perhaps a glass of brandy will help you?' I nodded to Indira, who turned to the bottle and glasses we had earlier placed in readiness on the long table running across one end of the room.

'It's bloody tight!' Molly moaned, pressing her hands against her sides as if to emphasise the statement.

I laughed and patted her shoulder. 'And it'll be a bloody sight tighter before we're done,' I warned. 'We haven't even started lacing it yet.'

Her eyes widened, but before she could utter another protest, Indira handed her a glass with a generous amount of what was a very strong spirit, especially when compared with the sort of stuff we're used to drinking in pubs nowadays. Molly gulped a greedy mouthful, swallowed, and coughed, tears welling up in her eyes. 'Fuck!' she exclaimed when she had recovered enough breath to talk again. 'That's got a kick on it like a carthorse!'

'And so it should have,' I retorted. 'I paid a lot of money for that, or rather, Erik did. Now, Indira, perhaps you would do the honours?'

Indira smirked and nodded, moving around behind Molly, where she undid the loose knot at the ends of the laces and began steadily pulling at them.

Molly groaned and took another drink, though this time she exhibited a great deal more respect for the fiery liquid. 'That's far too tight,' she protested as Indira completed the first pass up and down her spine. 'I can't bloody well breathe now!'

'Of course you can,' Indira chided her. 'Why, I've barely started. Look, there must be another three inches to go yet.'

'You black bitch!' Molly all but shrieked. 'You think it's funny to take the piss out of a white woman, do you?'

'That's enough,' I snapped. I stepped in front of Molly and raised a finger to her face. 'Listen, you stupid little trollop,' I hissed, 'if you ever mention anyone's skin colour again, I'll have Erik flay yours off you with a horsewhip, do you understand?'

The tone of my voice must have surprised Molly as much as it surprised me, but in truth I was very angry and it was all I could do to stop myself from slapping her face. I tried to calm myself with the thought that our Victorian ancestors had been brought up with a different outlook where other races were concerned, but at least my outburst served to chasten Molly.

'I'm sorry, miss,' she mumbled, 'but she's hurting me.'

'So would you rather go back on the streets of London?' I suggested. 'That's where you could really learn all about what it means to be hurt. You'll like as not even end up in the Thames with your throat cut if what I've heard is anything to go by.'

She looked down and shook her head.

'Right then, Indira,' I said in my firmest voice, 'get that corset closed up and let's get on with this. You'll get used to it, Molly,' I continued, turning away to get myself a drink, 'and you'll like what it does for the figure. You'll have men crawling at your feet if you pay attention to what I'm going to teach you.' *When you're not the one doing the crawling, that is*, I added to myself, for Molly's training still had a long way to go and these things would be best tackled one step at a time.

Half an hour later we had Molly more or less ready, thanks to a lot of pulling and tugging by Indira, who was much stronger than I was in this body, and thanks to the smelling salts I had thoughtfully put close at hand before we started. Still struggling to come to terms with the correct way of breathing in a corset, Molly stood before us, red-faced and unsteady, but apart from that she looked perfect for the role and would have reduced most men to a sticky surrender almost at first sight. To be honest, the sight of her was doing things to me and I could see my lover was just as appreciative.

'You see,' Indira said, demonstrating with her hands, 'I can very nearly span your waist now, Molly. A man could probably make his thumbs and fingers touch on both sides.'

It was a bit of an exaggeration, but Molly was visibly unimpressed anyway. Neither did she seem at ease in the high boots, which reached almost into her still bare crotch and which Indira had laced so tightly I was pretty sure the poor girl would not be able to bend her knees more than the slightest fraction. The same was probably true of her arms and elbows, for the leather gloves were equally close fitting, so that even her fingers were as good as useless. I thought back to those other gloves Megan had forced onto Angelina's hands and arms, the satiny ones with the fingers sewn together so they acted like mittens and made delicate tasks impossible for the wearer. She would appreciate these creations, I knew, except if she one day ended up wearing them, a prospect I hoped would eventually be realised.

The final touch to Molly's bizarre outfit, apart from the masking hood I did not yet want to introduce her to, took the form of a neck collar that was itself really a corset, for it laced at the back and was contoured so it forced Molly to stand with her head erect, and made turning her head more than an inch or so in either direction completely impossible.

'Excellent,' I announced.

Molly scowled. 'I feel stupid,' she grumbled. 'What man would find this attractive, eh? Why, this damned thing even covers most of my titties.'

I smiled and stepped forward, stroking beneath the leather-covered orbs. 'You'd be surprised how many men, and women too, prefer to see a pretty girl dressed so rather than simply naked.' Gregory Hacklebury, for one, not to mention generations of other men down through the ages, both before this time and ever since. I was maybe half a century or more ahead of this time in my innovations here, but I was willing to bet the early Victorian man would find this sort of fetishist display equally as appealing, as would a goodly number of men and women back in my own era.

'Now, please place your hands behind your back, Molly,' I instructed.

She did so obediently, and Indira pounced, buckling a cuff about her left wrist with commendable speed and efficiency. Immediately Molly pulled her right arm back around in front of her and tried to spin away out of Indira's grasp.

'Molly!' I warned. 'Please, let's not have any foolishness. Of course, if you'd rather leave us after all I'll understand, but it would be a great pity.'

The girl hesitated, looked at me uncertainly, and then slowly put her arms behind her back again, where Indira quickly completed the task of fettering them together.

'There, you see,' I said in a soothing tone, 'that wasn't so hard, was it. And who knows, I think you might just be a bit surprised at how much fun this can be. Of course, as the saying goes, *there's no pleasure without pain*, but in this case we're only talking about a *little* pain.'

'And a very great deal of pleasure,' Indira added, smirking behind her victim. 'Should I gag her now, mistress?'

I shook my head. 'No, not quite yet, Indira.' I turned away with the intention of refilling my glass.

'G-gag? ' Molly stammered. 'No one said anything about a gag!'

'Oh, no need to worry, my sweet,' I told her as I raised the brandy bottle and began pouring. 'It's just so you don't make too much noise from all the pleasure we're going to give you. We wouldn't want to alarm the other girls, would we?' In fact, the other girls were probably several hundred yards along the riverbank by now, for I had given Erik instructions to take them out for an evening stroll once we began Molly's tutorial session, but that information was on a 'need to know' basis and, at the moment, quite frankly, Molly didn't need to know.

I put down the bottle and picked up my glass once more, walking slowly back over to stand in front of my first student. 'You need to know *this*,' I told her, 'that whatever happens here I, we, would never hurt you, not really. A little sting or two, a smack or a slap, but nothing that would damage you, and only that which I hope you will come to enjoy as much as the ultimate pleasure we will give you.'

'But why?' she protested. 'Why any sort of pain?'

'Because you need to learn and to experience for yourself before you can hope to know how to give the same to others,' I explained.

She looked at me, aghast. 'You mean I'm supposed to *hurt* people?' she squeaked. '*What* people?'

'Men, and some women too, probably, the sort of people who will pay us well for the services we'll be providing here.'

'I thought I was just supposed to fuck the customers!'

I laughed at her shocked indignation. 'Oh I dare say there'll be some of that, too.'

'A lot of that, I should imagine,' Indira interjected.

'However,' I added, ignoring the interruption, 'you are about to learn a totally new set of rules and skills. By the time we're finished you three girls will be to normal prostitution like sewing a handkerchief is to hand stitching a wedding gown, if you get my meaning.' I could see she didn't, but I also didn't let her ignorance worry me. She would learn soon enough, I told myself, hopefully as quickly as I had done, and I just hoped I could be half as good a teacher for her as Anne-Marie had been for me.

'Well now, let's have a good look at you again.' I had all but forgotten about Carmen and her contest with Anne-Marie, but now, as suddenly as ever, I was back in my own time and once more securely within her clutches. It seemed we had been led away from the main crypt during what I supposed had been a few moments in this time, for we were now in a smaller room, though I was still convinced we were deep underground. How my body managed to walk while I was off controlling Angelina's body, I had no idea. Some sort of motor response, I presumed, or maybe a vestige of my mind remained behind in the same way it appeared a vestige of Angelina's remained present, if undetected by me, whenever I was being her.

I looked around, searching for my two friends, but besides Carmen, who had dressed once again in her dramatic black with white trimmings rubber, there was just one other occupant of the chamber, a thickset fellow whose identity was hidden behind a leather hangman-style mask, but whose gender was on open display amidst a complex harness of the same material. He stood silently to one side and I wondered if he too was gagged, not that it made much difference to me. More importantly, or at least more relevantly, I wondered if he was there to employ a manhood that looked as if it ought to be quite something once aroused. I felt that familiar little tingle deep in my stomach, but for once I didn't hate myself for it.

Strange how quickly some people can change or adapt. Here I was, completely at the mercy of a woman I hardly knew, and likely as not about to find myself riding an anonymous cock, and I didn't find the idea repugnant. Rather, I was actually anticipating it, and I knew why, for now I had learned to accept that when someone else has removed all control from you, then you are free to indulge without guilt. If this prime specimen of manhood was to be my fate, then I was bloody well going to enjoy it.

Carmen's plans, however, were nothing as straightforward as that, which I should have guessed. She began by stroking my rubber face, smiling all the while.

'Yes,' she said at length, 'as I said earlier, these are very nice. I must ask Anne-Marie where she got them. If the manufacturer hasn't got an exclusive patent in this country, then I think they would make a very popular extra line. Oh, didn't she tell you?' Carmen smiled behind her mask, for I saw her teeth revealed and her upper lip disappear momentarily from view, and I looked at her passively as she continued. 'I thought dear Annie would have mentioned it,' she said, 'only I own a large share of a company that specialises in manufacturing and distributing all sorts of interesting items. Hector's harness here is one example, though not one of our more imaginative or interesting lines. We make lots of rubber and leather suits, hoods, cuffs and special boots. We have nearly two thousand separate lines now, believe it or not.'

'In fact,' she chuckled, stepping forward to examine my hood beneath the wig, 'I have one very new line I intend to try out tonight, and the three of you are going to be my guinea pigs. It's going to be very popular, I'm sure, and there's even a version that will suit dear Andrea. I'm assuming you're actually Teenie underneath all this lot and that the cock thing on the other one was just a double bluff?'

I nodded dumbly.

'Well, I'll see to you first, and then you can come along with me and watch as we sort out your dolly friend. Yes, you're both going to remain as dollies and it's quite a coincidence that Annie was thinking along such similar lines already.' Her laughter echoed around the cold stone walls. 'Of course, my idea of a useful dolly is a mite different, as you'll shortly find out.' She reached beneath my false hair and began unfastening the neck of my mask.

'Now, I know you're going to be very good for me,' she said quietly. 'I know you're a bit of a novice, but I'm also sure you've got a good idea of the sort of rules we work by. You two are Annie's slaves, and Annie lost a fair contest to me, so now you become my slaves until you leave, and you'll obey my orders as you would hers. The three of you are now equal, with each other that is, not me. No, I am now your mistress, and I have decided that all three of you are going to be my dolly slaves. This is going to be very entertaining and also very good for business. If you three dollies perform properly, I anticipate taking quite a few orders over this weekend.'

Of course, I still had no idea what she was rambling on about, but I knew it wouldn't be long before I found out. What was obvious was that we were going to be used as part of an exercise to promote a new product line, and the news that Carmen owned, or part-owned, a company that manufactured fetish gear explained why she was willing to go to so much trouble to stage events like the one tonight and why she was so 'in' at the club we had visited. She was a one-woman marketing campaign, except that tonight she had extended her marketing department by three, or so it seemed.

My mask was quickly removed, but I knew better than to try to speak without being told to, so I stood quietly while Carmen began stripping me of everything else I had arrived in. As ever, given the amount of lacing and buckling that was used in getting me into this sort of outfit, it was not a quick process, but she seemed unhurried and her hooded companion - was he a slave or a master, I wondered? - remained almost as immobile as a statue, only the gentle rise and fall of his broad chest indicating he was a living, breathing creature.

Eventually Carmen's patience and diligence were rewarded and I stood before her naked, pressing my thighs together in an effort to prevent the rubber dildo from sliding out of me, and not wanting to remove it myself without her say so. I saw her smirk, and understood that her leaving the invading shaft inside me until last was a deliberate move to add to my humiliation and to emphasise my situation as her slave. Having made the point, she then relented.

'You can take the cock out now, Teenie,' she told me. 'We've got something much better than that for you, anyway. My, but you still seem to be very wet!'

As ever, I thought, but I reached down and collected the slippery rubber phallus as it slid out of me. I held it uncertainly, not sure of what I should do with it. Carmen solved this dilemma, but I can't say I found her solution quite to my liking.

'Suck it,' she instructed. 'Go on, put it in your pretty mouth and taste yourself, you randy little dolly bitch.'

I hesitated, but only for the space of two heartbeats, for I had seen the rack against the wall whilst being stripped and noted the selection of straps, canes, tawses and crops that hung from it. Not that I thought Carmen would use any of the implements too harshly, for this wasn't the Hacklebury house and she was no Megan Crowthorne, but at the moment I was naked, and without a protective layer of rubber, I could imagine how much my bottom would sting from even a light application of any one of those weapons of punishment. I swallowed hard and raised the tip of the dildo to my lips, gently inserting it at first and then taking half its length. I could taste myself, but it wasn't as bad as I expected, and if I could use my tongue and lips on another female's most intimate parts, what was the difference if I sucked my own juices off a length of inanimate rubber?

Satisfied she had established the proper control over me, Carmen was now anxious to get on and she quickly took the dildo from me, tossing it onto a shelf running above the whip and cane rack. I waited as she stooped to open a box that stood on a stool in the corner, and I smelled the unmistakable odour of new rubber as she drew out a pale bundle I knew could only be latex. I saw also that there was some sort of hair, a wig, within the bundle, and caught a glimpse of a staring blue eye as she began shaking out the garment.

'Now then, Teenie dolly slave,' she said when she was holding up what turned out to be a pink cat suit, 'this is your dolly outfit, but you'll see the idea better once we have it on you, so I won't bother explaining just yet.'

I thought there was something ominous in both her words and her tone and I was soon to discover just how right I was.

The first thing I noticed as my right leg was powdered and guided into the suit was that the foot section was formed in perfect anatomical detail, with a little tubular section to accept every toe individually, and that on the outside, these rubber toes were finished with red painted toenails. Once the rubber was in place and smoothed out evenly, there was hardly any difference between this foot and my own, now sheathed inside it, save the thickness of the latex, and I noticed it felt slightly denser than that used in the black suit I had recently been wearing.

Whilst still engrossed in admiring the craftsmanship that had gone into the manufacturing process, my other leg was similarly treated, and having drawn the suit up above my knees, Carmen set about pulling it up even further. For the first time I saw and felt the one feature she had been cunningly contriving to prevent me from noticing, and my eyes opened wide in astonishment when I saw the thickness of the dildo I was expected to accommodate.

'You won't get that inside me,' I wailed, but Carmen wasn't about to accept either my word or ultimate defeat.

'Nonsense!' she exclaimed, and a hand delved down between my thighs. 'See,' she said, 'you're still nice and wet and just a little extra persuasion...' She stopped speaking as her fingers found my clitoris, still swollen from earlier and yet still able to respond even more to this intimate contact. I groaned, but she was clearly not intending to bring me to an orgasm.

'Steady, girlie doll,' she whispered. 'Let's take our time over this, shall we? We just need these muscles nicely relaxed and this pretty little cunt as lubricated as we can manage. Ah yes, that's starting to feel better already.'

I began swaying and had to reach out to grasp her shoulder in order not to topple over. At this, the previously immobile Hector sprang forward and grasped me by the upper arms, steadying me in a powerful grip, but I hardly felt his fingers. I was more concerned with the monstrous phallus that was now pushing its way inside me, or rather, that was being pushed inside me by Carmen. I gasped and moaned and was sure it wasn't going to fit, but to my amazement my muscles began to stretch incredibly, and after just a few seconds the whole thing was inside, leaving me with a feeling of being completely stuffed, yet at the same time by an invader that felt surprisingly soft and yielding. Carmen tugged the suit up tightly about my waist and drew the rear zip up the first few inches to keep the shaft in place, and then she stooped down in front of me and reached between my rubber-clad thighs.

I felt a curious sensation of movement within me, but movement that was in some way distanced, and then she straightened up again and I saw she was holding a more life-sized pink penis in her right hand.

'Just need that to provide a little stiffening,' she explained.

I looked at her blankly.

'To fit your new pussy cunt,' she said, smiling. 'What you've now got inside you is an artificial rubber vagina, a soft rubber lining about half an inch or so thick, but with a membrane in it that also acts as a barrier to a lot of sensation. There's also a shaped piece that covers your clitty.'

'But why?' I asked naively, peering down at the rather overly developed looking sex lips that now protruded from between the tops of my thighs. Apart from their unnatural size, they looked horribly realistic and there was even a little triangle of dark blonde hair immediately above them.

'Why?' Carmen echoed my question. 'Well, because we're making you into a proper sex dolly, Teenie, and sex dollies don't get any fun out of being sex dollies, do they? They're just dollies, aren't they?'

'That's gross!' I gasped, understanding now what she meant, but she simply giggled and grasped my arm, which she proceeded to dust with talcum powder. A few minutes later, when both had been guided into arm-gloves and she was drawing the rubber up over my shoulders, I saw she had taken the 'no fun' bit to even greater extremes, for my breasts now snuggled within foam padded cones of a rubber that was quite rigid, and although these outer breasts were tipped with huge nipples, my own smaller ones would feel very little when touched.

'Face time, dolly,' Carmen announced.

For a second or two I contemplated trying to stop this, but I guessed any complaint from me would probably only be regarded as an extension of the game, and that even if I did manage to convince my temporary mistress I had changed my mind, she wasn't likely to release me now. No, she had made up her mind and she was going to play out her little drama whatever I thought about it.

The head of the suit was drawn up and over my own, and I had a brief glimpse of a moulded interior into which my features were to fit. I also saw the gag there, but it was so close to my eyes I could not focus on it properly, and so the surprise, when it came, was complete.

'Open wide, dolly,' Carmen instructed.

I took a deep breath and obliged. After all, I reasoned, she would get the gag in my mouth one way or the other, and the other might prove to be somewhat painful. A moment later she was pushing the thing between my teeth and I almost gagged at its diameter. It also felt hard and unyielding, and what was more, I could still draw air in through my mouth even though my jaw was distended far beyond my ability to talk.

I felt the back of the mask being zipped closed and the hair brushed back into place, hiding the closure efficiently, and then Carmen decided it was time to show me exactly what she had done to me. She stepped across the room, to what I had assumed was a curtain, though why it had been hung halfway along the side wall was anyone's guess. My guess was that it probably covered the doorway to an adjoining cell. I couldn't have been more wrong, because as she drew it aside I had just enough time to register that it had been covering a large mirror before I saw my reflection. Had I been able to, I would have screamed. As it was, I let out a throaty howl of horror.

Facing me was a parody of one of those blow-up sex dolls that can nowadays been seen or found in a myriad sex shops throughout the country, or ordered from any one of fifty mail order companies. If you've ever seen one, then you will know they are mostly made to be crudely functional rather than overly authentic.

In the case of the rubber doll I had been used to 'inflate', the detail was a lot more realistic, but the crude functionality was all the more obvious because of that. The tall doll creature was proportioned well and the eyes that looked back at me looked quite real, save for their inability to blink, but the gaping sex between its thighs was all too obvious, and the mouth - my mouth inside - was forced into a permanently rounded 'O' shape, and because there was some sort of rigid reinforcement in the tube that kept my jaw wide open, I was powerless to do anything about it.

Carmen had produced her first doll of the night, and as I stood there, rigid with shock, I knew only too well that she had not done so merely for artistic effect. That rubber vagina and that inviting mouth were going to be used for the purpose for which they had been so artfully designed. I wondered whether Anne-Marie and Andrea were going to be subjected to the same treatment - whether indeed they already had been - and wondered also just how my former mistress would react to being not only a submissive, but one who just like me had been reduced to the status and appearance of a basic sex toy.

Chapter 5

'Mistress? Mistress! Are you all right?'

I opened my eyes and nodded, seeing first Indira's worried face close to my own and then the black-garbed form of Mandy, still standing where I last remembered. I groaned inwardly and laid a reassuring hand on Indira's shoulder. The sudden switches in time were hard enough to contend with, but now I also had to cope with a just as sudden switch in roles. From pink rubber sex doll to stern teacher and mistress in the blink of an eye, more or less. 'Yes, I'm fine,' I muttered.

Indira did not look convinced. She grasped my arm and turned me away from our 'pupil', drawing me towards the furthest corner of the room. 'Did you go back again?' she hissed, her mouth close to my ear.

I nodded. 'Yes,' I whispered. 'Yes, I went back, or rather forward.'

'For how long this time?' she asked.

I frowned. 'Not long,' I answered, trying to calculate how long it had taken Carmen to complete my transformation. 'An hour, maybe just a bit more, but not much.'

'You looked... empty... your eyes, but only for a few moments.'

'I know,' I said. 'The time I spend in either place doesn't seem to have any relationship to the time I'm away, if you know what I mean. Last time I was away from here for nearly a month, but that was only hours in my own time. This time, I've apparently come straight back to where I was, and that was about an hour or so in nineteen seventy-five. Don't ask me to explain it, though.'

'No.' She patted my arm. 'No, and besides, we have work to do here, if you are feeling well enough?'

'I feel fine,' I assured her. 'The feeling of displacement only lasts a few seconds.' I looked down at myself and at the emerald-green dress. 'Perhaps I should change into something more suitable,' I said, smiling.

Indira grinned, flashing her brilliant teeth at me. 'I think perhaps I should be the one,' she said in a tone that made me realise she had already decided. 'Perhaps I should be Molly's mistress and you should watch and instruct if I do not do it correctly.'

'You want to pay her back for what she said to you,' I replied. 'That may not be such a good idea. We don't want to really hurt her, after all.'

'Oh, I shan't hurt her.' She chuckled darkly. 'At least not her pale pink skin. No, if

I am right in understanding the things you have explained to me, it is her spirit that needs to be disciplined.'

'And you reckon you're the girl to do that?'

She nodded, perhaps a shade too enthusiastically. 'Indeed,' she assured me. 'Besides, you will oversee and you will tell me if I become perhaps a little too energetic. And now, should I find something more suitable to wear whilst I deliver my first lesson?'

Twenty minutes later, having left Molly sitting on a stool to which she had to be helped due to the fact that her new boots prevented her bending her knees even far enough to reach the high seat, we returned from the adjoining room, me still in my original gown, but Indira now looking like something straight out of a twentieth century fetish fashion magazine.

Our bookmaker-come-leatherwear worker had done us proud in the intervening weeks, and I suspected when all this was over, if he had any business sense and remembered all the design ideas I had suggested to him, he might go on to become the founding father of quite an empire of alternative fashion. I remembered the trunks in Amelia's loft and wondered what would become of everything we were collecting here in the old mill house. Was there perhaps somewhere in the twentieth century a hidden horde of boxed bondage and discipline equipment that had lain undiscovered for a century or more?

I shook my head and concentrated on the present - or the past, if you prefer - and Indira, who had adapted to walking in the ridiculously high-heeled platform boots I had selected for her, and whose waist compressed easily into the matching white corset. With long white leather gloves on her arms and a white studded leather choker about her neck, the contrast between her outfit and her skin was stunning. Even Molly seemed impressed, though her initial expression soon gave way to one of concern when she realised she was now to be at Indira's mercy.

'Quiet,' I snapped when she began to protest. 'Slaves who speak out of turn will be gagged. Besides, you already know she won't really hurt you.'

'Just a little encouragement,' Indira smirked. In her hand she carried a short leather switch, which she flicked through the air now, smiling as Molly started visibly. 'Now,' she said, stepping behind her intended victim, 'let's have you back on your feet.' She grasped Molly beneath her armpits and lifted her upright with astonishing ease. Molly staggered a little for balance, but quickly recovered, only for Indira to prod her towards the end of the bed and the high footboard, the top of which was roughly level with the bound girl's waist.

'This should do to begin with,' Indira said, tapping the heavy woodwork with the end of her whip. 'Let's have you bending over this, I think.'

Molly shot me one last, pleading glance, but when she saw that I remained immovable, she surrendered to the inevitable and slowly bent forward.

'Further than that, white slave meat!' Indira barked.

I opened my mouth to admonish her for breaking my rule about colour references, but stopped myself. Just this once, I decided, it might do Molly some good to know what it felt like to have the hue of her skin used as a further insult.

The tight corset made bending at the waist difficult, but not impossible, even though there would have been no way Molly could have gone over as far as I knew she could do when unhampered by such a restrictive garment. She finally managed an approximate forty-five degree angle, which had her upper body leaning over the footboard parallel with the mattress. I stepped forward, picked up several pillows from next to the headboard, and arranged them beneath her shoulders and breasts. She tried to turn her head upwards to look at me, but the neck corset made that impossible. Until Indira permitted her to stand upright again, her field of vision was restricted to a flower-patterned counterpane just a few inches from her nose.

'Legs apart, slut,' Indira commanded, inserting her crop between Molly's thighs to emphasise the order. Awkwardly, the girl shuffled her feet to comply, but Indira was not satisfied at her first attempt. 'Further,' she hissed, tapping one taut buttock with the stiff leather.

Molly jumped, but the flicked contact had the desired effect and she increased the gap between her ankles by a good seven or eight inches.

'Now, what do we have here?' Indira asked, her tone teasing. She stepped closer and inserted her free hand between Molly's thighs, and from the bound girl's reaction, I realised she had gone straight in for the kill. Without withdrawing her hand, Indira used the other to flick down with the whip, bringing a squeak of pain from her hapless victim. 'I asked you a question, whore!' she snarled, though when she looked across at me I saw she was actually smiling.

I winked encouragement and nodded, but said nothing.

The whip rose and fell again with a sharp crack. This time Molly's squeal was a good deal louder and I saw a red mark appear across her buttock.

'Tell me what it is I have my hand in, slut.'

Molly groaned and I saw her eyes close. 'M-my f-fanny,' she gasped.

Indira laughed. 'Your *what?*' she retorted. 'You're a whore, a slave, and slaves don't have fannies, they have cunts, don't they?'

I was somewhat taken aback by Indira's sudden use of the most base vernacular, but the word had the right effect on her victim when she repeated her question.

'It's my c-cunt,' she whimpered.

Indira laughed and again snapped the crop down on unprotected flesh. 'It's your cunt, *what?*'

Molly was quick to understand, as quick as Indira had been to slip into this unaccustomed role. Anne-Marie and Carmen would have been most impressed with her, and for a moment I wondered if Andrea had suddenly returned to take over.

'It's my cunt, mistress,' Molly sobbed.

Indira nodded. 'Then answer me properly, whore-slave,' she persisted. 'What do I have my fingers in, eh?'

'My cunt, mistress.'

Indira winked back at me now. 'You see,' she said, addressing Molly, 'that wasn't so difficult, was it? All you need to remember is that your role here is as a slave, and a slave exists to serve and pleasure and, sometimes, if she's very fortunate and if she earns it, to be pleasured in return. Now, I shall give you one taste of what an errant slave should expect.' She stepped back and without warning swung her arm. It was not a particularly vicious blow, but it was far harder than anything she had so far delivered. The crack of leather on stretched flesh was like a pistol shot in the confines of the bedchamber, but its noise was more than matched by Molly's howl of pain.

'Oh, shut up,' was Indira's only reaction. 'Shut up and stand up. I have a duty for you to perform.' She grasped the back of Molly's neck collar and used it to help the weeping girl regain a standing position. 'Turn around, slave-slut,' she ordered, stepping further back herself. 'Now then,' she said, letting one white-gloved hand trail slowly down towards her own exposed sex, 'you, a whore, have a cunt, and I, a lady and a mistress, have what we prefer to call a cunny, or even a minnie. Do you think my cunny is pretty, slave girl Molly.'

Poor Molly. She blinked and tried to nod, but the restriction about her neck made the gesture impossible, so she was forced to answer out loud. 'Yes, mistress,' she said hurriedly.

'Then ask if you may kiss it, slut.' Indira deliberately moved her own legs further apart and pushed one gloved finger between her already glistening lower lips. 'Come on now, don't be shy.'

I could see the idea shocked Molly, and I could also see a practical problem in what Indira wanted her to do, but for the moment I decided not to interfere. For a few seconds nothing happened and I thought Molly was going to refuse outright, but the sight and threat of the crop, which Indira now flexed deliberately between her hands, proved a strong incentive. Unsteadily, the bound girl moved forward and tried to stoop and bend, but even though she was still able to get her back parallel with the floor, her boots meant she was just a few inches too tall to bring her head low enough, which was exactly what I suspected would happen. Indira allowed the poor creature to struggle for several seconds, pushing her sex against the bridge of Molly's nose and rubbing herself up and down, while her victim manfully tried to get lower and raise her head to even greater degree, a feat made doubly impossible by the corsets about her torso and neck.

At last Indira relented. Pushing Molly away temporarily, she turned and began arranging the pillows I had placed under our student a few minutes earlier, draping the final one over the top of the headboard with the others piled behind and beneath it to form a more or less comfortable seat, which she lifted herself onto and perched on with her legs wide apart. 'Now,' she instructed, 'let us try that once more, my pretty doxy, eh?' The arrangement lifted her at least another six inches and she was also able to offer herself at a more convenient angle now.

Molly, very red in the face, both from shortage of breath and from shame and embarrassment, tottered forward and once again bent stiffly forward. This time she was able to comply with Indira's wishes and, as her head disappeared between the brown thighs, I saw my exotic lover stiffen with pleasure.

'Ah, yes,' she crooned. 'Yes indeed, Molly... and now your tongue, girl. You know what to look for, I'm sure. I... oh yes!'

I smiled. Obviously Molly *did* know what to look for and had found the target first up.

Indira's eyes rolled and she lifted her legs and draped them over the stooping girl's shoulders, grasping her head and holding her firmly in position so she could not retreat. 'Lay on, my pretty pink slut,' she gasped, and began slowly rocking her hips back and forth.

Now I decided to take a hand in the proceedings and stepped quietly across the room to take up position just behind Molly, who standing with her legs apart for balance offered an easy target. I stretched forward one hand and gently cupped her sex from behind. It felt hot on the outside, but when I began to probe with one finger, I found she was still fairly dry. Quickly I began rubbing my finger back and forth as I would have done with either myself or Anne-Marie, and was rewarded first with a muffled moan from between Indira's legs and, a moment or so later, by a rapid moistening from within, so that I was now easily able to insert two fingers and establish mastery over that one weak point I knew would guarantee our reluctant trainee's ultimate capitulation.

It made quite an erotic tableau, I realised, and similar scenes would one day be captured on photographic plates and paper for the delectation of discerning gentlemen. For about thirty seconds we all remained like this, but the sights and smells were becoming too much for me. I dropped to my knees and pressed my own face between soft feminine thighs, my tongue eager where Molly's had earlier been hesitant.

Fortunately I had not bothered to wear any drawers beneath my skirt and shift and I scrabbled at the folds of fabric, clawing them up into my lap, so that the hand I had first employed to stimulate Molly could now perform a similar task on myself. I was already wet and my nubbin throbbing and swollen, and my self-ministrations drove me to redouble my efforts on the hot little box in my mouth. I heard several groans - Indira's and Molly's, it was impossible to distinguish the one from the other - and then suddenly I felt our joint victim starting to shake and tremble. A moment later I began to come myself, burying my face as deeply as I could in order to stifle my own cries.

And then it was done and somehow I was standing up, Indira too, with a red-faced and even more breathless Molly between us. I reached around and stroked her buttocks gently, noting that she was still quivering and possibly still in that state I always think of as 'aftershock', where although the main wave of the orgasm has passed, little miniature climaxes continue, in my case for anything up to three or four minutes, although I know now that I'm somewhat of an extreme case.

'Now, was that not quite nice?' I asked gently. I looked across at Indira and could see from the expression on her face that 'quite nice' didn't even come close, but Molly managed to nod. 'Good,' I said, 'so we'll do it again in a little while.'

'But surely, mistress,' Molly rasped, 'this is sinful, is it not?'

'What?' It was all I could do not to laugh out loud. Instead I said, 'You silly girl, it's no more sinful than anything you've ever done in your short life up until now, and quite probably a lot more enjoyable. And it's certainly not illegal,' I added with a chuckle, remembering that quirky story about how, when her ministers took before Queen Victoria a bill that would outlaw homosexuality and lesbianism, that grand but in many ways unworldly old lady asked how it was possible between two women. Rather than face the embarrassment of a graphic explanation, the officials struck out the passage referring to Sapphic activities and so the allegedly weaker sex enjoyed an immunity not enjoyed by their male counterparts until that insidious piece of legislation, that was to be the cause of so much agonising for so many decades, was finally repealed in the nineteen-sixties.

'No,' I said, leaning across and kissing the embarrassed girl on the cheek, 'you've committed no sin in my eyes. But there are those who have, and we should comfort ourselves with the thought that everything we do now is dedicated to bringing upon them the retribution their foul depravity has earned them.' Brave and noble words, I told myself, and tried to ignore the fact that in the meantime it looked as if I was going to have a most enjoyable time with my trio of acolytes, not to mention Indira and, of course, Erik, who I suspected I might have been neglecting for far too long. And, as I thought of Erik, a cunning idea began to form in my head. I grinned to myself as I left the room. So far this was all going very well and, if we continued as we had begun, my plan to deal with the dual menace of Hacklebury and Megan Crowthorne might be able to happen a good deal earlier than I originally anticipated.

When I returned to the present this time around, it was to find Carmen starting to really enjoy herself with her latest creation, in the same way that pre-teen girls become entranced with their Barbie dolls and all their various outfits and accessories, except that her ultimate aim was not to produce a finished ensemble reflecting the latest fashion craze, but rather to present me to her waiting audience in the way certain lonely males might try to give their inflatable bed companions the appearance of the girl of their more elaborate private dreams.

First she wrapped a waist-cinching corset around me, a garment that was not intended to even support, let alone cover, my rubber breasts, which in any case did not need any additional support, thanks to the hardened layer within the latex. This corset, to my surprise, was made from neither leather nor rubber, but black satin with red piping and lacing, the sort of thing it is possible to buy over the counter in one of the more discerning lingerie establishments.

The stockings she then drew up my legs were black fishnet, so that my painted toenails were clearly visible through the mesh, and this illusion was maintained by the addition of red sandals with thick platform soles and wickedly spiked heels. Red satin gloves were then drawn up my arms, but I saw they were fingerless, exposing my plastic fingernails. Finally, a black and red satin choker was fastened about my throat and there I stood before the mirror, the epitome of a high-class tart in her boudoir, though perhaps the allusion to class was somewhat spoiled by the gaping mouth that was plainly inviting only one thing.

I had half expected I would now have to wait around while Carmen transformed Anne-Marie and Andrea as she had done me, but in making that assumption, I had underestimated the devious dominatrix's ability to play psychological games. Where she was quite happy to spend her time turning me into one of her new sex dolls, having beaten Anne-Marie in what I still suspected was a fixed contest, she had now decided to emphasise her temporary superior status by consigning her defeated opponent's preparations to someone else, probably someone who could best be described as an 'underling'. As a result, no sooner was I pronounced ready than I was led out along a narrow passageway and into a slightly larger version of the room in which I had been dressed, to find myself confronted with one mirror image of myself, and one other that almost made up an identical trio, but for the far too obvious presence of a large pink penis jutting up from where the first two of us sported our oversized female genitalia.

Larger though it was, this second room was now quite crowded, for in addition to the three dolls there were their various creators - Carmen, Hector and a total of five identically rubber-clad women in deep red latex cat suits, matching high-heeled knee-high boots and enveloping hood masks. The scene was eerie and yet at the same time exciting, though in a way that had my stomach turning, for I was only too aware that all the trouble that had gone into preparing us in this way had not been taken merely to display us as trophies. I looked across at my identical twin, wondering just what was going on inside Anne-Marie's head, but the blank face and staring blue eyes of course gave no hint of emotion.

'Well ladies,' Carmen declared, and I guessed she wasn't talking to the three of us, but to her assembled helpers, even though one of these was the all too obviously male Hector, 'I think we can congratulate ourselves tonight. These three dolls are perfect, absolutely perfect. It's a shame we can't mass-produce and sell them just like this,' she added, laughing. 'The demand would be amazing, I think.'

I shuddered at the prospect of such a fate, for it was all a little too close to something Megan Crowthorne might have done, always assuming she'd had access to the latex and technology that went into creating our outer shells, which of course she hadn't. I supposed the world, and me in particular, should be thankful for the small mercy that Megan hadn't lived in the latter half of the twentieth century. On a desirability scale of one to ten, that prospect ranked somewhere in the very heavy minuses.

Meanwhile, role-playing fantasy or not, I was still stuck in Carmen's clutches and, whilst I could comfort myself with the fact that in what would only be a matter of hours, I would eventually end up warm and snug in my own bed, first there would be a 'scene' to contend with that had been created in the depths of a mind that was in its own way every bit as warped as those of my nineteenth century tormentors. To make matters worse, I had walked reasonably happily into this with both eyes open.

No, I consoled myself, that wasn't entirely accurate. What *I* had happily walked into was a scene with Anne-Marie and Andy in his Andrea role. It had then been Anne-Marie who walked - driven would be more accurate - both of us into this, and whilst part of me was whirring away towards sexual overdrive as I stood there gaping my stupid sex-dolly invitation, the sensible, feet-on-the-ground part of me was resenting every second I was spending here when I had so much to finish back in the real world.

For a few seconds everything in the underground chamber faded and the sounds about me, dull enough anyway from the effect of the rubber stretched over my ears, grew fainter still. My immediate reaction was that I was about to go back again, but then I realised that wasn't the way it happened and that what I was experiencing was something different, a sort of revelation. I realised what I had just thought, and what I would have just said, had my mouth not been filled and distorted by that awful gag.

Back in the real world.

I couldn't believe I'd actually said that - well, *thought* it - because eighteen thirty-nine was actually...

The *real* world.

Yes, eighteen thirty-nine *was* the real world. Maybe it wasn't *my* real world, but it was real enough to Angelina and Indira and real enough to me while I was there, even if I was really nothing more than a displaced person in the whole affair. In fact, eighteen thirty-nine and what we had been doing in Arundel was a damned sight more real than what I seemed to have been spending most of my time doing since my first encounter with Anne-Marie, leaving aside my attempts at playing Philip Marlowe with various records offices. And it was not only a damned sight more real; it was also a damned sight more urgent.

I closed my eyes and willed myself back in time again and...

And, of course, nothing happened. That is to say nothing happened in the time travelling department, though something did happen in the small, stone walled subterranean cell under a ruined priory. I felt a sharp slap across my rubber-clad backside and jerked my eyes wide open again, although wide open or peering didn't make a whole lot of difference, given that I could only see through the centre sections of the lenses covering my eyes.

'And of course,' Carmen was saying close to my ear, 'while number three dolly here can fuck as well as being fucked, I'm afraid you two dollies mostly just have to be happy with being on the receiving end.' She stepped away from me and I watched as she seized Andrea's monstrously jutting shaft. 'Sadly, though,' she continued, and I could imagine the smile on her face underneath the rubber mask, 'poor Andrea dolly here won't really get much out of all the fucking she's going to be asked to do tonight. You see, there's a very hard layer of plastic between the two softer rubber layers, so whether she's rock-hard inside this, or whether she's a total flop won't make any difference to any of us and certainly won't make any difference to her, poor love.' She flicked her tongue between her lips, a pink snake gliding between two carmine ribbons bounded by black and white rubber. 'My bet is she's actually hard as a stick of Brighton rock underneath, but then that doesn't earn me any bonus points for shrewdness. Give this girlie the girlie treatment and straightaway she starts acting like a dirty little boy, don't you Andrea, my sweetie doll?'

I felt a barely controllable urge to plant my heavy platform sole straight between Carmen's legs, and yet I knew she was dead right in what she said. I didn't pretend to really understand what it was about being dressed as a female that appealed to Andy - he'd been perfectly capable of rising to the occasion and satisfying me in a perfectly normal situation the night before - but there was something about it, especially when the feminine outfits in question were comprised either wholly or largely of either rubber or leather, or a mixture of both, that rendered my erstwhile lover a helpless slave to emotions and urges that went way outside the normal chemistry of sexual attraction, lust or even love. In much the same way that being bound and gagged and dressed in all manner of bizarre outfits seemed to have the same effect on me, I had to admit. Even this doll routine was doing something to my hormones, or at least to a trigger in some part of my brain that carried the authority in that little bit of my brain where the sign read *Hormone Department - Over Production Section*. Brought down to its basic components, mask equals anonymity (include heavily and bizarrely made-up face in the category of mask) and cuffs, chains and/or ropes equals 'not my fault', which in turn equals 'not my responsibility'. Result, off comes the handbrake labelled *Decent Moral Standards* and the automatic gearbox shifts straight into overdrive, with the result that the Teena mobile careers headlong down whatever hill of depravity happens to lie in its path.

'Come on then, dollies dearest,' Carmen trilled, 'time to show you off to your adoring public. And, oh my, aren't they just going to *love* you!'

And as we started to move towards the door, this time I *did* have just about two seconds' worth of warning before I was zipped back through time yet again...

73

Some things never change, and if you want a benchmark of stability it's rain in autumn in England, or more precisely, mucky, penetrating, dismal and chilling drizzle, the sort of stuff that seems innocuous enough when you watch it through the window from the warm comfort of your living room, but try walking outside in it for even ten minutes and you come back looking like a rejected extra from the set of *Titanic*, that bit of the film when everyone ends up in the water, either inside or out of the stricken liner.

It was drizzling and, of course, I wasn't inside in the warm looking out, I was walking along the riverbank with Erik, the stiff breeze finding every chink in the cape I had wrapped about me and my eyelashes doing creditable impressions of eucalyptus leaves in a monsoon. I looked round and upwards at the shimmering features of my Viking consort, but if he found this awful weather depressing, he was made of sterner stuff and wasn't about to show it any more than he was given to showing any other sort of emotion. A man whose forebears managed to discover America - and show the strength of will not to tell anyone in Europe when they got back - by braving the Atlantic in a ship not much bigger than a Ford Transit with the roof cut off, was hardly going to be put out by plain ordinary English autumnal weather.

'Going well it is with Molly?' he asked.

I nodded and a large drip of water flew off the tip of my nose. 'Very well,' I confirmed. I hoped now that things would be progressing equally as well with Milly, who was next in the queue. I had met Erik and the two girls just outside the mill house and despatched the unsuspecting girl inside, into the clutches of the waiting Indira and a newly polished version of Molly, who I was confident would be only too eager to play a part in imparting some of her recently acquired experience to her colleague. Mandy, meanwhile, had been despatched to fetch milk from the farmhouse that was halfway between where we now lived and the town itself.

'I should congratulate you on your choices,' I said as we halted before a stile. 'If the other two respond as well as Molly, we'll be able to say we're ready for business by the end of the week.'

'Yourself, you will not the same be doing?'

I peered cautiously at Erik. His features were as impassive as ever, but I sensed something behind his question.

'The same not be doing as what?' I replied carefully, determined to draw him out a little further.

He swallowed, perhaps nervously. 'As the girls,' he replied levelly. 'Not the thing that these people paying for will be,' he added, the closest he was going to come to clarification, I realised.

So that was it, protective or jealous, or maybe a combination of the two. I smiled and turned my head away, fixing my stare ahead as I carefully climbed atop the stile. 'No,' I said firmly, 'most certainly not. I have a different role to play, as I thought you would realise.'

He made no reply, but reached up to steady my elbow as I climbed down onto the wet grass.

'I have to create a character that will provide an aura of mystery and intrigue,' I elaborated, 'Madame X.'

'Madam X?'

I grinned, but was careful not to let him see. 'Well, maybe not Madame X exactly, but something along those lines. I have to make sure no one can possibly recognise or even describe me, for a start, which is why I've used that veil for our initial interviews. It's almost as good as a mask.' *Though it doesn't seem to have quite the same effect on me personally*, I thought.

'What I need,' I continued as Erik jumped over the stile to land alongside me, 'is some sort of alias, a different name, and to establish a reputation, at least among our own little circle of clients, of being a strict, authoritarian sort of person, if you get what I mean.'

'Like Miss Crowthorne?' Erik nodded.

I cleared my throat. 'Well, something like that,' I said. 'Maybe not quite such a nutter, though.'

'A nutter?' Erik raised his eyebrows. 'This something to do with trees is not, I am guessing?'

I tapped one forefinger against my temple. 'No, nothing to do with trees,' I agreed, mirroring his look. 'Nutter means mad, screw-loose, bonkers, not quite the full—'

'Krona?' Erik suggested. 'Ah, knowing what the driving is I now am.'

'So, first I need a name.'

'The name you have using been is wrong? No good?' He was referring to the name of Mrs MacIntosh, under which I had bought the house and conducted my business since our original escape. And as far as the prospective clients I had seen so far were concerned, they had been politely but firmly instructed to address me as Mrs Smith, at least until they were contacted again. I hadn't even confirmed to them I would be the final person they dealt with, suggesting merely that I was a go-between who could assist them in their quest to add flesh, or *more* flesh, I should say, to their particular fantasies.

'That name's all right as far as the official side of things goes,' I conceded, 'but I need a stage name, that's what I need.'

'A stage name?'

'You know, like actors and actresses have, a name to perform under.'

Erik looked at me blankly and I saw he had no idea what I was talking about. He obviously thought the thespian brigade used the names they were born with, so I quickly explained. He caught on quickly.

'Countess, you must be a countess,' he said.

I liked the sound of that. After all, there were tens of thousands of counts and countesses strewn across Europe, more so in those days even than now, when Italy and France especially have more than a share of them. 'Yes,' I said, 'a countess. How about Contessa di Ventura?' In my own time there had recently been a lot of advertising publicity concerning a car of that name and it seemed to roll off the tongue with just the right ring to it. Erik appeared to like it and so the Contessa Sadie Christa di Ventura was born. I'll leave you to work out how I settled on those particular names.

'I hate this rain,' I declared, by way of keeping the conversation going on a lighter note.

Erik gazed up at the leaden skies. 'Yes, and for a good time set now it is,' he announced.

'Like the next hundred and fifty years,' I quipped, forgetting in the way of most English people that we do actually have a dry summer period. 'Perhaps we should turn back?'

'There is shelter just up ahead,' Erik said, pointing along the path. 'An old barn used now not much, I think.'

'You've been exploring,' I said. 'Been having some nice walks with the girls, have you?' For the first time, at least I *think* it was the first time, Erik blushed. 'Ah, but I think that's nice, showing the poor city girls the beauty of the countryside, and other things,' I added wickedly.

His cheeks went two shades of red deeper. 'Go back then we ought,' he said, halting.

I shook my head. 'Oh no we don't.' I jabbed my finger forward in the direction he had just indicated. 'This girl wants to see the beauty of the countryside, and other things too.' I glanced down at the small satchel he carried slung from a rawhide shoulder strap. 'Do you have the things I told you to keep in there?'

Erik seemed taken aback, but quickly recovered. 'Yes, I do,' he replied, 'but needing them I have not been.'

'No, you wouldn't, not with Milly Molly Mandy, anyway. Cast off knickers fore and aft at the first murmurings from the cockpit, that trio. No, don't look so worried, Erik, you've only been doing what I told you to do. Got to keep the troops exercised, after all.'

I think it was at about this point that my Viking hero began to hear the tinkle-tinkle of the Krona dropping somewhere close by. Well, who in her right mind would go trudging along a draughty riverbank in crappy English autumn weather just for the hell of it, eh? And I knew precisely where that old barn was, having found it myself whilst out for a walk a few weeks earlier on a much more pleasant day, I might add. Or had that been Angelina? Never mind, whichever of us had been at the helm for the discovery, it was obviously etched clearly on our joint navigational charts.

It certainly didn't look as though it was getting much use nowadays, I saw as we approached it after rounding the bend in the river, for the sides were overgrown and one of the huge front doors was hanging by one hinge, and only just hanging by it at that, but the roof seemed largely intact and there were no glass windows to have broken over the years. Come to think of it, there probably weren't any vandals about to chuck stones through them had there been any, I mused as we trudged forward through grass, that was now above knee-high and adding to my soaked-to-the-skin factor by a multiple of two.

Inside the barn were the remains of what had once been three or four bales of straw, though weeds had encroached over nearly half the ground floor area now. I peered through the half-light and saw that someone - no prizes for guessing who - had heaped some of the straw in a far corner and draped what looked like sacking over it to form a rough bed. A *very* rough bed.

I tossed back the hood of my cape and began scrabbling at the ties that held it about my neck, letting the sodden cloth drop to the ground before, as an afterthought, scooping it up again and draping it over one of the misshapen bales. I ran my fingers through the hair of my wig, surprised to discover that apart from the fringe bit at the front it was near enough dry, and that even the lacy headdress I used for keeping the wig in place was only damp at the front. I turned to Erik, who had taken off his satchel and was now draping his own cape over a broken cartwheel that lay against one of the uprights supporting what had once been a raised area for storing loose hay.

'This is a bit better,' I said, looking around further, my eyes slowly growing accustomed to the shadows and picking out a handcart abandoned against the further wall, two pitchforks, one broken, a large rake and a stack of assorted timber lengths standing upright in one corner. 'I wonder who owns it?'

'Oh, you do,' Erik replied quite nonchalantly.

I blinked. 'I do?'

He nodded. 'Checking the titles I have been and all land from the house to here, belonging to the mill it was and still is.'

'But I only bought the house,' I said. The mill itself had been disused for so long there was hardly anything left worth talking about, and I'd assumed I'd just agreed on a price for the residential part. Apparently, I'd been wrong.

Erik shook his head. 'No, buying the mill and all its grounds you were,' he said. 'A chart there is with all the papers.' He grinned proudly. 'Charts I am knowing about,' he said.

I looked around the barn with fresh eyes, my brain slipping up two gears. 'Bloody Norah!' I exclaimed. 'This must be nearly half a mile from the house and you mean to tell me I own all that ground?' Mind you, it was probably only a narrow strip of ground, I realised, and Erik confirmed this when I asked him. However, he also confirmed that my narrow strip ran for another half mile upstream. My mind went back to that day in the solicitors' office in Chichester. This was the second time in my life I'd discovered I'd become a landowner... well, the first, if we're going by the standard calendar and not chronological events as experienced by me personally, of course.

It then occurred to me that this thought was quite possibly erroneous anyway. The whole motivation for Hacklebury's machinations was for him to get his claws into Angelina's fortunes, and the likelihood was that Angelina's wealth comprised land as well as hard cash, and I suddenly realised that I had absolutely no idea exactly how wealthy she was. There had to be more than the estate Amelia bequeathed to me, handy as that was, but just how much more and what had subsequently become of that wealth was a mystery, and likely to remain so, at least for the foreseeable future, I told myself, and instantly dismissed the thought. For the present, there were more urgent matters to attend to.

I turned to Erik. 'Strip,' I ordered, and he looked just a bit taken aback. 'Go on,' I said, 'you heard me. Take them off, the clothes, all of them.'

He opened his mouth to say something, but one look at my expression was enough to silence him. Slowly, he bent over and began removing his right boot.

'Everything,' I said, though very softly now, as he hesitated at the shirt only stage. Carefully, he reached down and began drawing the garment over his head, letting it drop to the straw beside him so he stood before me completely naked.

I stepped forward and reached out one hand to cup his manhood, which, to his everlasting credit, had remained flaccid and apparently unimpressed. However, my first touch was too much even for Erik's will, and I felt the beast begin to stir in my fingers. I looked up and smiled into his eyes. 'Up, Rover,' I whispered. 'Let's give the bone a dog, shall we?' Of course, he didn't understand what I was saying as such, but he most certainly had the gist of it. The thick shaft quickly grew thicker still, rising steadily until it stood proudly upright in my small hand. I stroked the length and then cupped his full balls with my other hand. 'Is this nice?' I whispered.

He grunted confirmation and I began working his length, drawing his foreskin back to reveal the shiny purplish knob that would soon be leading the charge into me. Quickly I stooped, opened my lips and drew it into my mouth, flicking my tongue wickedly back and forth and drawing a shiver from my towering partner. And then I stopped, stepped back and began taking my own clothes off, barely able to restrain myself from tearing them off in undignified haste. With an effort I managed to control myself and laid my gown, its lower skirt sodden from the rain, over a small heap of straw that had probably once been another bale. I stood in my shift, my corset, stockings and boots and held out my hand.

'Knife,' I rasped. 'Give me your knife.' He passed it to me, and without ceremony I used the razor-sharp blade to hack away the skirts of my shift from just below the hem of my corset, revealing stocking tops and garters and the fact that I wore no under-drawers. With great deliberation, I reached under my chin and pulled apart the ribbon that held the lace kerchief over my head, tossed it aside, and then slowly lifted my wig clear, placing it on top of my discarded gown. All the while, although I did not look at Erik once, I knew he was watching me intently and I could almost feel his eyes burning into my flesh. At last I looked up and took three steps towards him.

'Get the bag,' I whispered, and as he stooped to retrieve it, I slowly turned my back on him, crossing my wrists behind me in an unmistakeable gesture of submission. A moment later I felt the narrow leather strap being wound about them, securing my arms where I held them. I drew in a deep breath, my breasts rising so that my nipples rose above the top of the corset. Then, as I slowly exhaled, Erik began turning me back to face him.

'What you want, this is it, true?' he asked gently.

I swallowed and nodded, leaning closer towards him as if to emphasise my confirmation. Deep within me I could feel the fires beginning to fan themselves into life, the distant heat rising rapidly to become a furnace. I could feel my own hot stickiness and knew that any moment now it would be leaking onto my thighs, betraying me further, if that were possible. *Bitch in heat*, I thought idly. *Me or you to blame, Angelina?* I thought I knew the answer to that one, but it hardly mattered. 'Finish it properly,' I whispered.

Erik blinked twice.

I closed my eyes. 'The mask, you great ox,' I urged. 'Do it as you did those times before, for pity's sake.'

And then he was pulling the soft leather over my head, adjusting the eye and mouth openings, tightening the laces at the back until the kid hood hugged my skull like another layer of skin. I peered out at him, faceless now and ready for my surrender, a helpless slave in the hands of her powerful master. I felt tiny, powerless, but more than that, I felt liberated, as if I were now someone else and the destiny of this anonymous person was beyond not only my control, but hers also. Without a word I slipped down to my knees, craning my neck, my tongue flickering out through the slit in the leather, sliding wetly up and down his entire length. Then the throbbing shaft was inside my mouth and I was drawing it deeper and deeper, until I was all but choking on it.

I felt hands on the sides of my head, first encouraging and then restraining, as Erik pulled himself from me. I was drawn to my feet, lifted, my thighs spread wide as I was held above his fleshy spear.

'Oh yes!' I heard myself gasp, and I threw my legs about his waist as he cupped his huge hands under my taut buttocks, steadying me as I sat helpless on my human throne. I felt the heat pressing against my entrance and I wriggled slightly, groaning in pleasure as warm flesh caressed moist flesh, and then he was entering me, pushing me apart as he lowered me down, until finally I was little more than a mounted specimen of desire.

'Bastard!' I hissed, my lips searching in vain for his and finding only his thick neck. 'Oh you great, awful, beautiful bastard!' I looked up through misted eyes and saw he was watching my face intently, an expression somewhere between awe and bewilderment floating across his features. 'What are you waiting for?' I managed to gasp. 'I can't do anything like this, can I?' I couldn't prevent a high-pitched snigger from escaping my lips. 'Look at me,' I giggled, contracting my inner muscles so a spasm of icy heat shot up my spine, 'just look at me, the grand lady, all stuffed and mounted like a prize specimen.' I bit into my lip so hard I tasted blood, and groaned again as Erik lifted me slightly, and then let me back down again, the movement of his impossible shaft within me making every nerve-ending turn a triple backward somersault.

'Quiet now,' he said so calmly that I could not believe it. 'Quiet now you will be, for Erik is in the charge, is he not?'

I nodded dumbly and let out a long sigh. 'Yes,' I breathed, 'Erik is in the charge...'

Our reappearance back into the main crypt area was greeted with a mixture of applause, cheering, disbelieving gasps and shrieks, and one huge fellow's raucous laughter all but drowned out everything else. I peered across the heads to where he was standing, close to the wall on the left, and immediately I thought of Erik. For whoever this was, face hidden behind a glossy black leather mask, muscles bulging beneath a short-sleeved T-shirt of the same, was a giant of a man, taller even than I was despite my extreme footwear, a man who not so much stood out in a crowd, but who stood out *above* a crowd, and I was certain he had only arrived while we were being dolled up. I knew I would have noticed him had he been there earlier, and I had not.

My stomach did one of its peculiar gymnastic feats and I looked away, casting my eyes downwards as we were ushered centre stage, but I could feel his eyes upon me, yes, *me*, of that I was sure, for something told me I was going to end up with him in much the same way I had ended up with Erik, though where my Angelina self had appealed by her very lack of stature, the figure I now cut had an appeal for all the opposite reasons. With my natural height emphasised by several inches of platform sole and spiked heel, and my breasts hidden beneath a pair of much more prominent, albeit artificial ones, I knew I represented quite a striking trophy as surely as I somehow knew this Hercules was going to make sure he was the one who ultimately lifted me.

'Well now, ladies, gentlemen and others,' Carmen said, her voice booming over the speaker system. Somehow a microphone had appeared in her hand, but then I had been distracted for several seconds, so it almost certainly wasn't magic. 'Tonight we have several more special events and, as most of you know, our efforts here are dedicated to raising money for good causes - in this case St Beryl's Orphanage in Mattley Green. Several of you have already donated on the way in here tonight, but now we have what I'm sure will prove a most popular and profitable feature.' She paused, waved one arm for dramatic emphasis, and then pointed towards the three of us, not that she needed to draw any attention to us, as we were still the centre of attention visually.

'Friends and slaves,' she cried, 'may I present the epitome of sexual fulfilment, the answer to more than one wet dream, the Dollies Dearest!'

This time there was a concerted ovation accompanied by a variety of cheers and whoops. Behind my mask I would have grinned if I'd been able to, despite the apparent precariousness of my situation. Mask equals anonymity, bondage equals lack of responsibility, dolly equals... someone else's problem.

'Our dollies here are the ultimate love companions,' Carmen continued when the noise abated, 'and as such they are valuable commodities. Only partly trained, and that's going to be all part of the fun, I think, they are nevertheless capable of offering total satisfaction to all who need it.'

There was a ripple of laughter at this.

'And so, knowing that you're all going to be queuing for their services, we have decided the fairest way to prevent everyone getting trampled in the rush will be to auction our lovely creations. The auction will take place in three stages, each stage just over two hours after the previous, during which each of our dollies will be up for the highest bid, the highest bidder on each getting the dolly of his or her choice for one hour, the second highest getting that dolly for a further hour. After each two hours, all dollies will be auctioned again in the same way.

'As you can see, and as I have already said, we have three dollies for you this evening. Number one dolly,' she pointed to Anne-Marie, 'is called Tamsin. She used to be called something else, but I'm afraid she lost the right to that name for the rest of this event as she lost the rights to a lot of other things. As you can see, she is perfectly formed in every way, open and willing... well, I'm sure she'll be willing enough in any of your hands.'

More laughter and a ragged cheer.

'Dolly number two,' Andrea, 'is now called Poppy. She has a slightly different feature, as you can see.' Carmen paused again for the inevitable cackle of mirth to die down. 'So Poppy will obviously appeal in ways that her two sisters might not.'

'And then we come to dolly number three, who we've called Desirée, because she is most desirable. Tall, elegant, with the longest legs anyone could wish for.'

I suspected I ought to be blushing by now, but curiously I felt detached from my own persona and found I was trying to stand taller and straighter than ever.

'So now, good people, and bad, let us begin the first auction with dolly number one.'

The bidding was keen and rapid and reached sixty-five pounds in less than a minute, the lucky punter, or was it just that she had more money than some of the others, being the lady in red herself, Lady Davina, with the second bid secured by a blond-haired fellow in a black leather cat suit wearing a highwayman-style mask. Attention was then turned to Andrea and the bids once more came thick and fast. To everyone's apparent surprise, Davina was again in the thick of the action, and once more landed the bid, this time at eighty pounds, much to the chagrin of two blondes in white leather outfits who might well have been sisters, though their half-face masks made that impossible to judge with any degree of accuracy. They had to settle for second bid and second use.

Now it was my turn and I wondered if Davina might be trying for the clean sweep, but she seemed content with her first two prizes and stood back while others joined in. As before, Carmen started at twenty pounds and the early bidding was between a gangly fellow who was dressed as a sort of leather Count Dracula, complete with swirling cape and heavy face paint that made it impossible to tell what he really looked like, and a short, stocky older man who looked like a medieval executioner complete with a very realistic looking axe.

The bids went in five-pound stages until they reached fifty-five pounds, at which point an older, redheaded woman joined in and immediately raised the ante by jumping up to seventy pounds. The headsman dropped out, but his earlier competitor gamely raised his hand for seventy-five pounds, which her of the red hair immediately topped by a further ten pounds. A few heads swivelled at this, for eighty-five pounds was a considerable sum of money in nineteen seventy-five and it was obvious the bidding was some way away from finishing.

'Ninety quid!' Count Dracula called, waving a long thin arm above his head.

'One hundred,' his adversary announced in a silkily calm voice. One ten, one twenty bid with the lady with the hair and the toe-length skirts. Dracula hesitated and raised a further five. The redhead added five more. Dracula shook his head, acknowledging defeat and prepared to accept seconds, so Carmen looked around, raised her arm and prepared to sell.

'One fifty!' The powerful voice boomed over the heads of the throng, almost as loud as Carmen's amplified commentary. I didn't need to look to know who its owner was. Hercules had entered the fray and with a bid so heavy it reduced the crowd to total silence for several seconds.

'Any advance on—' Carmen began, but the redhead had reached her limit. I saw Dracula apparently considering again, obviously disappointed he had now been relegated to third place and another round of bidding later on, but apparently one hundred and fifty pounds was beyond him, or at least beyond his willingness to part with.

'Sold!' Carmen cried and there was a polite ripple of applause. The audience began to move, turning away, content to get back to whatever it was they had been doing before our entry, and to wait for the next auction session, but Davina stepped up onto the stage, nodded to Carmen and took the microphone from her.

'People,' she said, 'please remain as you are, although perhaps some of you would prefer to make yourselves more comfortable? I believe there are cushions stacked over on the side there, if any of you have slaves you would like to instruct to hand them out. As you know, I offered the top bid for the first two dollies, but not for myself or for my own gratification. As a gesture of my appreciation for all the good work that goes into arranging these functions and as a gesture of appreciation for the support you all show, our first two dollies are for your entertainment. As you can see, they are ideally suited,' Davina continued as black-clad figures moved away in the direction of the cushion pile. 'Poppy is endowed with one of the finest cocks it has ever been my privilege to see and Tamsin, well Tamsin has just the ideal places for it to go. So my friends, before our dollies go into more general action, I shall have them stage a little pleasant diversion for you all.'

The audience began to settle, those at the front squatting onto cushions, whilst further back they either knelt or stood. Meanwhile, Hercules stepped forward, looped a collar about my neck, to which was already attached a leather leash, and drew me from the stage, half lifting me down as a concession to my perilous footwear.

'We'll just watch this for a little while, dolly girl,' he whispered close by my ear. 'It won't take an hour for what I need from you, and besides, I'll have you again later, before this is all over.'

I wasn't particularly surprised at this declaration, for this anonymous giant had made no attempt to disguise his interest in me from the moment he first set eyes on me, but for now I was more interested in what Davina was planning to do with Anne-Marie and Andrea, for I was certain her scheme was going to involve something that was about to take my two friends beyond a particular boundary they had rigidly observed until now.

Not that they were actually related by blood directly, but I knew that, no matter what else they got up to between them, whether it involved other parties or not, Andrea had never until now actually had sex with her mistress. It was never mentioned, but then in its own peculiar way, it didn't have to be. Anne-Marie might masturbate her transvestite slave, and Andrea might well find herself with her head buried between Anne-Marie's thighs and her tongue working overtime, but Andrea's male part had never penetrated Anne-Marie's female part and now that was about to change.

Or was it? Looking at Andrea in her Poppy guise, there was no way I could truly relate that huge, bobbing phallus with the reality of the one I had enjoyed so intimately, and neither was that swollen sex between Anne-Marie's thighs anything but a parody, although I knew from my own identical situation that anything that penetrated its opening would ultimately penetrate her as well. I wondered what was going on in their respective heads as Davina shepherded them into position. Were they both resigned to the inevitability of it all? Did Davina herself know she was overstepping an invisible boundary marker? And, if she did, did the red bitch care?

Of course, as I understood only too well, all this was now superfluous speculation. The other two 'dolls' were powerless to prevent the inevitable, unable to protest, mere puppets in this staged play and, I assumed, only too aware of the vicious looking crop Davina now grasped in her right hand. No amount of latex protection was going to prevent that wicked weapon hurting if it was laid on with anything like true intent, and I was prepared to bet Davina would be only too ready to do just that if her 'purchases' did not perform to expectation.

The performance started fairly low-key. Andrea's arms were freed and Davina encouraged her first to play with her artificial erection and then to begin stroking and caressing Anne-Marie's exterior femininity, first her jutting breasts and then her sex. Of course, as I knew only too well, Anne-Marie would feel little, if anything, of this supposed foreplay, but to the watching crowd, myself included, the scene held an erotic charge that is hard to describe. We were mesmerised by the sight of two bland-faced creatures with gaping mouths, the one doll apparently seducing the other, and all the time the promise of that gigantic erection, which seemed impossibly large to be able to fit into any normal sized bodily orifice.

And yet fit it did, and first into Anne-Marie's rounded mouth opening as she was forced to kneel before her partner, who took hold of her head at either side and meekly followed as Davina grasped the shaft and guided it into the waiting hole. For a brief instant I thought it wasn't going to work, but then I realised the outer layer of latex was soft and slightly compressible and, with Davina snapping at Andrea's buttocks with her whip as encouragement, the initial thrust buried about a quarter of the length. Raucous barracking and cheering erupted, but then just as suddenly subsided as Davina reached down and freed Anne-Marie's arms. I half expected my friend and mistress to pull back at this, but she did not.

Instead, she reached around behind Andrea, grasping her buttocks one in each hand, and began drawing her closer. Slowly, ever so slowly, the pink rubber penis continued to disappear and I felt myself starting to gag at the impossibility of what I was watching. Surely, I thought, Anne-Marie would rebel any second now, and yet she continued swallowing the great length until, in my distorted imagination, I imagined the bulbous purple head must be somewhere close to reaching her stomach.

Of course it wasn't, and neither was she really able to engulf the entire length, but she had made a brave attempt and now, as a slow handclap began, she proceeded to give her partner fellatio with a steady, insistent rhythm. Andrea, of course, or so I assumed, could feel next to nothing from all her efforts, but outwardly the scene worked. Bobbing head, staring eyes - it was at one and the same time powerfully sexual and obscenely comic.

I felt something pressing against the lower part of my face and snapped back to my own predicament. Hercules had inserted what I thought had to be two fingers into my mouth opening, and was using them to turn my head towards him. I felt leather-sheathed fingers against the tip of my tongue and let out a throaty gasp.

'Your turn soon, dolly girl,' he whispered, 'and your efforts won't be as wasted as that one's obviously are.' I felt the pressure of his other arm against my lower stomach, and as I peered downwards I guessed he was probing my outer opening with his fingers, though at this stage I could feel little beyond more exterior pressure. The artificial padded vagina was holding me open, the rigid cup preventing any stimulation of my clitoris. Anything Hercules did would do nothing for me, but then that was what Carmen had intended. I was a sex doll, and sex dolls need no gratification. Sex dolls serve only for the gratification of their owners and, for the next hour or thereabouts, Hercules was my owner and he would gratify himself without any thought for me or my feelings or needs.

And then, to my utter surprise, that thought did what he himself would not be able to do. One moment I was standing there, erect and unresponsive, the next my knees were like jelly and I fell back against him from the sheer force of the orgasm that exploded with the force of a small atom bomb in my pelvis.

'Well, fuck me sideways,' I dimly heard his voice near to my ear. 'I've bought myself a dolly with hidden extras!'

The next few hours passed as in a dream, or as though I was mostly just an observer watching proceedings from behind a smoky glass screen. I watched as the Anne-Marie doll figure was laid out on her back. I watched as the Andrea doll mounted her, guiding her massive shaft into the rubber vagina and then into her body, which could feel virtually nothing. I watched in awe as the Anne-Marie doll bucked and writhed, and then again as the Andrea doll in her turn was laid prone and the Anne-Marie doll straddled and mounted her, riding her with increasing energy until Davina finally declared the performance at an end.

Did either of the mute figures feel or experience anything from their couplings? I know whether they did or not, because they told me afterwards, but I'll leave you to guess for yourselves. For my own part, I confess, I came twice more, even though the powerful hands that cupped my bulging breasts felt as if they were distant feathers and no amount of frigging of my own rubber cunt was ever going to have any effect. It was all in my mind, all of it, reactions triggered purely by the spectacle and by something inside me I knew would always be able to rise and take control, no matter how hard I tried to fight against it or deny it. I felt, as Hercules turned me around and began leading me towards the back of the crypt, that it didn't need a rubber skin and artificial mouth and sex openings to turn me into a sex doll - I was one already, a helpless marionette dancing on the strings of abandonment to a tune that was as old as the world itself.

Chapter 6

'Understanding I think I am,' Erik said, breaking the silence that had hung between us for several minutes. He was sitting, cross-legged, by the side of the makeshift bed, while I was lying on my side, still masked, still bound, and feeling as if someone had pulled a plug somewhere and let every bit of me drain out. Erik leaned across me and gently stroked my leather-covered cheek, a curious expression on his face.

'The game you need to play and pretend that things still as they were are,' he said. 'She has you infected with her wickedness, I think.'

I grunted, shifting my position slightly and shook my head. 'No,' I said, 'Megan hasn't infected me with anything. The infection was there already. I think it's something that's in all of us, but some of us manage to resist it and keep it under control. All Megan did, if she did anything at all, was to break down my resistance, though I couldn't say for sure it might not have happened anyway.'

Erik continued to look at me without expression, but his fingers wandered all over the mask. 'This is the key?' he asked. 'Unlocking a gate it is, I think?'

'It's part of it,' I conceded. 'Behind the mask, and all that. We all wear masks of different kinds throughout our lives, I think. This just happens to be a physical mask rather than an emotional one, if you can understand that?'

He nodded gravely. 'Yes, understand that I can,' he said. He reached over and touched my bound wrists. 'Uncomfortable you must now be,' he suggested.

I grunted again. 'But don't untie me yet,' I whispered. 'Let things stay as they are for a while longer. I need to be punished for my wickedness, I think.'

'Punished?'

'Yes.'

'Ah!'

I nodded, but turned my head sideways to avoid his unblinking scrutiny. There was another silence that lasted maybe ten seconds, and then I heard him stir. I closed my eyes, listening as I heard the rustling of straw followed by the sound of heavier items being moved. They were random sounds, as if he were searching for something. Finally, I heard him returning.

'Stand!'

I opened my eyes and turned my head back towards him. He was holding what seemed to be a length of strap in one hand, with the other hand stretched out to me. With his assistance I managed to get to my feet, and he held the strap out for me to see. It looked as though it might have been part of a harness once, the leather stiff and cracked in several places.

'For your wickedness,' he announced simply.

I nodded. 'Yes.'

Erik grasped my arm and turned me around so I was facing the doorway, and then I felt the pressure of a large hand between my shoulder blades. Suppressing a series of small tremors, I obeyed the pressure and bent forward, moving my feet further apart to maintain my balance. The hand ran down and along my back, past my bound wrists, and rested upon my right buttock. For a few seconds he stroked my taut flesh and then drew the hand back to deliver a sharp slap. I let out a small gasp, followed by a grunt as he spanked the other globe.

'Pretty,' I heard him murmur. I felt the fingers stroking again; twice, three, four times, and then they stopped. This time there was a longer pause before I heard the hiss of leather cutting through the air. It was a short swing, but the strap landed right across the middle of both my cheeks, sending a shockwave surging up to my brain that lit tiny red lights before my eyes.

Again the hiss, followed by another bolt of fire. I took half a step forward to prevent myself from toppling and at the same time Erik grabbed my bound wrists to steady me. I jerked upright, pressing back against his chest, looking up and craning my neck to try and see his face.

'Bastard,' I whimpered. 'Beautiful bastard!' I could feel the heat and pressure of his erection pressing against the small of my back and squirmed around to face him, slipping down onto one knee as he released his grip on me. His manhood stood stiff and proud, just asking to be worshipped, and I came to the altar willingly, almost gagging as I swallowed more than half his length. I sensed him trying to relax, the arm holding the strap dropping to his side. The fire in my backside had spread to ignite little blazes that now consumed my entire body and I could think now of only one thing. I let the slippery rod slide from my mouth and staggered to my feet, facing him squarely.

'Fuck me, master,' I begged. 'Fuck me!' Although I was by far the smaller, as well as bound and wearing the mask of a slave, there was no doubt now which of us was in charge as he scooped me up, spread my thighs and lowered me onto his sacrificial spike. I groaned as he filled me, encircling his hips with my legs and sinking my teeth into the flesh of his shoulder just as the first of a new series of climaxes reared up to claim its prize.

'Let's see if you're really worth your money then, shall we dolly?'

I blinked, peering through the shadows to where Hercules now stood, legs astride, an impressive flesh coloured column rising from the opening in his black leather breeches. He pointed to it, and then made an O shape with his mouth.

'C'mon, dolly,' he urged, 'that mouth of yours can only be intended for one thing, so don't be shy.'

I tottered forward and crouched in front of him. My hands were free now and I reached out with both of them to stroke carefully down each side of his shaft, testing it for size to see if the touch matched up with what my eyes were telling me. It did, and now all that remained was for me to see if Carmen's calculations when designing the doll suit's oral feature were generous enough.

They were, but it was a most odd sensation as I guided the gleaming head into the opening, for although I knew I was taking a cock into my mouth, my mouth itself could feel nothing beyond that awful jaw-stretching ache imposed by the rigid ring embedded within the softer latex. And then, without warning, I felt warm flesh against the back of my tongue, but Hercules was far from satisfied yet. He thrust forward and I made a gurgling, throaty protest as he all but gagged me.

'That's a good doll,' I heard him laugh. 'Nice little rubber mouth and very soft.'

Glad you like it, I thought grimly, and slowly began to move my head back and forth. I heard a heavy sigh of pleasure from above and felt his gloved hands grasping at either side of my skull, but now he seemed content to let me take the lead, for there was no attempt to force me to take his entire length again.

Foolish, I thought, how bloody foolish. You've got a live girl inside here with a live mouth and yet you get your rocks off fucking a plastic and rubber mouth in the middle of a stupid latex dolly face. And, in a few minutes, you're going to stick this great big cock inside a rubber cunt and pump and pump until it empties itself. Might just as well have stuck with a real dolly.

But then I *was* a real dolly, a real flesh and blood and rubber and plastic dolly that moved and breathed, and right now I was coming very close to experiencing something my inflatable counterparts would never know. Closing my eyes and biting hard against the plastic, I did my hardest to resist, knowing that nothing I could do was going to help and hating myself for being so bloody weak.

I had no idea how long we remained in the derelict barn, but outside it had grown dark long before we started back. Inside, Erik produced a lantern he had previously hidden away behind the timber stack in the far corner, and by its flickering orange light we made love twice more. I say 'made love', but in reality we simply fucked each other's lights out, which served to keep the steadily chilling night air at bay, if nothing else. Finally, however, even Erik seemed to have reached his limit, and when we finally emerged to stand looking at the moonlit river, I at least did so on very unsteady legs.

'Beautiful, is it not?' he asked softly.

I gazed at the silvery ripples as the water flowed past and at the darkened silhouettes of the trees on the opposite bank, and nodded. Beautiful and quiet, with only the soft whispering of the current against the banks to break the silence. I looked down immediately in front of me, where the grass suddenly gave way to the water a few inches below. 'This will be a river in a few years time,' I observed.

'This is a river,' Erik said, not understanding.

I shook my head. 'No, where we're standing,' I explained. 'The river is eating into the bank on this side and piling up mud on the other bank as it comes around the bend here. Bit by bit, the river's course is moving this way. A hundred years from now it could be over there, behind us.' I jerked a thumb to illustrate my point. 'I think that's why there's so little left of the mill building itself and the wheel is missing, in case you haven't noticed. The house is still all right because it sits back a way from the bank, but even that will go in time. Once,' I sighed, 'this pathway was probably a proper lane, but the river has eaten away and eaten away and now it doesn't go anywhere.'

'A bridge there was,' Erik said. He nodded upstream. 'Finding it I was when first we came, but gone mostly it is now. As you say, the water takes away.'

'And with no road to it on this side worth talking about,' I observed, 'no one would have bothered keeping it repaired. Was it stone or wood?'

'Wood, but now all rotted is all that is left. As you say, all changing is.'

'And changing I must be,' I mimicked. 'This dress is still damp at the front and the cape's no better.' It had at least stopped raining, but the air was heavy with moisture and I was beginning to feel chilled.

Erik lifted the lantern and by its light briefly studied my face. 'Yes,' he said. 'Warm we must be getting you, or the ague will come.'

More likely a common old cold, I thought, and that prospect, without aspirin, let alone even a basic antibiotic, did not appeal one iota. I had work to do and ending up sniffling and coughing in bed for two weeks wasn't in the script. 'C'mon then, tiger!' I exclaimed. 'Let's get back and see how Indira's been getting on, shall we? With a bit of luck, we'll have two out of three of the girls underway now and two out of three ain't bad, as the saying goes!'

'It does?' Erik shook his head, indicating his confusion, but then he was quickly getting used to some of my curious speech patterns, even if he *was* trying to be too much of a gentleman to say so. Mind you, in his case, an expression containing the words 'kettle', 'black pot' and 'calling' came easily to mind.

'I think you must be raving mad!' Anne-Marie exclaimed. We were finally on the way back home early on the Sunday evening, and she had unscrewed and removed our gags as Carmen finally removed hers. The hours we spent with our poor jaws distended had taken their toll, and she knew we would be feeling it, as she was herself.

However, the three of us remained inside the doll skins, for Carmen's final twist of devilment had been to insist we dress over them and drive off in the car, waved off by a gaggle of our earlier admirers. There was nothing we could do to extricate ourselves until we reached the sanctuary of Anne-Marie's house, for we would either have to find somewhere discreet enough for us to strip off and remove the latex suits completely, or else we would have to just take off the heads, which would then hang under our chins, complete with hair, and that would be even more likely to draw attention to us than a fleeting glimpse through the car windscreen of three females with big eyes and O-shaped mouths. I just hoped we wouldn't be stopped by a police patrol car.

'If anything happens,' Anne-Marie growled, 'we'll just say we've been to a fancy dress party and we're driving back like this to win a bet, okay?'

Andrea and I nodded; there wasn't much else we could do anyway. Besides, we weren't breaking any laws, so it would only be an embarrassment thing.

None of us really wanted to talk about our respective ordeals at the hands of our devious hostess and so, in an effort to distract us all, I began bringing Anne-Marie and Andrea up to date on my latest time jaunts. However, I had only got as far as outlining my plan for trying to turn the tables on Hacklebury when Andrea almost drove us into a ditch in astonishment.

'You're mad,' she repeated. 'The man's a monster and Megan is lethal. You should just concentrate on getting as far away from the pair of them as possible. Arundel is not much more than one hundred and twenty miles from Hacklebury's place. Try Yorkshire, Scotland, France even!'

I shook my head. 'If they're looking for us, they'll find us,' I replied. 'They'll start with London, if only because Angelina's family had some contacts and even some distant relatives there, which I know because Indira told me.'

'A young woman travelling with a bloody great Viking and an Indian girl are hardly anonymous.'

'Plenty of people had Indian servants then, you'd be surprised,' I said. 'Besides, you're forgetting, they don't know where to start looking and a hundred odd miles might not sound much to us nowadays, but back then there wasn't that much of a rail network, no telephones and almost no photographs to show around. The best Hacklebury might have would be some sort of portrait of me, but I don't think there was one. And we already know he's not exactly flush with money, so he's hardly in a position to hire an army of private detectives to search for us. It'll take them months, maybe even years.'

'That's exactly my point,' Anne-Marie persisted. 'If it's that hard, just keep getting further and further away and eventually he'll have to give up.'

'He won't give up,' I replied grimly, 'and even if he wanted to, Megan Crowthorne wouldn't let him. She'd keep searching if it took fifty years and she'd find us in the end, I know it.'

'But you're talking about actually bringing that bastard to you!' Anne-Marie exclaimed. 'That's as good as committing suicide.'

'Not if I do this right,' I reassured her. 'Hacklebury won't have any idea that it's me and neither would he expect it to be. Like you, he'll think we'll be trying to keep as far away from him as possible, so when he gets his invite to Lady Sadie's establishment - and it'll come from someone who shares his tastes and whom he trusts - he'll come a-running like a puppy dog chasing a kitten. Except when he gets there, he'll find the kitten is a cat and that she has nasty claws.'

'Lady Sadie?' Anne-Marie burst out laughing and the car swerved alarmingly yet again. 'You've gotta be kidding! Talk about a rotten pun.'

'Yeah, well,' I grinned, 'it'll be lost on him. The Marquis de Sade's writings didn't get that much exposure until a lot later, and Sacher-Masoch couldn't have been much more than a toddler in eighteen thirty-nine. It's just my little joke.'

'Well, let's hope Hacklebury doesn't have the last laugh,' Anne-Marie muttered. 'You're playing with fire here, my girl.'

'I'm being very careful, but I need to run a few ideas and thoughts past you and as quickly as possible. I reckon I've been a fast learner, and so are my three girls, but I want to make sure I've thought of everything so our trap ends up with just the right bait in it. On the other hand, now that I've got everything more or less set up, maybe I won't be needed back there, especially as Angelina seems to have some idea of what I'm doing, and Indira is well in on the act now.'

'Yeah?' Andrea cut in. 'And like you really believe that?'

I sighed, closed my eyes and settled back in my seat. 'No,' I said. 'No, I don't. I'll be going back there all right, and unless something's suddenly changing in all this, I shan't have to wait very long, either.'

Our first client did not come to Arundel. A letter arrived at the shoemaker's asking if we could supply the services discussed earlier, but at an address in Chichester. The note went on to explain the gentleman in question, a Mister Archibald Henderbrick, who had rented a house from friends of friends in order to escape the unpleasant winter atmosphere in the capital. Together with a companion, he would be happy to receive us for the fourth weekend in October. I showed the letter to Erik and read it out loud to him, in case his grasp of written English left any gaps for misunderstanding.

'What do you think?' I asked.

He shrugged his massive shoulders. 'Careful we should be,' he replied slowly. 'Better it might be if I went with two of the girls first and around the place looked.'

'You don't think it might be some sort of set-up, a trap, I mean?' We had to be wary of anything that might be a cover for Hacklebury and Megan, even though I remained convinced I would somehow receive warning if they were getting near to finding us, and the dream flashes had ceased since my last glimpse of the poor girl who was now being held in my stead.

'Dealing with strange people we are,' Erik said. 'Possible could almost anything be.'

I hesitated, considering the possibilities. I had found little in Archibald Henderbrick that was threatening when I first interviewed him; in fact, he was a quite unremarkable individual, in his late thirties, I guessed, somewhat overweight and with thinning, sandy-coloured hair and a ridiculously straggling moustache that was unevenly trimmed. He had money, and he would need it at the prices I had quoted, but it came from a doting, aging mother whose family had made their fortunes trading with the New World and, reading between the lines, probably shipping slaves from Africa to the Southern States. He had spent some time in Georgia himself, he told me, and I guessed he probably developed a taste for playing master and slave by experiencing it for real there.

'See if you can find out anything about this address,' I instructed Erik.

He took the single sheet, folded it away and headed off to find one of the two saddle horses we had bought only two days earlier and which we were now stabling temporarily in the old barn. He rode off immediately and did not return until after nightfall.

'The house is belonging to a Mr and Mrs Henry Strode,' he informed me. 'Mrs Strode is American and to New York they have gone for most of the winter. Doing this they have been for three years now,' he added. 'Henderbrick is known to a grocer and a wine merchant. Every winter he is at the house while his friends away are and also visiting them during the summer is. Then I calling on him was.'

I raised an eyebrow. 'Was he surprised?'

Erik shook his head. 'No.' He grinned. 'Expecting a reply he said he was. He also was saying that the partner is a new friend and not wanting to bring him yet to Madame's establishment was he, not sure of how to trust him as he is.'

'Oh no!' I exclaimed. 'Did you meet this friend?' Thoughts that this unknown friend might be Hacklebury immediately crossed my mind.

Erik shook his head. 'No, but describing him the gentleman was and it is not who thinking it might be you are. Only young, this one is, about twenty-two years and so high.' He illustrated with his hand at a height of about five feet six, which was definitely not friend Gregory. 'Also, his friends of the house have tastes most similar.' He grinned. 'Showing me he was, a large cellar.'

'A dungeon?'

'Yes, with barred walls and places for chaining and punishing. Many straps, chains, whips, most impressive. You would approve, I am thinking.'

'So he seems genuine enough,' I mused. 'Fair enough. Let him know that we accept.'

Erik nodded and his grin widened. 'Already I have done so,' he replied, and then reached beneath his jacket and drew out a small leather bag. 'Part payment this is,' he said, opening the end of the bag and tipping the contents into the palm of his hand before showing it to me.

I saw the unmistakeable glint of gold. 'There must be twenty guineas there!' I gasped.

He chuckled. 'Five and twenty, and five and twenty more afterwards.'

'But that's a lot more than we discussed originally,' I said incredulously. Fifty guineas was a small fortune by the standards of the day.

Erik made a sound in the back of his throat. 'To travel to Chichester is inconvenient,' he replied. 'Six people in the coach...' He shook his head. 'Most inconvenient.'

'So you've negotiated expenses as well?' I laughed.

He tipped the gold coins carefully back into the bag and drew the string tight again. 'Yes,' he said, and patted his left pocket. I heard a muffled jingling sound. 'Five pounds I have here.'

'On top of the other?' I was flabbergasted. 'I thought—'

'So did he,' Erik said, 'but firm I was. The ladies, I said, would not want to be travelling and entertaining on the same day.' This time, I noticed, Erik's English phrasing was immaculate and I realised he must have practiced it carefully for Henderbrick's benefit. 'Therefore, rooms I have reserved in a hotel nearby there and we shall travel on the Friday. Overnight we rest and back to the hotel on Sunday morning. A friend I now have at this hotel, and if returning we are not, he will raise the alarm.'

Ah, a friend by means of a healthy bribe, I realised. Clever Erik. Slow of speech, lumbering in action, but I made a further note not to underestimate whatever brain lay inside that broad skull.

'You assured me that your man would find them and yet we still have no clue as to their whereabouts, do we?' Hacklebury glared across his desk, but Megan Crowthorne was unconcerned by his obvious anger.

'Gordon Marjoribanks has three men in addition to himself working on this,' she replied calmly, *'but there are a lot of places for them to look. So far they have concentrated on London and Birmingham, but they could have gone further than that, possibly even across the Channel into France.'*

'Four men to search an entire country and maybe even half a continent?' Hacklebury snorted. *'How in the name of hell does the fool expect to find them like that? Finding a needle in a haystack would be easier, I venture. He needs twenty or thirty men out there looking, or he'll never find them.'*

'And for twenty or thirty men, he would also need six or seven times as much money,' Megan said. *'I'm sure I don't need to remind you of the perilous state of your finances?'*

'Damn it! Of course not!' Hacklebury slammed the palm of his hand down onto the inlaid leather surface of the desk. *'And d'you think it doesn't grind on me that there is so much money just a fingertip away and I cannot touch it yet?'*

'Of course I do understand.' Megan nodded, her tone almost sympathetic suddenly. *'But patience, my dearest one, patience. There is not long to go now. Her birthday is just before Christmas, and then the balance of the inheritance passes to her, and through her to you. Then we can afford to hire an entire army to find the other little bitch and that treacherous bastard Erik.'*

'Yes, Erik.' Hacklebury's features formed themselves into a thoughtful arrangement, his eyebrows beetling together. *'Yes, when we get our hands on him, I think we shall have to find a special way of punishing him.'* He looked up and smiled, but there was no true mirth in the expression. *'To begin with,'* he hissed, *'I shall take the greatest pleasure in castrating the great ox and feeding his genitalia to the girl without telling her what she's eating. We'll save that information until she's cleared her plate, I think.'*

'Revenge is generally regarded as a dish best served cold,' Megan chuckled, *'but in this case, perhaps the dish should be served piping hot!'*

Despite having apparently dozed off in the car, I was feeling completely exhausted by the time we got to Anne-Marie's, but if I was expecting to strip, shower and sleep, I was quickly disillusioned. Before I could even think of trying to remove my doll exterior, Anne-Marie had grabbed me and cuffed my wrists behind my back.

'What—?' I started, but she held a hand up to my open mouth to silence me.

'I like the pair of you like this,' she said, 'though I don't think the image really suits *me*, so while I have myself a bath and find something more suitable, you two can just wait down here for me. Andrea! Get yourself back in here, you little slut!'

Andrea, who had headed in the general direction of the toilet, reappeared looking somewhat sheepish, the bulging artificial phallus plainly visible beneath her tight skirt.

'Get the top clothes off and come here,' Anne-Marie ordered. 'You two are staying as dollies for a while longer yet. By the way, were you able to pee through that thing?'

Morosely, Andrea nodded and began to comply with the instructions. Doubtless she was as tired as I was, and the prospect of now having to suffer further at Anne-Marie's hands was not as appealing as it might have been on some other occasions.

Within a few minutes we were sitting side-by-side on the long sofa, hands cuffed behind our backs, our attire as it had been during our extended performances in the crypt. The only difference now was that the centre sections of our gags had not been replaced, so that although outwardly our faces looked the same, behind the rigid O-shaped openings we were still able to use our mouths as normal.

'She's taking this too far this time,' I grumbled.

Andrea nodded. 'Yes, but she has to,' she said. 'It's her way of re-establishing the pecking order; her mistress, we slaves. Ergo, we have to play dollies longer; otherwise she's no different from us. At Carmen's, because she was daft enough to accept that silly bet, she ended up being as much a part of the entertainment as we were. Now, I think, we get to entertain her.'

'But none of that was our fault,' I protested. 'She took us there in a helpless condition and then used us as part of her daft wager. We had no say in anything.'

'Huh,' Andrea shrugged expressively. 'No change there then, is there? Our darling mistress doesn't expect us to have opinions, not when we're playing games, anyway.'

'I can accept the role-play rules,' I sighed, 'but I don't want to play any more games tonight. I'm shagged out, literally as it happens. All I wanted was to clean up and collapse, and maybe cuddle up with you for what's left of the night.'

'And you think she doesn't know that? No, think again, Teenie. We're in for it, and however and whenever we do get any sleep, it ain't going to be all nicely snuggled up together.'

'And we're not even doing it for charity this time,' I added darkly, glancing sideways at my companion. There was a moment's silence, and then we both began giggling helplessly.

I was a little surprised Erik had chosen a large hotel in the centre of Chichester rather than a slightly more discreet establishment, but when he explained his reasoning I couldn't fault it. To turn up anywhere in a party of five attractive women with a male escort who was clearly some sort of bodyguard, as well as the driver of the coach, and then to book into a cheap hotel would arouse more than just passing interest. The girls were supposed to be my maids, so it stood to reason I must be wealthy, therefore, if I was wealthy - as befits a countess - then I would want to stay somewhere with a bit of style. As I've mentioned earlier, my opinion of Erik was going up almost by the hour.

He had even given more than passing attention to our coach, which of course had originally belonged to Hacklebury, driving it to a village between Arundel and Brighton where he found a craftsman who not only made a few exterior changes to it, but who was also able to repaint it in cream and black and even add a small crest on each door complete with a convincing looking coat of arms. When Erik drove the coach back to the old mill house, it was even drawn by different horses, far lighter in colour than the originals and completely in keeping with the new style of the vehicle they were harnessed to. When we drew up outside our Chichester hotel we must have presented quite a sight, and anyone searching for a couple of runaways trying to keep a low profile would have been hard-pressed to make any connection between them and our splendid looking party.

Milly, Molly and Mandy were dressed smartly, but not ostentatiously, as might befit three lady's personal maids, and their training sessions seemed to have helped in their general behaviour as well as in preparing them for their main role, which would be behaviour of a totally different nature from that which was required of them in public. Indira, of course, looked and acted as serene as ever, adding just the right touch of the exotic at one end of the scale that made a perfect counterbalance to my character and appearance.

To be honest, until Erik returned with Archibald Hendrick's deposit, I had begun to wonder about our finances, for although we had been comfortably placed even after buying the mill house, we had since been spending quite heavily, not least on several outfits for me, which included a splendid collection of fake jewellery. The paste diamanté cost only a fraction of what the genuine article would have done, but still represented quite a heavy investment. However, if a job was worth doing, I reflected, it was worth doing well.

We occupied a suite of four rooms on the top floor, and all the windows afforded us a splendid view across rooftops to the rolling countryside beyond. Under different circumstances I might have been tempted to take a walk in the late afternoon sun, just to see whether or not I could recognise any landmarks from my own era. However, there was work to be done in the form of a final briefing for the girls, followed by dinner, and then a meeting with Simeon Marsh, who had written to say he had a whole sheaf of notes I would find interesting. A knock at the door of my sitting room at precisely nine- thirty announced his arrival.

The dapper investigator accepted my offer of a large brandy, seated himself comfortably in an armchair that made him look more like a little boy, and opened a case from which he extracted a large, stiff folder. He opened it, flicked quickly through the contents, and produced a single piece of paper, which he passed to me. I scanned the neatly written page and nodded approvingly. Simeon Marsh had been very busy, I could see.

'You will notice I have underlined several names there,' he explained. 'These are the, um, *gentlemen* who I now know share Gregory Hacklebury's particular tastes, and the underlined names that have that small star shape over them are also men who have extended hospitality to him on a regular basis. These fellows also do business with the man Pottinger, who apparently has something of a reputation.' He coughed nervously, as if trying to clear his throat, but I could sense his embarrassment.

I smiled disarmingly. 'I know all about Mr Pottinger and his artistic creativity,' I said quietly. 'I would like the opportunity to meet him in the right circumstances, but that is another matter altogether. For the moment it would be wiser to concentrate on Hacklebury and Megan. Have you found out anything more about her, by the way?'

Marsh shook his head. 'I'm afraid I haven't had the resources to devote too much time to the lady,' he confessed, 'but I fear that even if I had, we should not get too far. I have, of course, instigated some general enquiries, but it is almost as if the woman never existed. Of course, Megan Crowthorne might not be her real name, or else it might be and she has spent some years using another.' He spread his hands apologetically. 'I'm afraid I really don't know,' he finished.

'No need to apologise,' I assured him. I tapped the sheet he had given me. 'This is the important part of the job, at least for the moment, and what you have done is truly excellent. With these names I am now ready to move on to the crucial stage of my plan, once I have established my credentials in the right field.'

'Which I presume is the main reason for your being here in Chichester?' Marsh queried, his eyes twinkling. A shrewd man, Simeon Marsh.

I nodded. 'Yes, indeed,' I confirmed. 'We have an appointment with a certain gentleman, whose name I notice is also on your list. These small arrows I presume indicate some sort of links between the different names?'

He nodded.

I grinned a very wolfish and unladylike grin. 'Aha!' I exclaimed. 'Yes indeed. Our man here seems to have a strong connection with two fellows, here and here, who are obviously thick as thieves with friend Gregory. There's our way into the heart of the matter, I think. All we need to do now is impress our host tomorrow.'

Even with the leather outer skin as added protection, Maudie was beginning to find her underground prison very cold, especially at night. In fact, the temperature drops were her only real way of marking the passage of one day into the next, for with the heavy doors closed and bolted, her only light came from the small lantern her keeper kept hanging in one corner, the wick turned down low to conserve the oil between his twice daily visits.

To her surprise - although it had taken her many days to even realise it and even longer before she could bring herself to admit to it - those interludes during which she would be taken above ground to exercise her cramped limbs, trotting dutifully before him on her four limbs, and then given a little food and some water, became the highlight of her miserable existence. And although at first she found the rest of Burrows' treatment of her too terrible to even think about between times, eventually Maudie grew to enjoy the release that accompanied his vigorous sating of his carnality. Curiously, however, although he removed her mask head to feed and water her, and was even beginning to exchange a few words with her during his more affable moods, the head went back on and the canine identity was reinforced before he had his way with her, after which, having given her a final drink through her muzzle with the long-necked flask, he would return her to what he described as her 'kennel' and depart without another word.

What Maudie dreaded most of all was those mornings and afternoons when Miss Crowthorne came to check on her instead, for the woman never removed the head, insisting on feeding her by poking chunks of meat through the dog mouth. She was also given to fits of sheer spite, whipping Maudie's scarcely protected rump as she walked her to the accompaniment of a stream of most vile invective. Tears clouding her eyes, Maudie understood that, as far as this evil woman was concerned, she was in fact no better than a dog. Worse still, it seemed Megan had forgotten that the creature beneath the ruin was, or ever had been, human at all.

'How long am I to be kept like this?' she finally asked Burrows during one of her brief periods of respite.

Will Burrows simply gave a deep chuckle and patted her rump. 'As long as it takes,' he replied.

Maudie sniffed. 'As long as what takes?' she wailed.

'Whatever it is that sir and madame have in mind,' he replied evasively.

'And then I suppose she'll kill me? She's told me I ought to be put down, just like you would a sick hound.'

'T'ain't for me to say,' Burrows sighed. 'I just do as I'm told and you'd be advised

to do the same. You ain't opened that silly mouth when she's been here, have you?'
Maudie shook her head. 'And you'd better keep it that way, else she'll have your
tongue cut out and that'll be an end to your silly prattling.'

'But would you kill me just because she said so? That'd be murder!'

Burrows snorted. 'I've killed before,' he said. 'Orders is orders and it's the same
here as it was when I was in the army.'

'But that was war!' Maudie protested in horror.

'We wasn't always at war,' he retorted darkly. 'And when you've served as long as
me, you learns to do as you're told, keep your mouth shut and draw your money on
payday. That's all there is to it.'

'But I'm not your enemy,' she persisted desperately. 'I've never done anything to
hurt you. I've never done anything to hurt no one, in fact.' She paused, thinking
hard. 'Don't you feel even the smallest thing for me?' she went on eventually. 'I think
I could quite like you, you know.'

'Until it came to a magistrate, you mean,' Will Burrows chuckled. 'Then it'd be a
different story. I'd swing on a rope for sure, though I reckon those two would
probably get off scot-free. Money and rank talks, and I'm just a humble soldier in
the line.' He slapped her across the buttocks again, this time much harder, and she
let out a surprised yelp. 'Well, let's get your bitch head back on and finish off your
exercise,' he said, stooping to pick up the mask. He jerked on her leash, turning her
around to face him. 'Then we'll attend to my exercise,' he added as he began pulling
the hood over her smooth head.

Archibald Hendrick's temporary residence was less than half a mile from the hotel,
an imposing, brick and sandstone Georgian edifice that stood within its own walled
grounds near what was then the edge of the city. Tall iron gates opened onto a short
driveway, which ran around and in front of an entrance flanked by two carved
pillars. I wondered how much it had cost its owners, and also how much it would be
worth in my own time, assuming it was still standing, which was more than likely.

The door was opened as Erik reined the horses to a halt, and two uniformed male
flunkeys stepped out. Inside the carriage I adjusted my mask, making sure the eye
openings were correctly aligned and that my elaborate wig, which was my latest
acquisition, was properly in place. The mask, a carefully crafted piece of paper
maché that had been studiously painted and then stiffened further with layers of
clear lacquer, was a nice final touch and saved me having to mess about with a
leather mask in order to hide my true identity. Of course, I had not worn this
disguise at the hotel, but having arrived there behind a lace veil, and not having
spent more than a few seconds at close quarters with either staff or other guests, I
was prepared to bet no one there could have described me beyond what I was
wearing.

In fact, if I had chosen to wear this new mask in public, it was doubtful whether it
would have elicited much interest. Throughout the sixteenth, seventeenth,
eighteenth and early nineteenth centuries there were all sorts of disfiguring illnesses
that were endemic, especially on the continent, with smallpox and certain venereal
diseases to the fore, diseases that could leave features scarred or pockmarked, so it
became a commonplace sight to see masked females at the theatre or opera house.
These masks were made from a variety of materials, including kid leather, carved

bone and, like my own, paper maché, and I find it surprising that so few have survived into our own time. But I digress...

We were shown through into a lavishly furnished rear room overlooking a garden that made up for in style what it lacked in size, with an ornamental stone fountain in the middle of a pond forming the focal point. It was all very predictable, but nonetheless elegant. A third uniformed footman appeared and served drinks to Erik and myself, and I waved him away when he made to approach the girls. I had allowed them a relaxant brandy before we left the hotel, but I didn't want them drunk for what was to come.

Hardly had I sipped at my wine - not an easy feat, given the rigid nature of the lip opening in my mask - than the door opened again and Archibald himself appeared. He was dressed conservatively, but I could see the flush of anticipation in his cheeks and his eyes darted over the girls as he approached me and bowed.

'Everything is ready, your ladyship,' he announced. Whether or not he believed I was nobility I neither knew nor cared, but if he guessed at my deception, he gave no sign of it.

I nodded to Indira, who ushered the girls towards the door. As if at a given signal, one of the original footmen appeared and bowed them through.

'Now then, Mr Henderbrick,' I began in what I hoped was a passable 'noblewoman's voice, just to make sure there are no misunderstandings concerning our arrangement...'

He blinked, but nodded.

'Good,' I said. 'Well, my assistant here, Mr Johannson, is sworn to protect my person at all times and will shoot anyone he considers to be endangering my safety. That is, he will shoot to kill, you understand?'

I saw Henderbrick swallow heavily as he again nodded.

'We are also expected back at our hotel by a certain time in the morning and, if we fail to arrive for whatever reason, word will immediately be given to the rest of my men, who are staying nearby. They know precisely where we are, and if we do not return safely they will come straight here and make quite a nasty mess, both of you and your friend and of this house.'

'I understand,' Henderbrick said, blinking faster now. 'But I assure you, Madame, you will be perfectly safe. You are my guest here and no one will harm you in any way.'

'And that goes for my girls, too,' I said firmly. 'There are certain limits, beyond which I do not allow anyone to go. I think I explained these to you previously?'

'Of course,' he said. 'Absolutely. And now, if your, err, lady assistant is competent to prepare the other, err, ladies, which I'm sure she is, perhaps I could offer you another drink.'

I looked down at my glass, which I had barely touched, and shook my head. 'Perhaps a small cigar, though,' I said, 'if you have such a thing here, that is?'

Erik had not exaggerated in his description of the converted cellar dungeon. Indeed, I quickly realised he had probably only seen half of it, for there were several chambers beneath the house, two linked directly to each other and five more leading off a narrow passageway I saw also led to a flight of steps, at the top of which I could just make out another door. Presumably it was an exit leading directly to the open air, which was a common enough arrangement and enabled supplies such as wine and cheese to be delivered directly without the inconvenience of having tradesmen tramping through the house itself.

Three of the smaller rooms were still in use for cool storage areas I observed as Henderbrick led the way along the passageway, passing their open doors, but the owners of the house had given over the vast majority of the space down here to the enactment and enjoyment of their fantasies. The remaining two smaller rooms had been arranged as dressing areas, with racks of costumes of every imaginable kind, whilst the two large interlinked chambers were clearly the stages upon which the performances took place, and as much thought, if not more, had gone into them as had gone into Carmen's subterranean theatre.

As we walked through into the second of these cellar rooms, I realised there was a figure standing at the very far end, the shiny black leather of his outfit rippling slightly in the flickering lantern light as he moved towards us. He was unmasked, but from the neck down he had been laced into a cat suit that looked as though it had come straight from the pages of a nineteen seventies fetish magazine. I smiled behind the anonymity of my mask. As I had observed many times before by now, some things never change and there are few genuinely new ideas, just variations on a few old, tried and trusted ones.

The young man - for the figure proved to be male - stopped a few feet in front of us and bowed stiffly, not that he could have done anything other than stiffly in that get-up, which I could now see was little more than a collection of corsets sewn together, and probably as restrictive as that damned dog suit Megan had forced me into. Pottinger again, perhaps, I reflected, but this youthful fellow looked anything but aggrieved at being constricted so. His fresh cheeks were flushed and his eyes, although looking just a touch unfocussed, gleamed with what could only be anticipation.

'May I introduce my young friend, Contessa?' Henderbrick said with a formality that was almost ludicrous. 'Paulie, this is the Contessa Sadie Christa di Ventura, our honoured guest for this evening.'

Paulie bowed again and extended a black-gloved hand, which I took lightly in my own white-gloved one and then released, perhaps a shade too quickly.

'Delighted, Contessa,' the young man trilled. 'Archie has told me all about you, of course.'

I made a harrumphing noise in the back of my throat. 'No one could tell you *all* about me, young man,' I said in the haughtiest tone I could muster, 'excepting for myself, of course. My clients know only what is necessary for them to know; no more, no less.' It sounded ridiculous to my ears, but the effect was right on the nail.

Paulie flinched visibly and Archie stiffened.

'Apologies, Contessa,' Archie declared. 'I'm afraid young Paulie here is a little raw. I'm sure he meant no offence.'

'In which case there is none taken,' I replied smoothly, 'but I nevertheless think that a salutary lesson is required before we proceed any further. I cannot tolerate any indiscretions and I am sure you would prefer for the proceedings not to be marred by youthful inexperience.' I eyed Paulie with a steely gaze he could not see. *You wanna learn, buster, I'm gonna teach you and then let's see how fucking eager you are.* 'Do you have a cane?' I demanded. 'A good stout one, the longer the better.' I was already eyeing a piece of equipment to my left, a sort of vaulting horse, except the arrangement of straps on its legs and sides indicated that anyone who went over it was supposed to stay over it and not continue to the other side.

Archie, who had noticed the slight turn of my head, was quicker on the uptake than I'd expected him to be. 'Of course,' he said, turning and striding across to a rack from which hung a variety of sticks and crops. 'Perhaps you would care to correct Paulie's attitude whilst I go through and change into something more suitable?'

At this point a penny dropped somewhere in Paulie's head. His eyes grew wide and round. 'I - I say!' he stammered. 'I say, Archie old man, that's a bit rich, surely. You can't mean—?'

'Be quiet!' I snapped, my voice echoing around the brick and stone walls like a manic tennis ball. Paulie actually jumped as I pointed one gloved finger at him. 'You want to be a part of this,' I said silkily, 'then you will learn from the very beginning. Besides, that leather will offer you more protection than my girls will be afforded later on. Plus,' I added wickedly, 'I'm sure you've been beaten before, at school, no doubt?'

'Well, err, yes, but never by a - a...'

'Never by a woman, no,' I said it for him. I allowed myself a smile that he could not see. 'Perhaps the experience will be good for you,' I added evilly. I had seen the way he had been eyeing me as opposed to the way he looked at Archie. Whether he yet knew it or not, I suspected this young man's preferences leaned away from the female sex, but then the English public schools system had much to answer for in that respect. 'Just consider this an extension of your education,' I said as Archie handed me a long bamboo cane. 'The Contessa's finishing school for effete young men, if you like. Now drag that horse this way and let's have you over it. Normally I would have my girl strap you down, of course, but as she is still engaged with her other duties, perhaps your master here would do the honours?'

Archie looked surprised at this, but quickly recovered and nodded, managing not to look too eager, even though I suspected otherwise.

With Archie's help the whipping horse was quickly manoeuvred into the central area. I examined it, nodding my approval at the craftsmanship. Good solid joints, nailed and bolted through, the heavy top padded and covered in tough looking leather, the weight of the whole thing more than sufficient to prevent it bouncing around from the bucking struggles of its victims. I tapped the top of the padding with the bamboo rod and nodded at Paulie. 'Up, you snivelling wimp!' I barked. 'Get yourself on here and be quick about it.'

He now looked genuinely frightened, but more frightened of disobeying me than he was of what was about to come. Actually, I realised he was in a state of complete shock at the rapid turn of events, and the quicker I had him immobilised the easier this was going to be, for me, at any rate. As for him, well, I hadn't got him into this, so as far as I was concerned, it would do him good to be on the receiving end before he got to being on the giving end. The only way to appreciate what a cane or whip can do is to experience the effects firsthand.

He struggled to haul himself up, but eventually sat straddling the horse. I motioned to Archie with the cane and he quickly moved in, dragging Paulie's ankles back and buckling them into the heavy straps. Initially the young man tried to keep himself in a semi-sitting position by using his hands to support his upper body weight, but as soon as I saw his ankles were secure, I rapped him smartly across each set of knuckles in turn. He got the message and laid himself down so that his head hung just over the front end. A few seconds later and he was stuck in that position, his wrists buckled to the forward legs.

I smiled to myself and jabbed the tip of the cane at the wide strap hanging midway down the side facing me. 'And that,' I ordered curtly.

Archie nodded and quickly drew the leather band over the small of Paulie's back, walking around to the far side to bring up the matching strap with the buckle.

'Good and tight,' I commanded. 'I don't want the little gobshite to be able to twitch so much as an inch.'

Paulie turned his head, an expression of sheer terror on his face. 'Please!' he wailed. 'Please, Contessa, I think... I think I've changed my mind!'

I laughed and flicked the cane against the bottom of the front leg nearest me. Paulie flinched and would have jumped, but for the broad strap that was now buckled tightly across his back.

'Changed your mind, have you?' I mocked. 'Well, I haven't, so that's just too bad. Archie, you may now go and change.' I looked up at the ceiling. 'One final thing, first. This place is probably soundproof, but my ears are a little sensitive today, so perhaps you would be so kind as to gag the whelp?'

I could see Archie's excitement level was mounting and he was only too willing to oblige. Yes, I could see our host was starting to enter into the spirit of things, and Paulie's predicament and impending punishment was as much of a turn-on to him as if he was one of my girls. Ah well, I thought, it takes all sorts, and whatever poor Paulie got in the course of events, it would be a bit less for Milly, Molly and Mandy to endure. The only problem was, when Archie forced the leather wedge gag into his young friend's mouth and finished buckling the strap behind his head to hold it in place, I saw he was now more than a little reluctant to leave.

'You go ahead,' I urged him, patting his shoulder. 'I'll just be warming him up and I'll leave him here for you to give him a couple of good swats when you're properly attired, yes?'

Archie hesitated, but then nodded enthusiastically. 'Oh yes,' he breathed, 'yes indeed. Most kind, Contessa, most kind.'

Paulie stared at him, his eyes bulging above the gag strap, and made a plaintive mewling sound, but if he thought that was going to do him any good he was very much mistaken. I waited until Archie had departed and then walked over to stand alongside the helpless figure. I shifted the cane from my right hand to my left and then ran my right hand gently over the leather-covered target area.

'My, my, Paulie,' I chuckled, 'but you have such a pretty bottom. The leather suits you so well and the strap across your middle has much the same effect as a corset does on a lady. There's many a girl would be pleased to have such a nicely rounded arse. Are you sure you're really a boy under all this, Paulie, eh?'

He nodded vigorously, trying to say something through the gag, but of course the only sounds he could make bore no resemblance to intelligible speech.

'Yes,' I said, deliberately drawing out the ritual, 'this is a very pretty body indeed. Reminds me of someone I know, as a matter of fact. Hmmm, I wonder if we oughtn't put you into petticoats and stockings and then let Archie punish you along with all the other naughty girls, eh Paulie?'

This time he shook his head so violently I thought he might be in danger of inflicting permanent brain damage on himself.

I patted his head. 'No, maybe not,' I said reassuringly. 'Not this time, anyway, though I suspect you might like it, eh you naughty young thing? I'll wager the thought of being made pretty and then sucking on Archie's fat cock makes you feel all hot and sticky, doesn't it?'

Again he shook his head, though I noticed it was less forcibly, but then maybe it was just that his neck muscles were getting tired.

I moved backwards a pace and thrust my hand between his splayed thighs, forcing it beneath him, palm uppermost. I felt a satisfying bulge under the leather. Men can't help but betray themselves, yet I always find it funny when they do. I moved my hand in a truncated circular motion and was rewarded by a long groan from behind the gag, and further exploration revealed something more.

'Oh dear, Paulie,' I sympathised. 'It would appear there isn't an opening down this end.' I eyed the row of lacing tracing the shape of his spine up to the nape of his neck. That represented a lot of time and effort. 'It would seem Archie has sealed you in here, in this suit, I mean. This poor piece of meat is going to have to wait quite a while, I fear.' I withdrew my hand and patted his buttocks again.

'Ah well,' I sighed, stepping back and transferring the cane again. 'I suppose you shouldn't really enjoy this anyway. After all, this is supposed to be a punishment, isn't it?' I gave the cane one testing swing, adjusted my grip and braced myself.

Of course, the leather of the suit prevented any real damage, ensuring his skin wouldn't be broken, but even so, I think I went pretty easy on Paulie. It was, after all, his first proper punishment. Whatever he had suffered during his school years would have been brisk, brash and to the point. This, as I knew only too well from my own experiences, was a different kettle of fish entirely.

Crack! The first cut produced a very pleasing report, even though I did not give it full vent. A mangled gasp blew out around the gag and despite the straps, I saw the shiny black backside rise from the horse at least an inch.

Crack! The second stroke landed a little lower, cutting across the crease between his buttocks and the top of his thighs, a much more painful area. This time, a high-pitched wheezing squeak echoed around the walls, chasing the echo of the cane. I paused, eyeing his upper back and shoulders, but decided against. Instead, I landed the third cut about an inch higher than the first. He moaned, his head tossing from side to side, and I saw he was crying. I considered for a moment and then stepped up and stooped alongside him, grasping his chin in my hand and turning his face towards me.

'Bloody hurts, doesn't it?' I whispered. 'Well, just you remember this, Paulie, when it's you on the other end. How does it feel to be helpless, eh? Not nice? No, but exciting at the same time, eh? Is your cock getting even harder under there? Well, don't you worry, young man, we'll let it find its own release before long.' I straightened up, moved back again and resumed the beating. By the time I reached the eighth stroke, and well before Archie returned, Paulie unloaded all his frustrations in a manner so explosive I thought he had passed out. I quickly undid the gag-strap and wrenched the sodden leather from between his teeth.

After about another thirty seconds he groaned, shook his head slightly and opened his eyes. It took him a few seconds longer to focus and then, when he saw me stooping alongside him, my face only inches from his, his expression suddenly changed, assuming what could only be described as a beatific look.

'Oh, Mistress Contessa!' he gasped. I saw that his entire body was still quivering from tiny aftershocks, something that is quite common in women, but which I had, and have since, rarely seen in men. I smiled, and though there was no way he could see this, his own mouth wreathed into a crescent of contentment. 'Oh Mistress,' he gasped again. 'Oh Mistress, I adore you. I love you!' I'm sure that, in his chaotic mental state he really did love me, at least for those few minutes before I decided to give him another two cuts just for good measure, making absolutely sure I delivered them at such an angle that they would land right across the welts I knew were already rising on his youthful skin beneath that gleaming black leather.

Chapter 7

The remainder of our Chichester assignment was somewhat low-key, to be brutally honest. With Paulie reduced to little more than a slavering mass prepared to throw himself under my heels had I demanded it, his interest in what happened afterwards between Archie and our three girls was minimal. Archie himself seemed more than a little confused. I suspected he had been hoping to draw Paulie in to a mutual session where the girls were a common bond for excitement, but after that punishment session Paulie appeared to be almost withdrawn, and certainly paid little heed to anything that was going on that didn't give him the opportunity to fawn over me. Which, I was forced to admit, was quite a shame and certainly a waste of the facilities at our disposal. Archie's friends were obviously both rich and inventive and had spared neither money nor artistry in their efforts to turn the cellar region into a fetishist's dream world. Archie should have been content with that, and the fact that my little troupe were more than compliant, but somehow, when confronted with a totally different version of Paulie from the one he expected, the gloss seemed to go off the proceedings for him and he went through the various scenarios like an automaton.

For my part, whilst I detected the mood shift from the outset, I was still determined we would give Archie no grounds for complaint when it came to our input. And whether or not Archie was getting from this what he expected, the facilities here were far in advance of our own and it would have been a shame to waste them. I therefore resolved that, if nothing else, the session would prove to be an invaluable training addition for Milly, Molly and Mandy. With Indira's eager assistance, I brought our trio on by leaps and bounds over the course of those next few hours and, at the same time, began formulating a few improvement ideas of my own.

The sight of Mandy and Molly sitting in identical chairs facing each other, their lower orifices filled by twin polished wooden shafts attached to the seats, their wrists, arms, legs, and even their necks, strapped to the woodwork, whilst Indira and Archie whipped their breasts with lightweight multi-thong cats, was both erotic and at the same time educational. When I then had Paulie suckle their nipples - Indira whipping his backside while he did so - until they each climaxed, I not only had the outline of what I was convinced would be my final plan to finish off Hacklebury, I was pretty sure I had me a new recruit.

Forget business ethics. Long before we finally met the dawn light for our short trip back to our hotel, I had added Paulie to our team, although poor stupid Archie had no idea, and I knew Paulie would not tell him in the meantime. Not that Archie really appreciated what he had held in his hands, but then that's men for you. Lead them by the balls and the hearts - and everything else, for that matter - and they are bound to follow. As our coach rattled down the street and a watery sun struggled to climb above the rooftops, I knew we had left behind a more than satisfied first customer, or at least a customer who was too exhausted to know the difference.

'I'm actually doing this for your own good.' Anne-Marie stood over us, hands on hips, her facial expression set somewhere between neutral and grim determination.

I peered up at her and yawned behind my mask. 'How do you work that out?' I protested. 'All we want to do is crash. I feel like I've been run through a combine harvester and my brain has turned to mushy peas. Can't you just let us sleep?'

'Oh, you can sleep all right, if that's what you want,' she said, 'but you'll sleep the way I want.'

'Can't we just do this tomorrow?' Andrea whined. 'I need a shower and I'm ready to fall over. I've been in this doll skin thing for hours now.'

'Listen, you pair of silly cows,' Anne-Marie snapped, 'stuff has been happening back there, right Teenie? You've flipped out several times in the past few hours. I'm getting so I know the signs, even though you haven't had the chance to tell me.'

'Yeah, okay, you're right,' I admitted. 'But so what?'

'So you've been going back on your own, haven't you? Our dear little Andrea here has been left very much in our own time.'

'So what?' I retorted.

'Yeah, so what?' Andrea echoed.

'So,' Anne-Marie said, 'you can call me Miss Silly, but I reckon it would be a lot better if both of you were back there when things start coming to a head. I take it I'm right when I say the crunch is coming soon, eh Teenie?'

I nodded, almost without thinking. 'It's getting close, certainly,' I confirmed.

'Right then, so you need all the help you can get.'

'Well, the real Indira is doing okay so far,' I said. 'She seems to have a good idea of what's going on and she's adapted to it pretty well, all things considered.'

'Yeah, okay, but Andrea would be a better bet, wouldn't she?'

'Possibly,' I admitted. 'Particularly with what I've got in mind now.' I quickly related what had happened during my last time flip, keeping the details to a minimum, but stressing what I thought would be the importance of Paulie's role in what I was now planning. Andrea found it particularly funny, and would have had trouble keeping a straight face had not the doll's head mask been doing it for her.

'Well then,' Anne-Marie said, '*my* plan is this. I'm going to keep you two sweet dollies together for as long as this now takes, as it seems Andrea goes back with you mostly when the pair of you are, well, connected at this end, as it were. If that Davina bitch had paired you together instead of being intent on humiliating me the way she did, it's odds on the fact Andrea would have gone back with you earlier, in my opinion.'

'And what happens if we don't time flip?' I protested, visions of what Anne-Marie intended flashing before my eyes. 'You intend we play fuck-a-dolly together *ad infinitum*, is that it?'

She shrugged. 'If that's what it takes,' she replied simply, 'though I think we all know it won't be that long. Things back there are speeding up out of all proportion to the passage of time here, aren't they?'

'Yes, but—'

'No buts. Besides, I seem to be the one here who's in the position to call the shots, so let's have no more crap. Let's get things set up properly and then see what happens. Worse scenario is you spend the rest of the night shagging each other silly, and you aren't going to try to convince me that would give either of you much trouble?'

End of argument.

Archie may not have got quite what he was expecting from our visit, but he was certainly well pleased enough to add a bonus of ten guineas when he paid Erik the balance of our fee and booked us to return on the following weekend. He also passed us a brief letter from a friend of his from Oxford, who would be visiting Brighton the weekend following, who wondered if we could accommodate him for an afternoon and a night if he extended his stay. Back at the hotel I penned a brief affirmative reply, together with instructions for the fellow to rendezvous with Erik at the hotel in Arundel, and Archie undertook to ensure it was conveyed to him in good time.

'Not bad at all,' I said to Indira and Erik when we were finally back at the mill house. 'One very satisfied customer and one new one and we've hardly started up yet.'

'Another letter there is,' Erik said. 'Collecting it from the shoemaker I was as we coming through this morning were.' He took out the packet, unfolded the contents and passed them to me.

There were two large five-pound bank notes and a sheet of paper, which I saw was a brief note from Julian Corner-Browne, requesting an 'appointment' at the earliest possible opportunity. 'We'll need to start a proper diary,' I chuckled. 'I'll write and let him know we can fit him in just after we get back from Archie next time. Perhaps you could make sure it gets delivered, Erik? Oh, and I have another little job for you, but it will mean riding to London.' No wonder the railway was greeted so enthusiastically in the next decade, I thought, but Erik seemed unperturbed at the prospect of several hours in the saddle.

'I have a name from Mister Marsh,' I elaborated. 'The gentleman in question is French, but he speaks very good English. He has a device that is available for sale I need you to bring back. It is very delicate, so it will need wrapping very carefully. You may need to buy another horse to bring it back on.'

Erik nodded and did not question me any further. As I have said, our funds had taken quite a pounding over the weeks, but I had put some cash aside for this particular phase of my plan as soon as it started forming in my head. The sudden appearance of young Paulie on the scene could possibly be an unexpected bonus, but it all depended upon whether what M. Delascier had to sell us, and on whether it could be made to work properly in the circumstances in which I wanted to use it.

As I considered this, I realised it was time to do a quick sidestep and try for a slightly different approach. 'On second thought, Erik, take the carriage and I'll write you a letter for the gentleman. It could be useful if we could persuade him to come down here for a few days, even if we have to pay him a bit extra. Nothing like having an expert when it comes to new technology.' That last word flummoxed not only Erik, but Indira as well. 'It's a new invention,' I explained. 'It's a sort of box for taking pictures of people. They call it a camera, but at the moment it's very new and probably very tricky. This Frenchman is one of the very few people who knows anything much about it, so we'll need his help and advice.'

'Why do we need a box for this?' Indira asked. 'What is wrong with an artist? Surely there must be a portrait painter living in the town?'

'I'm sure there is,' I replied, smiling, 'but a portrait takes time to be painted, whereas this box of tricks does it in about two seconds and it's a real picture, not something someone's painted. And we can have lots of copies made too, all of the same thing.'

At this Erik suddenly looked very alert. 'Ah!' he exclaimed. 'Believing I am that I know what it is you plan, mistress.'

'Yeah,' I said, sure he had caught on. There was so much more to Erik than met the eye and he was still surprising me. 'It's called blackmail,' I said, 'and if this works, we'll be setting a trend that will continue for centuries to come, unfortunately.'

By now I had realised, as I'm sure you have too, that Anne-Marie's plan to get Andrea back in time with me hadn't worked out, because Indira was still most definitely Indira. As to why the plan had failed, I entertained my own ideas, but more of that later. In the meantime, the real Indira was turning out to be a great help, and with Erik's calm Scandinavian attitude and apparent natural instinct for management and organisation, we were turning into a formidable team. In addition, pieces of the plan were falling nicely into place and luck seemed to be favouring us, so the original strategy was almost refining itself as we went along. Paulie was a perfect example of this, and I discreetly obtained an address where he could be contacted directly, without having to use Archie as a go between.

Meanwhile, my various artisans - the shoemaker, dressmaker and the young carpenter - were completing the various projects and tasks I had assigned them. I just wished we had a usable cellar at the house, but shutters, heavy curtains and the application of a lot of black paint eventually turned what had been the large rear sitting room into an acceptable substitute. As a fallback position we also had the barn, which now that we had extra horses, Erik and the builder had given a bit of a facelift. Even with five horses stabled inside there was still plenty of room, and so I had two hoists installed and the main beam strengthened, just in case.

'If this doesn't all work out the way I intend,' I confided in Indira, 'then at least you and your mistress will have the basis of a profitable business here. Of course, I hope we'll get her fortune back for her eventually, but then who knows, she might want to continue with a profitable hobby?'

At this, Indira burst out laughing. 'When you are not here - not in her body, I mean - she talks to me of this,' she explained.

'And what does she tell you?'

'That she thinks you must have corrupted her mind, but that she is helpless to do anything about it.'

'That's funny - funny as in curious, I mean. I was wondering whether or not that was the case, or if perhaps it was the other way around.' I sighed heavily and lowered my eyes. 'Ever since all this started,' I continued quietly, 'I've been thinking I must have inherited some family trait from the past, which is the present here, of course, and that it was the Hacklebury genes to blame.'

'You seem sure you are descended from Miss Angelina,' Indira said.

I nodded. 'Pretty sure, yes.'

'And you think Hacklebury must have fathered a child with her?'

'Yes, of course, at least—'

'Well, it hasn't happened yet,' Indira stated. 'I can swear to that. Don't forget, I am with my mistress, or with you, very nearly all the time. I would know, and what I do know is that you are most definitely not carrying Hacklebury's child at this time, not unless one certain rule of nature has changed drastically.'

I pondered this statement, understanding exactly what she meant, and although this cheered me in one way, in another it did not bode well, for it indicated Hacklebury might not yet have finished where Angelina was concerned and that was a far from pleasant prospect.

The days passed by steadily, punctuated by further lessons for the three girls, making sure they remained 'match fit', and interspersed with other matters so routine as to be humdrum. It was about now I found I had enough time on my hands to sit back and consider properly what was happening here, and as the weekend approached for us to return to Chichester, for the first time I reflected on how truly unbelievable all this time tripping was. This time around I had been back here for nearly two weeks and yet, back in my own time, I was pretty damned sure I was exactly where Anne-Marie had left me only a matter of minutes before my last jump. At this rate I was going to end up effectively living through a couple of hundred years back in the past whilst living maybe seventy or eighty in my own time.

As events since have unfolded, this proved to be more than true, and that was before I came to realise my time in the past seemed to be adding credited time to my life expectancy in my present existence.

I opened my eyes and immediately realised I was back in nineteen seventy-five. It should not have come as a surprise by now. In fact, the actual time jumps did not, but what did catch me on the hop this time was the fact that I had been many days back in Angelina's body, with little of import apparently happening, and then suddenly, just twenty-four hours before we were due in Chichester, I reverted to being myself again. Or rather, I reverted to being the helpless doll Anne-Marie had left impaled upon Andrea's huge artificial cock with my arms bound about her as hers were bound about me, an unbreakable embrace of coitus Anne-Marie had been convinced would be the answer to the pair of us making the next jump in unison.

Wrong.

I knew why, but the frustrating thing was, I could not tell her, for apart from the fact that she had left us alone in Andrea's bedroom, she had replaced our dolly gag inserts, twisting them to engage the snap fitting securing them, so that we remained locked in silence, me filled to bursting by an outsized inanimate phallus and Andrea with her own equipment trapped and feeling nothing within its soft lining and rigid outer layer.

Not that this lack of sensitivity seemed to be stopping my rubber lover from making a good attempt, for as I came back to consciousness, I could feel her making good use of the little slack our bonds allowed, pumping steadily in and out of me. It was then I remembered the vibrating plug Anne-Marie had inserted into her just before leaving us. I groaned silently and made a note that when I was finally loose from this impossibly stupid and unproductive situation, Anne-Marie and I were going to have words - lots of them, and few of them overly subtle.

If there was a way to get Andrea back to help me as the plan moved towards its climax, it was not this, and from now on, whether Anne-Marie liked it or not, things were going to happen in this timeframe as they were happening in the earlier one, *my* way and my way only. Meanwhile, all I could do was sit there with my legs wide open and think of England, nineteenth century England, as it happened, not that it would have made any difference to twentieth century Teena's situation.

I stood in the centre of our now completed 'torture chamber' and nodded in satisfaction. The room was not large, not by the standards of the cellar dungeon complex in Chichester, but it would more than suffice, especially as we had moved one or two items of equipment into the corner bedroom, leaving only the X-shaped cross against the end wall, and a faithful copy of the Chichester whipping horse in the centre of the floor area, with one of the two bondage chairs pushed back into a corner, where it stood in shadow outside the circle of light cast by the four lanterns now hanging from the ceiling.

In contrast to the black walls and dark wood of our bizarre furnishings, Indira, who stood beside me, was a vision in pure white, having chosen this moment to unveil the results of her many hours of needlecraft. From head to toe she was dressed in dazzling kid leather, a close-fitting bodysuit that showed every single one of her ample curves, with a hood and mask completely disguising the colour of her skin. She had even added a fine horsehair ponytail to the top of her hood, bleaching that to match the leather. When the time came, Hacklebury would never make any connection between this exotic creature and the hapless Indian girl he had so brutally banished from Angelina's company.

'You look stunning!' I told her in genuine admiration, and wondered what Andrea would have thought of the outfit had she come back this time. I imagined her strutting around the room, poised and full of attitude on those high heels, swinging the coiled whip, itching to be able to put her new persona to good use. But then again, I marvelled, that was exactly what Indira was doing now. The change in the former serving maid's personality since the night of our escape was incredible. In many ways, she was now the dominant personality in the household. Even Erik seemed wary in her presence, even when she was wearing her normal dress or sari. In this mood, and looking more like a modern day superhero, she was truly terrifying.

'I am glad you like it,' she said, offering me a mock little bow and clicking her heels together in military style. 'I wish to use it to practice my techniques with the young man.' I knew she was referring to Paulie, who was due to arrive within the next two hours or so.

I nodded. 'He's all yours, if that's what you want. Will you want Erik with you?'

Behind the mask, Indira trilled a laugh and shook her head. 'No, indeed, that will not be necessary.'

'Fair enough, if you're sure.' I smiled at her. 'Would you mind if I sat in, as an observer, that is?'

She seemed to hesitate and there was a silence of several seconds. 'Would you agree to *sit in*, as you put it, on my conditions? I wish to discover if I have the ability to exercise control, and your presence in the room as the Contessa would not make it a fair trial.'

'I could get a screen in here and hide in the corner behind it,' I offered.

She made a negative gesture. 'No, that was not what I had in mind. A corner, yes, but in full view.'

'Then how...?' I began and stopped, my jaw dropping and my eyes flickering towards the bondage chair. 'Oh!' I exclaimed, momentarily at a loss for words. 'You mean...?'

She nodded. 'You will pretend to be one of the girls. You are smaller than any of them, of course, but I doubt whether young Paulie will remember much about the other evening. Well,' she corrected herself, 'he will remember plenty, but the height and bosom size of the female company will not be that clear in his silly mind.'

I turned away from Indira, considering the proposal, feeling my pulse rate quickening as I pictured the scenario. I walked over to the cross and fingered the heavy straps I knew would soon be holding Paulie ready for whatever Indira had in store for him, and answered without turning back.

The chair could have been the model for what was later to become the electric chair in America, but this particular one would be generating electricity of a totally different nature. As Indira led me into the room and paraded me once around the helpless naked figure already stretched over the horse, I struggled to remain calm, breathing with difficulty due to the corset she had laced so tightly about me and tottering on one of the highest heeled pairs of boots we had.

My arms were clad to the shoulders in soft kid gloves, my wrists bound together in front of me with a wide satin ribbon tied off in a huge bow. My legs, apart from the ankle boots, were sheathed in black silk stockings held up by black and red lace garters. Between the tops of the stockings and the lower hem of the corset I was naked and completely hairless. From behind the mask hood I peered out at the brooding scene, reflecting that we had indeed done a good job with the room as I looked across at Paulie, wondering what was going through his mind. If it was anything like my thoughts then he was not, I suspected, about to be disappointed.

Indira drew me around in front of him and pushed me forward, so that I was standing with my denuded crotch only inches from his head. She reached out, grabbed his hair and lifted his head so his face was raised and he was looking straight at my already moistening jewel. I knew his nostrils would now be full of my scent, for I could smell my own arousal even over the dull musk of my hood.

'This is a low slave bitch,' Indira said, and for a moment I wondered which of us she was actually speaking to, until she continued. 'However, boy, you are even lower, a vile little dog, and you will demonstrate your lowly status by worshipping this slave as if she were a goddess. You will kiss and lick her temple until I tell you to stop and *you*,' she added, addressing me now, 'will control your urges. If you weaken, you will be whipped and this creature will be permitted to put his filthy little snake rod inside you later.'

I was stunned. The change in Indira was more than external, obviously, but it appeared to have gone much deeper than even I had suspected, and she was revelling in this new dominant role as if she had been doing it all her adult life. The expression on Paulie's face was quite something to behold, a mixture of fear, adoration and lust, and I wondered what he would have looked like had he realised the anonymous slave girl standing before him was in fact the same creature who had begun his re-education in that Chichester cellar room.

'Open your legs, slut, and step forward!' Indira reinforced her order by slapping me across my bare rump with the short-coiled whip. I let out a sharp yelp, but instinctively obeyed. Immediately, Paulie's mouth was there to receive me and I felt the wet heat of his lips on mine, the rough tip of his tongue pressing between the soft folds of my flesh. I groaned, gritting my teeth, determined I was going to resist what was usually the inevitable, for I knew now Indira's threat had not been an idle one. If I lost control and climaxed she would most certainly have me over the horse after Paulie, and Paulie would have me, and that was a complication I didn't want.

Satisfied Paulie was applying himself to his appointed task with due diligence, Indira stalked around and took up a position to his left, letting the whip uncoil as she went. For my own part, I found I was grasping Paulie's hair in her stead, and whilst I did not dare try push myself away from him, I did at least try to exert some sort of control over him. It was, of course, a wasted exercise. If I was going to pass this test, it would have to be by sheer power of will alone and, I reflected grimly as the fire gremlins began their ritual dance, in these sort of situations I had not exactly proved I had any will at all, let alone power over it.

However, Indira's pre-planned routine actually began to work in my favour, for the first slash of the braided leather across Paulie's upraised backside, besides producing a spectacular cracking sound also produced a reaction in him that made me suspect she had perhaps used a little too much force. Even though I was holding his hair, his head jerked up and backwards and he yelled out loud, his mouth gaping, his eyes opening wide in pain and astonishment.

'Get his mouth back down and covered!' Indira commanded.

I pulled his face back between my thighs and pressed against his lips, but his enthusiasm seemed to have melted. He blubbered against me, the vibration of his lips pleasant, but in no immediate danger of raising me towards the capitulation level. The whip hissed and cracked again and this time I yelped, for Paulie's teeth nipped me painfully. I staggered back, clutching myself.

Indira let the whip fall to her side and placed her hands on her hips in an attitude of sheer exasperation. 'Damn it!' she cried. There was a momentary pause, and then the braid snaked through the air again.

This time Paulie's yell was ear-splitting in the confines of the room.

Indira strode over to me and began unbinding my wrists. 'Are you all right?' she whispered.

I nodded, blinking fiercely, for although the initial shock had made me jump, Paulie had not done me any damage; his teeth had been some way from endangering my most tender and treasured possession.

'Stupid little bastard!' she hissed. 'No control over himself at all. And so noisy. We'll have to gag him.'

I opened my mouth to protest, for I knew she was losing the plot. Instead of exciting her prisoner, she had changed his perception so pain was not currently equalling pleasure, nor even indicating pleasure to follow. I pulled my wrists apart and tried to drag her to one side without alerting Paulie, who was in any case lying with his head slumped downwards, blubbering quietly to himself.

'You're hitting him too hard!' I whispered fiercely. 'He's supposed to enjoy this, don't forget.'

She snorted. 'He'll enjoy it all right,' she said with conviction, 'but he'll enjoy it my way and he'll earn his release. He's a weak, snivelling, spoiled, ignorant little English fop and if you think he would have any compunction were the boot ever on the other foot, then I think you have a lot to learn, my angel.'

'Oh, I know about his kind,' I agreed, 'but that's not the point. We're not here to exact revenge on him. This is all about finding a way to get to Hacklebury, and then we'll take revenge in a far more appropriate fashion.' For a few seconds I thought Indira was going to turn on me, for she drew herself to her full height and her shoulders stiffened. I stood faceless before her, but I did not waver, and then, suddenly, I saw her relax.

'Yes, of course, you are right,' she said quietly. She looked down at the whip as if studying the plaited braids for something. 'I will spank him with something less vicious then, but he will also learn that there are other ways of suffering at the hands of womankind. Wait here and I will be back. I have something to show you,' she added as she strode past me, opened the door and clattered out along the passageway beyond.

She was back in less than a minute, and for the second time in a short space, I found myself at a loss for words.

'Do you like it?' she asked, holding it up before my face like a trophy.

I stared at the double-ended dildo, blinking in astonishment at the cunning craftsmanship and the carefully made harness arrangement. Where she had got the inspiration for the design I could not imagine, but then I remembered the various conversations we had shared and how she occasionally prompted me about sex in my time. Somewhere along the line, I must have made mention of twentieth century lesbian sex. Or was the strap-on a lot older than I had previously thought? 'Where did you—?'

'The shoemaker, Faraday,' she replied. 'I found the wood myself, a broken piece from a tree, and took it to him with instructions of how I wanted it carved. He then covered each end with two layers of leather to give it a softer feel. The rest of it is only part of his trade skills.'

'Yes, but didn't he say anything about—?'

She shook her head. 'He was well rewarded. Very well rewarded, and is even now making three more of these.'

'Astonishing!' I wasn't sure whether I was talking about the device or Indira herself. Worms turn, they say, but this one had done a series of pirouettes, by the look of things. I then had a sudden thought. 'This... this is for me?'

'Yes.'

I looked past her to where Paulie remained inert over the horse. His position made the implications obvious.

Indira followed my gaze. 'Yes,' she said again simply. 'You, my temporary slave, are going to fuck him, that useless boy, and then, if it doesn't happen beforehand, we are then going to milk him until we drain every last drop from his balls.'

'But if he goes running back to Archie—'

'He won't,' Indira assured me. 'If he runs anywhere it will be to me, and by the time I've finished with him he won't be running anywhere for a while. Crawling, maybe, but definitely not running.'

I could see there was no point arguing with her or even trying gently to dissuade her. Besides, I could see she might have a point, and it would be interesting to observe just how Paulie ultimately reacted to being a helpless plaything in the hands of a dominant woman.

'Fair enough,' I conceded. I reached out and took the dildo arrangement from her. I studied it one final time and then stooped slightly, parting my thighs, and began pushing the female intended half up inside myself. The cool leather surface produced a pleasant enough sensation, and when the full length was embedded in me and I pulled out the straps, allowing Indira to complete the task of harnessing me, I had to admit to a satisfyingly full sensation.

'One thing,' I said urgently.

She looked at me through her mask slits, her eyes twinkling. 'Yes?'

'If I come now, no letting squinny-face there roger me, right? Until this is over I don't mind doing the rogering, but I don't want to be on the receiving end of any man.'

'Except maybe Erik?' The twinkle was fiercer than ever.

I coughed and half turned my head away. 'Except maybe Erik,' I admitted.

'Agreed. Now, if that feels comfortable, let us go and see if our blubber-baby there is still a virgin. I doubt he is, but let us see how he acts playing the woman's role to another woman, eh?'

Of course, with my hands now free I could have simply refused and walked away, but I could understand Indira's point of view and even sympathise with it. How long I would remain back in this era, how many more times I might revisit, I had no idea, but one thing was for certain - in some small way I had contributed to women's equality, and though it would be decades yet before anything like equal rights for our sex began to emerge, at least I would be leaving behind me a dedicated advocate. And probably, assuming Angelina was in some way assimilating some of my personality traits - call them defects, if you prefer - this once demur and sweet little Indian maid was not going to be alone in carrying the fight.

With slow deliberation, I walked back across the room and stood before Paulie, who all this time had been lost in his own thoughts and discomfort. I turned to Indira, who nodded, and then reached out and grasped the hapless young man by the ears. Without saying a word I lifted his face so the jutting portion of my recent acquisition rose immediately before his eyes. He blinked, struggling to focus, and then when he recognised the shape of the beastly looking thing, he gasped in horror.

'No, please!' he squealed, trying desperately to wriggle in his bonds, which were of course far too tightly secured for him to have even the slightest chance of escape. 'No, please, I beg you, not that!'

'And why not, indeed?' Indira demanded, and I realised she had moved quietly to stand just behind my left shoulder. 'I'll wager you've taken the real thing before now, eh my lad? I think you are a very wicked young fellow and should own up to your misdeeds, don't you?'

'No! I mean, yes... yes I have been wicked,' Paulie stuttered. 'But I did not know any different and Archie always told me—'

'I expect Archie told you lots of things,' Indira sneered, 'and yet Archie seems to like women as much as he likes young men, doesn't he? Well then, it is only fair you should learn to like us and also learn to like being like us, for you are like us, aren't you, Paulie?'

'No, no, I'm not like you, not like you at all!'

'Is that what you think?' She laughed harshly and slapped my shoulder. 'Hear that, slave-slut? The poor little baby thinks he's not like us, and yet I'll wager further that if we put him in a dress and rouged his pretty cheeks he'd make a fine whore and no one would know the difference.'

'No, please,' Paulie wailed, closing his eyes.

Behind my mask I was grinning wickedly to myself. Indira was playing this role so well, and yet I suspected she no longer regarded it as a role at all. This was now the real thing to her, taking revenge on male-kind and savouring every moment of it.

'Well, perhaps we'll put you in skirts another time,' she threatened, 'but to do so now would be a waste of time. Once you have a whore naked, why dress her again when she's lying there with her legs open?' She took my arm and drew me aside, ushering me down the length of the horse and guiding me around until I was positioned immediately behind Paulie's quivering backside. Then, before I had time to realise what she intended, she stooped, engulfing my leather phallus in her mouth and sucking it in and out with several vigorous strokes. When she finally stood up again the black shaft was glistening, wet with her spittle. 'That should ease its passage,' she remarked and nudged me closer, at the same time taking the artificial cock in her hand and guiding it towards its puckered target. 'Nice and slowly,' she advised as the tip touched home.

I saw Paulie stiffen, his back arching as best it could beneath the thick centre strap. I pushed forward slightly, meeting with what seemed impossible resistance, but Indira was not to be cheated. She raised her free hand and brought it down across his left buttock with a resounding clap. He let out a shriek containing as much surprise as pain, but at the same time automatically relaxed his sphincter. Immediately the first inch or so of the black rod pushed home. For a second he tried to tense again, but a second slap, this time to the other buttock, produced a similar effect, and now there were easily two and a half inches of dildo inside him. At this point either a sense of the inevitable or an automated switch to another time and another role seemed to take over. He let out a low moan, relaxing completely, and the remainder of what had to be at least a seven inch pole slid easily home, until my hairless mons slapped against the soft flesh of his glowing buttocks.

'There!' Indira declared. 'That wasn't so bad, was it? Now, pretty Paulie, you will ask this slave, who is now your mistress, to roger you until you come, d'you hear me?'

After a few moments, in which Paulie's wrestling match with his conscience and his ego finally ended in submission, that is precisely what he did, and I of course duly obliged, though in reality it was me who climaxed. It took a half hour strapped to the cross, and my deft manual ministrations, before he finally spurted forth in full subjugated glory.

Chapter 8

'You got it wrong, Annie,' I said as we sat over a breakfast of toast and coffee the next morning. 'I should have thought it might have occurred to you that doing the dolly fuck thing wasn't the same as doing it properly. There was no flesh to flesh contact anywhere, was there?'

Anne-Marie was unabashed. 'Well, it seemed like a good idea at the time,' she replied brightly, 'and you did both look so sweet there.'

'Like the two of you did back at Carmen's?' I retorted sourly.

She gave me an equally sour look and I knew I had hit a nerve. 'That was different,' she snapped. 'And it was completely out of order. I didn't mind afterwards, it was quite a good laugh, in fact, all those sweaty blokes poking away like fury and me not able to feel a bloody thing, but she shouldn't have made Andrea and me do what she did. You wait and see, I'll make the bitch pay for that one day.'

'I shouldn't bother if I were you,' I said. 'She's as cunning as a sack full of foxes, and you'd need to get up early to catch her out.'

'Well, I'm not *you!*' she snarled. 'And Carmen isn't as clever as either you or she seem to think. I'll have her when she's not expecting it, believe me.'

'Well, she was clever enough to rig those cock-and-mouth contraptions,' I pointed out.

Anne-Marie looked at me oddly and I realised she hadn't yet caught on to Carmen's subterfuge. Almost smugly I explained my suspicions. 'The chances of you getting her still long enough to line your dildo up perfectly must have been more than a thousand to one,' I finished, 'and yet she managed to get hers into your mouth at her first really serious attempt.'

'The bitch!' Anne-Marie shrieked. 'I'll expose her in front of everyone at the next event. She'll have to be my slave this time and she won't get away lightly.'

'Don't be so naive,' I said calmly. 'If you say anything she'll just produce two identical sets and you'll look either stupid or like a bad loser. You might even end up having to be her dolly again, and you wouldn't like that. And don't forget, the two of us will have to go through the same again and I for one have had enough of cocks down my throat.'

My bluntness seemed to sober her somewhat, and she quickly switched the conversation to an update of my further adventures in the past. I related the important parts and filled in a few incidental details, at the end of which Andrea in particular seemed more than impressed, and at the same time not a little disappointed.

'Good for Indira!' she exclaimed. 'I just wish I could have been there.'

'If you had,' I pointed out, 'then things might have happened differently. You make quite a good girl in a lot of ways, but there's a mean streak to a vengeful woman no man could ever hope to understand, let alone copy.'

'Oh, so you reckon you can handle the rest of this without my help, is that it?' Andrea's freshly made-up face creased into a sulky expression that would have done full justice to a petulant twelve-year-old schoolgirl, but which looked slightly incongruous on the features of what was supposed to be a mature young woman.

'I didn't say that,' I replied, 'but as neither of us has any real control over who goes back and when, the question is entirely academic anyway. All I'm saying is that, assuming your time travelling days are over, I've got a very good deputy back there already. When the time comes, Hacklebury won't know what hit him.'

'And when do you think the time will come?' Anne-Marie asked.

I gave a little shrug and reached across for the last slice of toast. 'I'm not entirely sure, though it shouldn't be long. Everything is more or less set up now, and all we need is to reach Hacklebury through his so-called friends. If we continue the way we've started they'll give us one hell of a recommendation, and dear Gregory won't be able to resist coming along to see for himself. Of course, as everything is more or less set up, maybe I won't be needed any more. Perhaps Angelina and Indira will be able to carry it all out on their own and I'm now surplus to requirements. Maybe my part is also finished now.'

'Do you really believe that?' Andrea asked, standing up and brushing crumbs off the front of her jumper with a vigorous action that made her false boobs bounce alarmingly.

I paused, the toast inches from my lips. 'No,' I said finally. 'No, I don't believe that. I'll be there at the finish, I'm sure. And I'm owed that much anyway. Fate, or whatever, wouldn't *dare* not give me the chance to see this through to the finish!'

Maudie stood resignedly, bracing her stiff forelegs as Will Burrows fumbled with his breeches behind her. High above the stars blinked and winked in a moonless sky, while the night breeze rustled through the nearly leafless treetops with a forlorn sigh that seemed to echo her own feelings.

She had been so long in this awful canine guise, she had almost forgotten what it was like to walk upright, to be allowed to talk properly and to eat with a knife and fork or even using her own hands, which now felt stiff, numb and useless inside their leather prisons. She was even beginning not to care what happened to her any more. She was quite content to stand splay-legged while her keeper thrust into her, as he was preparing to do now, feeling little until the more base reflexes began their work and then, afterwards, when it was all over, curling up as best she could in her subterranean kennel and crying herself softly to sleep.

'Hold there, bitch!' she heard Burrows' rough command, and a moment later felt the pressure of his blood-filled knob pressing against her sex. As she had learned to do, she relaxed, allowing him easy entry. He slid into her quickly, grasping her flanks and pulling her back, slamming into her with a grunt of satisfaction.

'Woof!' she said in a commendable imitation she knew now would earn her the odd extra tid-bit and the odd small kindness. When he first instructed her on this Maudie had felt ridiculous, but now it, along with everything else, seemed almost a normal part of her everyday existence. 'Woof!' she repeated, and then started a low whining. She felt him withdraw partially, and then thrust in again. Her whine became a howl, for she understood now that her performance could control the length of time she was forced to endure this humiliation. The more convincing she was, the quicker the keeper usually climaxed.

She felt him picking up the pace, in and out, in and out... she howled again and

113

felt her pulse beginning to quicken. She flexed her internal muscles, gripping and then releasing him in turn, an action she knew excited him and in some way also served to heighten her own pleasure, if pleasure it could be called.

'Good girl,' he urged. 'Good girl, now let's—'

His words ceased in mid-sentence as Maudie heard a dull thudding sound, followed by a short groan, and another heavier noise as she felt him slipping from her. She waited, her eyes closed, and then, when he did not renew his efforts, she tried to turn and look back. As she opened her eyes she was aware of a dark shadow looming alongside her, a hand reaching out for her neck, and a voice, a male voice, but softer, reassuring, not Burrows' voice.

'Steady girlie,' the figure whispered. 'It's all over now. Just take it easy and don't make any noise and we'll have you out of this god-forsaken hellhole. Everything is going to be all right now, you'll see.'

I - or rather, Angelina - had obviously been enjoying an afternoon nap on the long settle in the main living room. When I opened my eyes, I knew two things immediately without even having to think about them. The first was that this time I had been away from eighteen thirty-nine and Arundel for nearly a month. The second was that I could remember everything that happened during my absence. Furthermore, things had moved on apace and today was the day. I sat up, rubbed my eyes and looked around the room, my heart suddenly pumping wildly.

A moment later the door opened and Indira, dressed in a dark-blue sari, entered the room carrying a tea tray.

'Ah, you're awake,' she said, and then paused, looking me up and down. 'And you're back, aren't you?'

'How is it you can tell?' I asked.

She shrugged and placed the tray on the small table at one end of the settle. 'I don't know, you just feel sort of different from my real mistress, I suppose.'

'He's coming, isn't he?'

'Yes, tonight, with Lord Morlan and Mr Corner-Browne.'

'What time?'

'Eight o'clock.' She began pouring tea, completely calm and unhurried. 'It is now nearly four, so there is ample time to prepare. I have laid out your costume for you, complete with the special boots you ordered from Mr Faraday, though I must say they do look as if they will be very awkward to walk in.'

'Don't worry,' I assured her as another memory slipped effortlessly into place, 'platform boots are all the rage where I come from. The main thing is that the extra four inches the built-up sole allows on the heels will make me look so much taller than the real Angelina that Hacklebury will never guess the truth. Is everything else prepared as I instructed?'

'Yes, everything. Mr Faraday will arrive at six-thirty and will receive the visitors. He will be suitably attired, naturally.'

'Naturally.' I smiled. 'And he's quite prepared for his role?'

'Very much looking forward to it, I should say.' She smiled back. 'He is most keen.'

'Knowing you will suitably recompense him, I suppose?'

'He has had no complaints regarding his compensation so far.' She giggled, and I laughed with her.

'No, I'll bet. But what does the real Angelina think of it? Does she not feel jealous at having to share you, and with a man, at that?' I thought I already knew the answer, for there were all sorts of emotions swirling around just below the surface inside my head.

'Oh no,' she replied, confirming my assumption. 'Besides, I would not desert her arms completely, and in the meantime she has been continuing what I believe you started with Erik.'

'Then that's all right.' I smiled, taking the proffered teacup from her. 'And Erik is also ready for tonight's adventure? He knows to remain out of sight until the time comes?'

She lifted her cup. 'Of course,' she replied with a slightly superior look on her face. 'Everything and everyone is quite ready. We are well practiced and thoroughly trained. Hacklebury will suspect nothing until it is too late.'

I raised my cup in a toast. 'Then here's to us!' I exclaimed. 'To us, and to success.' I sipped my tea as Indira echoed my words. Then another thought struck me. 'What about Mad Meg?' I asked. 'Will she be coming with them tonight?'

She winked knowingly. 'No. By now I think she will have other things to occupy her attention, or had you forgotten the instructions you gave to Mr Marsh?'

'Of course,' I cried. 'How could I have forgotten? Was he successful? Is Maudie all right?'

'Well, she is safe, most certainly,' Indira answered gravely, 'but whether that is the same thing, I would not care to guess. However, we shall be able to judge for ourselves, for Marsh will be bringing her here in the morning, by which time our work should be completed. After that we can deal with Megan Crowthorne if we have to, but I suspect Hacklebury will draw her sting for us if everything goes to plan.'

'And it could hardly have gone better,' I said, taking the refilled brandy glass from Anne-Marie. 'Mind you, I was nervous as hell to begin with, and I felt sure everyone could hear my heart thumping, but thanks to Indira I got through it.'

'What about her voice?' Andrea asked. She was still very miffed she had missed out on the action. 'Surely her accent would have made him realise she wasn't English?'

I shook my head. 'Not a bit of it,' I replied. 'Indira is one hell of a girl, believe me, and a damned good mimic.'

The leather outfit Indira had prepared for me felt stifling, and I was perspiring profusely by the time I entered the room where Hacklebury and his friends were waiting for me. Despite the black leather mask covering my entire head, and the additional height of the platform-soled boots, I was suddenly certain Hacklebury would guess who I really was, but to my relief he seemed almost as nervous as I was.

'I thank you, Contessa,' he said, grasping my hand and bowing to place a brief kiss on my leather-sheathed fingers, 'for inviting me here this evening. I have heard much about you.'

I withdrew my hand from his - perhaps a shade too hastily? - and tried to make it

115

look as though I was giving him a thorough but impassive once-over. To one side Indira, resplendent in her all white costume, stood tapping a long riding crop on her booted calf as if she was impatient, and perhaps a little bored. Silently, I blessed her for her composure. 'You are welcome, Sir Gregory,' I replied haughtily, trying to keep my voice pitched low and speaking very carefully, like someone to whom English was perhaps not a first language. 'And you too, gentlemen,' I said, addressing Morlan and Corner-Browne, 'it is a pleasure to see you both once more. I trust your journey went well?'

'Indeed, Contessa,' Morlan said, bowing slightly and following Hacklebury's lead with a kiss of his own. 'Of course, things will become much easier for all of us when they finally complete the proposed railway line between London and Brighton.'

'Indeed,' I nodded, 'and profitable, too. I take it you have all invested in shares of the company building it?' In truth, I couldn't remember who was responsible for that line, only that it would finally get underway as a proper business concern in about another three years, but I was speaking only for effect and, in any case, I didn't expect the small talk to continue. I decided to hasten matters along. 'You will remember Cassandra?' I said, waving a hand in Indira's direction. 'You, of course Sir Gregory, have not had the pleasure of meeting her. She has lived some years in the Arabian lands and is very skilled in the disciplining of errant young slave girls. Watch and listen to her and you may learn something, I venture.'

On cue, Indira cracked the crop harder against her leg.

'Well, gentlemen, if you will follow Cassandra, she will escort you to our costuming room. I have taken the liberty of selecting outfits I think will be suitable for our little adventure. This evening I thought we might start with a little walk along the river. We have just completed work on very singular stables, which I believe some of you will find very much to your taste. Are you familiar with the work of Mr Pottinger?'

I saw an immediate light glint in Hacklebury's eyes and knew then we had him. I could imagine the images already whirling about in his head, and smiled to myself. If he could have seen the images *I* was seeing, he would have fled for his life, or else he would have tried to strangle me on the spot. Of course, I had not dared make any approach directly or indirectly to Pottinger, for he would surely have recognised Erik if he had not remembered me, but throwing his name into the conversation was a stroke of genius, even if I do say so myself.

Erik emerged from the corner closet unit as soon as the sound of their retreating footsteps had faded. I turned to him, clapping my hands together. 'I do believe this is going to work!' I exclaimed excitedly.

He nodded solemnly. 'But of course, a very clever lady you are as well as most beautiful being.' He stepped over to me, took me by the shoulders and bent to kiss my leather-lined lips, my padded bosom pressing hard against his massive chest. 'Brave for a little longer must you be,' he said, stepping back, 'and then it will be done. And remember, Erik will be close by and harm not shall come to you.'

In the barn I had already installed Millie and Mandy. We did not have any of Pottinger's artistry to help with the effects, but our tame shoemaker and now willing assistant, Milton Faraday, had excelled with the bridles they now wore, even if he had professed himself astonished any man would want to see a woman wearing such a thing. Having said that, when he finally saw the finished articles being modelled, I suspect he underwent a rapid change of heart.

The girls themselves played their parts to the full, obediently trotting around the inside of the barn with high stepping strides, knees coming up level with their waists, as the three men took turns at schooling them. Morlan and Julian seemed more than content with this horseplay, but I soon saw Hacklebury wanted more.

'You are growing bored, Sir Gregory?' I asked, as he stood detached from the main group, watching with fading interest and smoking a long thin cigar.

He turned to me, his face darker now in the flickering lantern light. 'Amusing games, Contessa,' he replied, 'but I was led to believe there was far more to your entertainment than this.'

'And so there is, Sir Gregory,' I replied coolly. 'Perhaps you would like to see something a little special? I think I can promise you an experience the likes of which you will not forget until your dying day.'

'A bold claim, Contessa,' he said dryly, 'but I am willing to be impressed, if you are that confident.'

'I am very confident, sir. Perhaps you would like to accompany me back to the house? Your friends can join us later, when they tire of this diversion. Cassandra, perhaps you could offer the gentlemen some wine. Sir Gregory and I are going back now. He seems eager to meet Molly, I think.'

'As would any man be,' Indira replied lightly. 'So why keep him waiting. The other gentlemen will be perfectly safe here with me for a while.'

Hacklebury said little on the way back along the river path, but I could feel impatience radiating from him. He was so eager to find a new way to sate his perverted lust that I imagined I could smell it as he strode along in his tight leather breeches and jacket, the new hide creaking with his every eager stride.

Upstairs, Molly was already strapped to the cross dressed only in boots, stockings and a tight corset. The gold rings clipped to her full nipples hung clear and unfettered and her shaven crotch was thrust wantonly in full view.

'She has already been beaten,' I said as I closed the door behind us, 'but you may beat her again later, if you think she deserves it. Meantime, I think you will find her the most entertaining and willing partner a man could want. May I offer you a glass of wine, whilst I prepare her for you properly?' I strode across to where Indira had earlier set the small side table with two wine bottles and several glasses. I picked up the bottle on the left and quickly filled two glasses. I passed one to Hacklebury and raised the other to my lips. 'Your good health,' I said, and then, as if suddenly remembering something, I lowered the glass and strode back across to the rack where we stored our impressive array of accessories. 'Pardon me, sir, but I should have checked her myself earlier. She should be wearing this until you are ready for her.' I picked up a long dildo that hung from a basic harness and made my way back over to Molly, leaving my glass on the table on the way.

I stooped in front of Molly, gently stroking my fingers across her sex, which I could see was already very wet. A natural for this, was our Molly, but then the same could now be said of her two companions. 'You will notice the extreme length of this implement,' I remarked as I raised it to her nether lips. 'I have yet to encounter any man who can boast he would match it, and yet, as you will see, Molly can accommodate it easily.' I pushed the shaft home and Molly, her head lolling to one side, groaned in appreciation.

'At the same time,' I continued, 'she is very tight and has superb muscle control, which Cassandra taught her. They have such interesting techniques in the Orient, don't you agree? There, hold that yourself for a moment, slut.' I straightened up, leaving the dildo inside her and the harness straps dangling between her legs. 'It will not slip out, as you can see,' I said smugly, 'even though the harness must way half a pound on its own...

'Why, Sir Gregory, you must have been quite thirsty. Let me refill your glass and you can test her muscle control for yourself. Try to pull it out of her and you'll be surprised at how much effort is required.' Without waiting for a reply, I took the empty wineglass from him and walked over to refill it.

Hacklebury, meanwhile, eagerly accepted my invitation. 'Quite impressive,' he agreed, accepting the glass I offered him. 'I think perhaps I would like to experience those muscles on a more intimate level.' He swigged another mouthful and I stepped past him, bending to withdraw the dildo, which slipped out easily enough when Molly relaxed her devilish grip on it.

'Let me take the glass,' I offered, reaching for it. 'You'll find that if you just undo those two buckles at the front, you will be able to drop the front of your breeches for convenience.' My instructions were unnecessary, however, for Hacklebury's fingers were already fumbling at the straps, and before I had need of saying anything further, the triangular crotch-piece fell away, revealing that long, slightly curving cock I remembered only too well. He massaged its length proudly and leered at me.

'You think your cock-piece there is so long now, eh Contessa?' he boasted. 'Perhaps you'd like to sample it yourself later; mine, I mean, not that wood and leather thing.'

'Perhaps,' I replied coolly. 'It is indeed a proud and impressive weapon you have. But first the girl. Let's see how you handle her.'

In the end it was almost too easy and was over before Hacklebury had time to realise it. At first everything proceeded exactly as he would have anticipated, with him turning to Molly, stooping slightly and shuffling in between her spread-eagled legs. He entered her without ceremony, driving in to the hilt with a vigour that brought a gasp from her, and immediately began thrusting, at the same time mauling her breasts and pulling horribly on her nipples so that for a moment I thought he would tear them from her body.

And then, as his heart pumped the blood faster and faster the drugged wine took effect, and so rapidly he had barely time to register something was not quite as it should be before he collapsed, dropping to his knees as his glistening member slipped out of its warm sheath with an audible plopping sound. He made one feeble attempt to rise, grasping at the strap that held Molly's waist, and then fell backwards and sideways, his eyes rolling up until only the whites were visible. His eyelids fluttered once, twice, and then closed as his head hit the floor with a satisfying thump.

I stepped forward, peering down at him from behind my mask, my own heart thundering madly. I extended one boot, prodded him in the side, and then flicked the toe across his shaft, which inexplicably remained as rigid as before. 'More fight in that than there is between your ears!' I exclaimed. I turned to Molly, who was slowly recovering from her own reverie. 'Well done, my girl,' I said softly. I looked at the red marks over her chest. 'You'll get the chance to repay our friend for that,' I promised. 'And now, let me release you and you can have the pleasure of preparing him for the *coup de grace*.'

'You gonna let me stick him with a knife, mistress?' Molly grinned as I stepped over to her.

I laughed as I reached for the first strap buckle. 'No, I've got something much better than that to stick him with, and unfortunately, neither you nor I are properly equipped to do the job. However, I know a man who can.'

Paulie entered the action rather reluctantly to begin with, mostly because he was cringing with embarrassment from the way we had prepared him for his role. He must initially have been convinced we were simply out to humiliate him, whereas the real object of the exercise was to inflict the maximum humiliation on Hacklebury, and Paulie was simply an instrument to that end.

With Erik's assistance Indira had made the young man ready beforehand and left him in one of the unused attic rooms until it was time to introduce him. The wicked girl had not missed a trick, first lacing Paulie into a tight corset and putting him into stockings, lacy frilled garters and a pair of high-heeled French-style shoes that must have been cramping his toes terribly. She had added long gloves and a velvet choker and then rouged his cheeks and painted his lips. But as the corset stopped well below his chest, and his hair, though longish was obviously cut in a masculine style, even without the fact that his male genitalia were left openly displayed, it was obvious this exotic creature was simply a man dressed as a woman.

While Hacklebury was unconscious, we stripped him of his leather and laced him into a corset that was the twin of Paulie's. After a brief consultation we continued to add to his costume similarly, although there were no shoes large enough to accommodate his feet.

'Don't bother much with his face,' I instructed. 'Maybe a couple of rouge patches on his cheeks, though even that's not important.'

Erik lifted the sleeping figure onto the horse and Indira and Molly quickly fastened the various restraining straps. A bucket was then placed directly beneath Hacklebury's head, in case the drugged wine resulted in him being sick when he first came round. The fellow from whom Erik had obtained the innocuous looking clear liquid had assured him the potion was completely harmless and caused no side effects, but I preferred not to take chances and time spent with a mop would be time wasted.

However, I need not have worried, for not only did Hacklebury regain consciousness without such problems, the way in which he did so was remarkable for its speed. Whatever the drug was I did not, and still do not know, but one moment the bizarre figure was slumped lifeless, and the next it was bucking and squirming in its bonds as the full realisation of his situation struck with the force of a sledgehammer, followed almost as rapidly by the realisation that struggling was pointless. There ensued from his lips a stream of the most foul abuse and threats, then he fell silent as Indira and I, still masked, simply stood and let our prisoner finish venting his spleen.

'That's better,' I said when I judged that the tirade was at least temporarily over. I stepped forward and stooped down, raising Hacklebury's chin so his face was level with my own. 'It really will be a lot easier for you if you accept there's nothing you can do to escape what's coming. And, who knows, if you're a good fellow and please us with your performance, you might even come out of this with your worthless, cheating, lying, bullying hide in more or less one piece.'

'What do you want from me?' he demanded, though the hesitancy in his voice betrayed utter fear.

I laughed and let his head drop, but he raised it himself, apparently desperate to keep me in view. 'That's a good question,' I replied easily. 'However, the answer is not so simple. What do I want? Well, for a start, I'd like to see you spend a year in one of those awful dog suits in a cold damp cellar and have some brute of a keeper fuck the arse off you twice a day. Then you'd know what it feels like to be Maudie. Oh, she's safe by the way.'

'Safe?' A look of puzzlement creased his features, for of course he had no idea of Maudie's suffering. As far as he was concerned, Maudie had run off with Erik.

I explained. 'You see,' I finished, 'your dear, loyal Megan lied to you. It was Angelina who did a bunk and Maudie who took her place as the human bitch. And Megan didn't even dispose of Maudie as she said she would dispose of Angelina. Instead, she kept the poor bitch in an underground hole you wouldn't want a rabbit to live in.'

'You're lying!' Hacklebury snarled. 'It was the stupid little peasant who ran off. Angelina was still there, I saw her. I—'

'You fucked her?' I finished for him, and laughed harshly. 'You saw what Megan wanted you to see and you fucked poor Maudie, who couldn't tell you, and couldn't do anything except stand there while you did it. The way you did to Angelina and the way you think you can to any woman you choose.'

'How do you know all this?' His features were frozen, his eyes wide and bulging. 'Who are you?'

'Haven't you guessed?' It took Indira several seconds to loosen the laces at the back of my mask and I think the penny was already rolling, even if it hadn't properly dropped, even before I pulled the leather hood off my head. He blinked, but even with my still quite short hair, there was no way he could deny the truth now standing before him. 'Surprise, surprise!' I mocked. 'Poor, helpless little Angelina now has the big bully-boy exactly where he had her not so long ago.'

'I - I don't—'

'You don't understand? You don't know what to say? You don't believe it?' I was beginning to enjoy this role reversal, determined to make the bastard suffer as much mentally as he was certainly going to suffer physically. I stepped back two paces and twirled around away from him, hands on my hips.

'Well, you started it with the leather thing,' I told him, 'but I think even you would have to agree that this outfit is far more becoming. Do you like what you see, Gregory, my dear?' I turned again and beckoned to Paulie, who had remained standing alongside Erik in the corner behind Hacklebury out of his field of vision. 'And what about this delightful creature, hmm?' I ushered the blushing young man around so he was standing immediately in front of Hacklebury. 'Don't you think he looks quite sweet, Gregory dear? Prettier in his frillies than you are, I'd say, but look at this, what have we here?' I knelt and cupped Paulie's balls in one hand, raising them slightly so his tumescent shaft bobbed and waved. 'Not so impressive as your tackle,' I said, 'but not bad for a little sissy.'

'I - I'm not—' Paulie stammered, his face growing pinker than ever.

'Oh shut it, Paulie!' I snapped. 'The fact that you fancy the odd woman from time to time doesn't change a thing, and why should it? You are what you are, so you might as well be proud and enjoy it for what it's worth. Now, let's see if we can wake this here sleeping beauty, shall we?'

It didn't take much effort on my part; a few gentle stroking motions and the odd encouraging squeeze of his ball sack and Paulie's little soldier started to grow, until within a few seconds it was standing straight to attention.

'Guess what he's going to do with this, Gregory?' I leered.

Hacklebury's face was a mask of horrified disbelief.

'Oh indeed,' I continued, 'it's such a terrible thing, isn't it? Shame you never thought of that before, but at least you'll have plenty of time to contemplate the error of your ways.'

'You bitch!' he hissed through clenched teeth. 'I'll kill you for this, all of you!'

I reached out and patted him on the head, and it was funny to see the way he flinched at the approach of my hand. The bigger the bully, the bigger the coward. 'In case it had escaped you, Gregory dear,' I said, 'you're not exactly in any position to kill anyone, quite the reverse, in fact, and if you continue to annoy me I might just let Indira cut your throat at the end of all this.'

'You'd have to kill all three of us then,' he rasped. 'You'd have trouble explaining—'

'There's nothing to explain,' I retorted. 'Your two friends are quite happily playing down in the barn. We drugged them too, though with a different thing. They'll just think they're very drunk and in the meantime, Millie and Mandy will give them plenty to occupy their docile minds. They'll eventually fall asleep, of course, and when they wake up they'll just think they had such a good time they exhausted themselves. I'll just tell them you couldn't wait for them and that you rode off before first light. If your body is ever found, it'll be miles from here and weeks from now, so the authorities will assume you were attacked and robbed on the road.'

I released Paulie's shaft and nodded at him to continue stimulating himself. 'Of course, things needn't come to such extreme conclusions,' I went on. 'All you need to do is sign a few documents I've had drawn up, and then write a note to get Megan to come here with that so-called marriage certificate and then we can all go happily on our separate ways.'

'Documents? What documents?'

'Nothing too involved,' I replied. 'Just a full confession of what you've done - which I won't show to anyone unless you make me do so in the future - plus a document saying you renounce all claims to my estate, now and forever, and that you will not seek to interfere in my life or the lives of any of my friends.'

'You expect me to do that?' Hacklebury all but shrieked.

I nodded. 'Only if you want to escape from here in one piece. Of course, we could always burn your body afterwards. People disappear so often on the roads these days. It's a scandal, really, don't you think? And if we don't have to worry about your body, then we don't have to let Indira kill you quickly. I think she said something about cutting off your balls and then your prick and feeding them to you. Oh, the lady in white there is Indira, in case you hadn't worked that out yet. And she owes you big time, buster.'

'You can't hope to get away with this!' he yelled. It was a line straight out of a bad melodrama, but people really do say such stupid things.

'Whether we get away with it or not,' I said firmly, 'you're not going to be around to know either way, so it's up to you. And don't think you can sign and try to say afterwards you were forced to do so. That might work, I suppose, but we're going to get ourselves some insurance. You won't have heard of photographs yet, or if you have I doubt you know much about them. The prints are still a bit rough, but they're good enough so everyone who sees them will recognise you and be able to see what it is you're getting up to. Here,' I said, taking the print that Indira, right on cue, held out to me. 'Here's one I prepared earlier.' I held it under his nose.

The print showed two young women standing outside a house - our mill house actually, for although the image was grainy, Indira and I were clearly recognisable, and although the light outside had been better than it was in this room, the magnesium powder I'd had Erik buy in London would take care of that. All we had to do was set it off, click the lever on the rather cumbersome camera, and our French friend, who was currently staying at the hotel in Arundel, would do the rest in exchange for a fat fee.

Hacklebury's head slumped and he groaned quietly, but I grabbed his hair, pulling his head up again. 'What did you say?' I demanded.

He swallowed and ran his tongue along his upper lip. 'I said I'll sign your damned papers.' His voice was barely more than a cracked whisper.

I released my grip and stepped back. 'A wise decision.' I turned slowly to smile at Indira and wink at Erik. I then patted Paulie gently on the backside before clapping my hands. 'Right then, people,' I announced. 'It's party time!'

Epilogue

And that, as I finished explaining to Anne-Marie and Andrea, was more or less that. The photographs we took were not top quality and the majority of them didn't even print properly, as we had trouble synchronising the flash with the shutter, but those that did come out were more than enough for my purpose. Hacklebury would not risk them being circulated in society, not when they showed him dressed the way we had dressed him, and one clearly illustrated the moment when Paulie first thrust into him, with another shot, taken later, showing him bound to the cross and Paulie bringing him to a climax with his hand.

In the end we kept Hacklebury with us for a total of four days, much of which time he spent strapped in the chair with the dildo preventing him from shifting about and the straps preventing him from rising. In due course Megan arrived, complete with the false marriage certificate, which I locked away as potential evidence, together with a statement from Maudie regarding her part in the deception. Megan at first refused to sign a confession to her own role, but when we showed her Hacklebury and threatened her with an identical chair and a few other assorted options, she finally gave in, though as she sat at the table carefully inscribing her signature, the look she gave me was pure venom.

In the end Hacklebury was released to go to London and instruct the bank, though there was little left of the initial dowry payment he had received. Erik accompanied him, and together they went to see the lawyer who would be responsible for releasing the balance of my inheritance on my coming birthday. Papers were drawn up and notarised and my fortune was removed from the Hacklebury clutches for evermore.

Meanwhile, as added insurance, we kept Megan with us. She spent the five days in the barn wearing the dog suit that first I and then Maudie had suffered in, for Simeon Marsh had brought the hateful garment with him in case we needed it as further proof of the cruelty that had been inflicted upon us. Paulie - who eventually entered into the spirit of things and expressed a desire to remain with us for a little while - was given the job of dog handler. I won't go into detail, but suffice it to say he carried out his duties with all diligence, and that by the time Megan finally left with Hacklebury, she was walking a little gingerly.

And so all was well that ended well, although I suspected this would not be the final ending. Neither Hacklebury nor Megan would dare try anything openly, but neither was the type to take defeat graciously, and Megan in particular was the embodiment of evil, so I knew we would have to be careful and watch our backs. Whether or not it would be Angelina on her own now, or whether I would continue with my back and forth existence, I had no idea, but I knew that in Erik and Indira I would be leaving my ancestor in safe and loyal hands.

'So that's it, is it?' Andrea asked me when I had finally finished my tale.

'More or less, though I still want to work on tracing my family tree properly. There are still too many unexplained gaps and I'd like to find out why, if it's at all possible.'

'Work out how the wicked Hacklebury genes found their way down to you, eh?' Anne-Marie chuckled.

I smiled back at her. 'Funnily enough, that doesn't worry me any more. That's the one other thing I haven't told you yet.'

My two friends looked at me, puzzled.

I grinned. 'Unless something happened afterwards, which I don't think it did,' I explained, 'then the one thing I now know is that Gregory Hacklebury isn't one of my ancestors.'

'What?' they chorused in unison.

I chuckled. 'Apart from Indira's assertion that she knew Angelina wasn't pregnant when she got away from Hacklebury, I now know who did father her child - her first child, anyway, as she could have had others. While we were waiting for Hacklebury to come back from London, I started throwing up everywhere and getting these weird cravings for pork with cream on.'

'Ugh!' Anne-Marie snorted and Andrea pulled a face.

'Yes, I agree, not a nice thought, but I knew it could mean only one thing. I, or Angelina, rather, was pregnant, and because Indira knew her mistress had had a period since the escape, there could only be one father. It was Erik who was my ancestor, not Greg Hacklebury,' I concluded, beaming happily. 'Good old Erik. Could account for why I'm so damned tall, I suppose.'

The End (Until Another Time)

Author's Footnote

Well reader, there you have it, the conclusion of our Teena's first adventure in time, and good eventually triumphing over evil, as it must surely do in every satisfactory story.

Of course, as our heroine herself said, much remained unresolved, but then life has a habit of leaving loose ends around to trip the unwary. Perhaps Teena will one day unravel the twisted branches of her family tree, perhaps she won't, only time will tell and she seems to have plenty of that.

Will she go back?

Yes, most certainly, but whether or not it will be to that time or another, I couldn't really say, as she hasn't confided in me as yet. As I said at the beginning of this book, our Teena is a wilful minx with a mind of her own, so we'll have to wait and see what she decides to do next, or what fate throws at her.

I hope you've enjoyed reading about her as much as I've enjoyed the writing, and once again we thank you, Teena and I, for your support and loyalty through the three books so far. And so all that remains now is a promise and here it is, in the words, more or less, of good old Arnie...

We'll be back.

Enjoy more of Teena's time-travelling adventures, also published by us and available on **AMAZON Kindle**...

I nodded and opened my mouth to say something, but immediately it was filled for me, as Anne-Marie pressed a soft rubber ball between my teeth and buckled a

retaining strap at the nape of my neck to prevent me spitting it out again.

'Oh, sweet,' she trilled. She came around and knelt down, so that she was looking up into my face. 'I'll have to let you see yourself gagged,' she said. 'A gag does make a girl's face look so gorgeous, I've always thought; makes those big eyes look even bigger.'

Born in the fifties, a child in the 'Swinging Sixties', Teena Thyme comes to adulthood in the even more outlandish seventies, a self-possessed eighteen year old with the ability to see the funny side of most things. Little does she know, when she inherits the estate of a great-great-great aunt she never knew she had, that she will need all her wits, resolve and downright bloody-mindedness in order to survive the trials of time travelling and the perils of being a woman in an age when men ruled - either with a rod of birch or a whip of leather.

Whisked back through the ages, Teena finds herself as the very unwilling pawn in the power games of the black hearted Sir Gregory Hacklebury, who is determined to marry another of her previously unknown ancestors and seize her inheritance, even if to do so means that he must kill the unfortunate Angelina Spigworth, whose body Teena is now inhabiting - a body constrained by corsets, abused by everyone she comes in contact with and finally, it seems, destined to be left to rot in a forgotten prison.

Thyme II Thyme

Jennifer Jane Pope

I struggled into a sitting position, no mean feat without the use of my hands, which were still trapped inside those awful disabling gloves, my wrists locked to the broad corset belt that was part of the suit. Then, grunting into the foul tasting leather gag that was strapped between my achingly distended jaws, I managed to stand up using the rough stone wall as support. Just as before, my feet were encased in those ridiculously high heels and I had to pause for a moment to re-accustom myself and balance before finally tottering across to where the top half of the stable door stood open, the bottom half locked and bolted against any hope of escape.

Eighteen year old Teena's apparent journey back through time into the body of her ancestor, Angelina, has left as many marks on her psyche as Sir Gregory Hacklebury's whip had left on her borrowed body 130 years earlier, and her encounter with the dominant lesbian Anne-Marie back in her own time in 1975 has asked even more dark questions and opened too many secret doors to the depths of her soul.

Has the Hacklebury gene left a permanent scar through the decades, or is it the Thyme side of the family tree that causes Teena to seek thrills through pain and degradation? Needing an answer more desperately with every passing day, Teena knows that she can probably only find it in the past, and once again must try to journey back into an era where women were merely corseted chattels and poor Angelina is still suffering an existence of bondage and suffering that her supposed husband and master would not inflict even upon his livestock.

www.ingramcontent.com/pod-product-compliance
Lightning Source LLC
Chambersburg PA
CBHW060939120626
46557CB00003B/1062